# WONDERFUL FEELS LIKE THIS

# WONDERFUL FEELS LIKE THIS

SARA LÖVESTAM

TRANSLATED FROM THE SWEDISH BY LAURA A. WIDEBURG

FLATIRON BOOKS
NEW YORK

This is a work of fiction. All of the characters, organizations, and events portrayed in this novel are either products of the author's imagination or are used fictitiously.

 Printed in the United States of America. For information, address Flatiron Books, 175 Fifth Avenue, New York, N.Y. 10010.

www.flatironbooks.com

The Library of Congress Cataloging-in-Publication Data is available upon request.

ISBN 978-1-250-09523-7 (hardcover)
ISBN 978-1-250-09519-0 (e-book)

Our books may be purchased in bulk for promotional, educational, or business use. Please contact your local bookseller or the Macmillan Corporate and Premium Sales Department at 1-800-221-7945, extension 5442, or by e-mail at MacmillanSpecial Markets@macmillan.com.

Originally published in Sweden in 2013 as *Hjärta av jazz* by Piratförlaget

Translation published in the United States of America by arrangement with the Pontas Agency, Spain

First U.S. Edition: March 2017

10 9 8 7 6 5 4 3 2 1

*Out of the blue, someone you meet*
*will be the friend you need.*

—Povel Ramel,
"Underbart är kort" (What Wonderful Feels Like)

# WONDERFUL FEELS LIKE THIS

# – CHAPTER 1 –

Steffi is becoming happy jazz. She lies on her striped bedspread, eyes shut, while deep down inside, she's turning into an upbeat happy blues, a going-crazy-with-happiness blues. All the stupid people vanish into a fog far beyond her window; they're nothing now as she walks the bass line with her guitar. She rubs away a few tears, which have mingled with the hair at her temples. Povel Ramel sings: *Just slap them away like a mosquito! Who cares what they say? Get on with your own show!* She's singing along with his hit "A Happy Blues." She takes a deep breath and no longer gives a damn about any of the other kids in class 9B. The bass player works the blues line like a madman. It's one of the most difficult walking bass lines on the whole record. As if there were no rules, as if you could play exactly what you wanted, but she hasn't yet figured out how.

When she finally leaves her room, nobody can tell that she's been crying. Mamma puts a dish of fish in white sauce on the table, Pappa is throwing out the box the fish came in, and Edvin is getting out the tableware.

"Can you get Julia?"

The door to Julia's room is closed. Steffi walks right in.

"Hey, would it hurt to knock?" Julia yells and then into the phone: "It's just my nerdy little sister." She turns her head to Steffi again. "One day you'll walk in here and see something you really don't want to see." A laugh comes from the phone.

"Time to eat," Steffi says.

"I need to finish this."

"She needs to finish her call," Steffi reports back to the kitchen, and her father gets up from the table with a sigh.

Edvin does not want to eat the fish or the potatoes. He swirls the sauce around with his fork and eats a little of it with a bit of lettuce and a tomato. The struggle to get Julia to the table transforms into a fight to get Edvin to eat at least one bite of fish.

"You're eight years old." Mamma sighs. "Eat it now and you won't have to eat it later. You can't live on gravy alone; you'll get dizzy."

Edvin laughs at the image. "Like thiiiiis?" he asks and flops his head from side to side again and again.

"Just eat."

Edvin clamps his mouth shut. Julia has started to text under the table. Steffi swallows a bite of fish with potatoes.

"Think of it like this," she says to Edvin. "Potatoes are precious like gold."

Edvin looks at her skeptically. "No, they're not."

"More like gold than tomatoes. Look at your plate. What looks the most like gold?"

Edvin cuts a tiny piece of potato and stuffs it in his mouth, swallowing it with exaggerated effort. "It doesn't taste like gold."

"That's because you're eating it all alone. If you eat some fish with it, it'll have more gold flavor."

Pappa gives her a grateful look. Mamma is asking Julia where she bought her mascara, and when Julia doesn't reply, Mamma asks Steffi about her day at school.

"Fine," Steffi mumbles. She's concentrating on her potatoes and fish. When the thought of the girls in class 9B forces its way into her mind, she slaps it away just like she'd slap away a mosquito. She is a happy blues, as cool as cool can be.

"I can tell our last semester is coming," she says. "We're getting a project."

"Sounds fun," Pappa says. "How exciting."

"Don't act so surprised," Julia says. "When I was in ninth grade, we had a project, too, remember?"

"Yes, well . . . ," Mamma says. "What fun that you get to do one, too. Have you picked out a topic? Or does the teacher assign one?"

"I don't know yet," Steffi says. "I'll have to see."

Edvin plumps both elbows down on the table. "This. Does. Not. Taste. Like. Gold."

Steffi has stopped logging in to The Place, although sometimes she'll go back just to see what's happening. But then she'll delete the guest book comments, trying not to read them, but she always does. She tries not to feel hurt by the words *whore, dyke,* and *disgusting,* but she is. She's never been a prostitute, she's never been in love with another girl, and she takes a shower every day, but the feeling of being dirty seems to come with the words. She's definitely stopped going to The Place. She's done that many times. Today she's not even going to start.

Instead she takes out her bass. Last week she'd taken "A Happy Blues" to her bass teacher, who hemmed and hawed at it doubtfully. He'd explained that a walking bass line goes from one note to another through three notes you choose yourself. Then they practiced it together for a while, but it never sounded right. She has seen through him already. All he really wants to do is teach classical guitar and sing Bellman songs. It's easier when she's alone. She goes from A to D a few times, testing different notes, grimacing when it sounds off, repeats. Nods her head to the rhythm when she gets going, ups the volume.

Finally, she puts on "A Happy Blues" again. She ignores the bass player on the record and does her own thing between the downbeats. It sounds passable, but nowhere near Povel's bassist. After eight measures, she gives up, stops playing, and falls backward onto her bed, her bass on her stomach. Listens to the rest of the song. Slaps away The Place's nasty comments just like a mosquito, gets on with her own show. Becomes happy jazz.

# – CHAPTER 2 –

Their project is supposed to explore some aspect of social or natural sciences in depth.

"They did a *fashion* show last year!" Karro protests. She rolls her eyes and looks around for affirmation. She's wearing well-applied eye makeup.

"That's why this year, we decided to change the guidelines," Bengt explains. "This is practice for *gymnasium*, when you'll have to study on your own. Take advantage of it!"

Karro rolls her eyes. Steffi can't stand Karro, but on this point she has to agree. She'd hoped to record some of her music.

"You can choose to do a project on your own or in pairs," Bengt continues. "Those who decide to work in pairs must give me a plan of who will be responsible for each part of the project."

The girls immediately reach out their hands to pair off like invisible magnets—Steffi is left out, as if she has as much magnetism as a block of wood.

"Project outlines will be due next week. More detailed information is on our class page, and part of your work is to understand the instructions and follow them. Any questions?"

Victor raises his hand. "Is there going to be a test?"

Some giggles break out.

Bengt remains calm. "Everything is on our class page. You will be required to prepare a written report with a summary, a table of contents, and a bibliography, as well as do an oral presentation during class."

As they all file through the classroom door, Steffi finds herself next to Sanja. Karro gasps theatrically as she grabs Sanja and pulls her away. "Watch out for Steffi!"

Sanja snickers and then sighs hugely in relief. "I didn't see her!"

"You'll have to wash your clothes in bleach, you know, if you get too close."

Sanja giggles at the laundry advice as Steffi rushes off, breathing hard and trying to distract herself by thinking of what subject to choose for her project. But the lump in her throat gets in her way. She knows her face has turned bright red and her eyes have filled with tears that will brim over if somebody talks to her. She slinks into the bathroom.

Surprisingly, her reflection in the mirror is not quite as ugly as she'd imagined. She meets her own eyes, pushes her hair behind her ears, and tries to smile. She will never show them that they'd made her cry, never. She can picture their snickering and their pointing fingers: *the slut's crying!* Never!

She flushes the toilet before she leaves.

She walks home with Povel Ramel on her mp3 player. The familiar notes open up that other world, where Karro is nothing more than Povel Ramel's wilted kangaroo vine—useless in every way.

The headphones are warm on her ears and she walks in time with the music. “Wow, How Lively the Band Swings!” gives her feet a beat that swings as the bass slides into the closest Povel ever came to reggae. Next comes “Look, It’s Snowing,” and she hears the intro even before it starts. Her footsteps are lighter, strutting. She moves her lips in Povel’s lightning fast patter: *“Look, it’s snowing, fireside glowing, flakes are whirling, everybody’s stirring. . . .”*

It had taken her an eternity just to figure out the lyrics. Like most of Povel Ramel’s songs, they aren’t online, and all the many words flashed by in an instant. Once, in the fifth grade, she’d performed “I’m Digging You” in music class and was met with forty-four rolling eyes. Her music teacher tried to make them more receptive by explaining that this was actually the first rap song out of Sweden, written by the hardworking and mischievous Povel Ramel. It didn’t help that her teacher pronounced “rap” as “repp.”

The batteries run out halfway home. Steffi stops and shakes her player; sometimes this squeezes out ten more minutes. Sometimes it doesn’t. For a second, she thinks she hears it start up again, but when she puts on her headphones, she doesn’t hear anything. She shakes the player again but realizes as she’s shaking it that she’s already hearing the music. It’s “Where’s the Soap?” And it’s not coming from her headphones. She furrows her brow.

Nobody is around. Other than the weak sound of music, it’s completely quiet. The streetlights shine on no one but herself. Still, she can hear the words clearly: *The wind’s stopped howling, the old aunt stopped growling. . . .* She stands stock-still and brings her player to her ear to make sure that the music’s not coming from it. Then quiet falls again. A handful of snow slips from a tree branch. She is just about to start walking again when the next song starts: “Jazz Is Calling.”

Steffi turns around. Then she turns slightly to the left and finally to the right to zero in on the sound. It seems to come from the short row of town houses a few meters back from the road.

Her feet leave silent marks in the snow. The notes of a string bass and a clarinet bubble out like champagne, slightly muffled, but coming closer. When she comes to the fourth window along the row of town houses, she sees it's slightly open. The music is coming from there, right next to her. Povel Ramel's high-pitched voice finds its way out into the empty February air around her. It's like being in a dream. She stands there until the clarinet has wailed up into a falsetto and then dies out. The wind is ruffling through a spruce tree somewhere, the dark sky seems to touch her head, and the yellow bricks in front of her are harsh with black shadows. Then there's a noise from the window above her head, and she jumps as if she's been slapped.

A voice, nothing like Povel Ramel's, rasps at her as the shape of a head forms inside the window frame. Steffi wants to run away, but her body won't move.

"So, answer me!" the voice barks from the window.

Steffi is breathless, even though she's been standing absolutely still. She has to swallow before she can say a word. "What . . . I didn't hear what you asked," she calls up to the window.

"Well, then, let me repeat myself! Why are you standing around down there?"

Steffi has to think for a moment. Why does *anyone* stand around outside someone's window?

"I heard someone playing Povel Ramel."

More noise comes from the window and then it's opened so wide that she can now clearly see the man's whole head. He's almost completely bald; his face has cheeks that are long and narrow, and his bushy white eyebrows are as white as the hair sprouting out of his ears. His lips turn up in an amused smile. "I'm sure you did, since I *was* playing Povel Ramel."

Steffi stares openmouthed at the man in the window. He's really old. Not like Grandma and Grandpa, who have just retired, but with wrinkly skin like parchment paper, like the old folks in the care center. He sucks on his lip and then lets it go.

"Do you know when he recorded this song I just played?"

Her heart starts to beat again, like when her teacher asks her a question she knows. Even more so, since she's standing in the snow and being questioned about Povel Ramel. She feels that her answer will change everything.

"Nineteen forty . . . the forties."

"Of course it was recorded in the forties. In 1946 exactly. Casper Hjukström on the clarinet. But that I don't really care about."

"You don't?"

Silence from above. She looks up, expecting his head to disappear back into the room, gone as if he'd been a ghost. But the man stretches his neck farther out so she can now see his chin and cheekbones outlined against the wall. He lifts his wild eyebrows.

"Well, are you going to give me pneumonia in this cold air or are you going to come up and introduce yourself like a normal person?"

The hallway reeks of soap residue and plastic mats. Steffi stands still just inside the entrance after she's been buzzed in. A picture showing a house in the forest hangs on the right-hand wall and on the left is a needlepoint with a phrase about God. She pulls up the shoulder strap of her school bag, which always slides down. A door opens down the hallway. The face from the window appears, followed by the rest of a body.

He's not much taller than she is, but once, maybe, he'd been taller. She takes his knotty hand and they shake. His hand is cool and dry, his handshake stronger than she'd thought it would be.

"Alvar Svensson's the name."

She wonders if she should introduce herself as Stephanie or perhaps give an imaginary name. But she is who she is. "Steffi Herrera."

Alvar Svensson leads her to his room. It is square and contains one bed, one plaid armchair, two chairs, one table, and one enormous bookcase. He folds into his armchair like a collapsing measuring rod, while nodding at Steffi to take a chair, which she does. It's already dark, judging from the lack of light through the window. She pictures the ground outside where she'd just been standing and listening to the music.

"Well, as I was saying," Alvar says and leans back so that his armchair squeaks. "I really don't care if it was Hjukström on the clarinet. I was more impressed by the wonderful vision that went by the name Anita Bergner. I don't suppose you've heard the song 'Letter from Frej'?"

Steffi wants to laugh. He's underestimating her, this old guy who enjoys Povel Ramel. She wants to imitate the bit where the woman begins to quiver in ecstasy from reading Frej's letter, but she doesn't know the words. Instead, she quotes from another part of the song:

*"Your mere nearness devastates*
*A fire flames in me that incapacitates."*

She's starting to sing as she reaches the end, but falters on the last note.

"Yes, that's just how I felt when it came to Anita," Alvar says, pleased. "Perhaps you've felt it, too." He states this as a possibility, but not a question.

"She was outside the studio when Hjukström showed up with his clarinet."

Steffi repeats his words in her head. *Was he there?*

"What do you mean?" she asks, feeling stupid.

"Oh, didn't I say that? I was hired for a recording . . . oh, I probably forgot to mention it. I was in Stockholm back then."

Steffi stares at the man in the armchair, the one who had been to Stockholm and had met Povel Ramel's clarinet player. Did he come from Stockholm? But what about his Värmland accent, then? She decided it would not be polite to ask.

"You had to go to Stockholm," Alvar reminisces without prodding. "Just look at the labels on the gramophone records."

He grabs the arms of his chair and heaves himself up. He walks to his bookcase and pulls out something very flat. Since Steffi did not immediately jump up, he pulls out another and waves them around.

"Look! Konserthuset in Stockholm! Odeons Studio, Stockholm!"

Steffi looks closely at the records. They are as large as plates, and their paper sleeves have nothing printed on them. Circling the center holes, she can make out Povel Ramel's name written in cursive. A gramophone record from Alvar's time. It is so very real it makes her seem unreal.

"You couldn't keep me away," Alvar goes on. He holds out a record in its sleeve to her and she takes it. The paper is rough. She feels a connection with the past—just then a cell phone rings into the swing music still coming through Alvar's large gramophone horn. Her cell phone plays a line from "A Happy Blues."

Alvar startles and looks around, then laughs as he sees her pull out her phone. "Jazz is calling," he says.

Steffi smiles. "Or the blues. The family is calling, my pappa, he's wondering where I am."

Alvar nods. The ears on his head seem so large they could have been bought at a costume shop.

"I'll tell you my whole story someday, if you want to hear it."

Steffi thinks there must be a pleasant polite phrase she should say, but she can't remember what it could be. "OK."

When she walks through the door at home, she wishes she could have stayed longer at Alvar's place.

"ADMIRAL!" Edvin is shouting, holding up his stick with a yellow flag, his imitation of a military gesture. When she doesn't respond, he marches into the kitchen, flag held high, turns, and then marches back to her.

She takes off her shoes. She should have thought to tell her father she was in the music room at school. Then she could have stayed longer.

"Hi, Steffita," her father greets her. He claps her on the shoulder.

Mamma asks her to help in the kitchen.

"Julia can," Steffi answers, but then she sees the extra pair of shoes in the hallway and knows she can't get out of it.

"Fanny's come over," Mamma says.

Fanny coming over is like having two Julias in the house. It's also like having a song on repeat, because they say the same things over and over even if someone eavesdrops on them. What idiots some other girls are; how to get rid of unwanted hair; how cute the senior boys are. Fanny would complain, "I can't stand the boys in our class. I want a real man!" And Julia would agree. "We girls just mature faster." And wonders if she should get Botox for the wrinkle beneath one of her eyes. "It's because you smoke!" Fanny would exclaim, and then the two of them would giggle so stupidly that Steffi couldn't stand it. She had to be really bored to even bother eavesdropping on them. Most of it was scribbled in Julia's diary anyway.

"How was school today?" Pappa asks.

An image of Karro and Sonja—*Watch out for Steffi!*—the bathroom, the song that came from nowhere, the bald old man in the window, the original gramophone records behind a plaid armchair.

"We were told how to go about choosing our projects," she replied.

Edvin leaps into the kitchen. He's exchanged his yellow flag for a golden sword. "*En garde!* A duel! What's for supper?"

# – CHAPTER 3 –

Kevin, Leo, Hannes . . ."

Sanja is ranking the boys, and Steffi is not there. She's not there because she's sitting on the farthest bench away, with her back to them, and she's concentrating on putting on her sweater. She's not there and that gives her a bit of breathing room.

"No, Kevin, Hannes, Leo," Karro objects. "Hannes is really hot, now that he's cut his hair, and Leo stinks."

"That's because he's always exercising."

"He still stinks."

"But he's so cute."

"That's why he's third. Or do *you* want him?"

Sanja pretends to hit Karro with her towel.

Steffi can see them reflected in the mirror on the wall. She has the song "Letter to Frej" running through her head.

Povel's bossa nova from the seventies gets entwined with Sanja's attraction to Leo and his aroma. Steffi smiles at the thought. They could start a song, she thinks. Sanja would begin:

*Your nose to me is so enchanting*

And Karro would reply:

*But your mouth spews only bantering.*

They'd giggle like the singer Wenche Myhre and trill the lyrics that Steffi hasn't yet figured out. Something about the gods.

"Excuse *me,*" a voice says too close to her ear and Steffi transforms back from air into flesh and blood. "Excuse *me,* but I think this slut has been laughing at us."

Steffi immediately checks her clothes and finds herself still half-dressed. At least she had gotten her pants on and her cell phone is safely in her pocket. But her tights and woolen socks are on the bench next to her.

Her shoes squish all through the last class, even though she'd wrung her socks out as well as she could and held them under the hand dryer for at least two minutes. When she's about halfway home, her feet have gotten so cold they hurt. She unties her shoelaces and pulls off her wet socks to walk the rest of the way home in just her shoes.

As she walks by the long, flat building that is the local retirement home, she sees that Alvar's room is dark. Even though she hits pause on her mp3 player, she doesn't hear any music from his window. Just as well, since her feet feel like tender blocks of ice. She walks a few more steps and looks back to see if he's turned on a light, but she couldn't turn back anyway.

Of course, according to Sanja and Karro, Kevin is the hottest of all the boys in their class. There's no room for discussion there. Everyone agrees. It's a fact, not an opinion. That Steffi disagrees with everyone else makes her a little worried. She knows she's old enough to understand why cute boys are cute, but she thinks that Kevin's eyes are too narrow and she doesn't like the way the ends of his mouth turn down. She can't see what makes him the cutest guy in class. This must mean that the others are right: there's something wrong with her.

Just before she reaches her block, her shoes really start rubbing on her bare ankles and she forces herself not to tear up by holding her breath. She's been through worse—and she is definitely going to learn how Wenche Myhre sings that trill.

At home, when she pulls off her shoes, her feet are bright red in the middle and white around her toes. They tingle as she pulls on some woolen socks from the dresser in the hall while she yells, "Hello? Anybody home?"

She gets no answer. But there's a sound from Julia's room.

A wheezing, a sigh, a human sound. Julia's door is slightly open. Steffi tiptoes up to it. She sees Julia on her stomach on her bed, completely still. Then a snivel followed by a long, halting exhalation. Steffi stands there, mouth wide open. Julia is crying. Steffi feels frozen in place as she watches Julia's shaking back and catches the sound Julia is trying to muffle. She feels tears welling up in her own eyes. She wants to ask what's going on, but this is Julia.

She leaps back when, without warning, Julia flips over and stares at her.

"What the *hell* are you doing here?"

Steffi backs away. "I'm just . . . I'm just . . ."

"You're so damn nosy! Go away and shut the door behind you!"

"What . . . what's wrong?"

Julia sits up in bed. Her eyes are red from crying and her anger makes them ugly. "GO AWAY!"

---

By dinnertime, Julia seems back to normal. She rolls her eyes at Pappa. He's been trying to understand the Swedish word *påbrå.*

"I thought it meant something else! I mixed up *brå* with *bra* and it wasn't until I realized that *å* and *a* were totally different letters in Swedish that I figured out why Swedes didn't understand me! But it was a logical mistake!"

"What does *påbra* mean?" Edvin asks.

Pappa starts a long explanation involving Pippi Longstocking, a Siw Malmkvist song from ages ago, as well as his own Caribbean Indian grandmother.

Steffi is chewing her fish balls, trying not to look at Julia. Julia is not a person who cries. She's the one who flips back her hair and tries on lip gloss. Julia rolls her eyes at last year's shoes and gossips with Fanny about twenty-year-old guys. There are never tears in Julia's eyes, only mascara on their lashes.

Edvin is eating for a change and Mamma asks Steffi, "How was school?"

Steffi stuffs two fish balls into her mouth and nods instead of answering. Outside, the winter night is black as coal.

After dinner, Steffi decides to get right to work. She tries to laugh like Wenche Myhre and attempts the hoarse sound of a laugh making its way all the way up through her throat. Wenche Myhre is Norwegian, and her Swedish has a Norwegian accent.

*Your mere nearness devastates*

*A fire flames in me that incapacitates*

Steffi sings along as well as she can. "Oh, oh, oh!" She trills together with Wenche Myhre, and Povel Ramel's lyrics become a dramatic duet between them. The trill is not so hard; it just doesn't rhyme. Once she's figured out the entire song, she pulls out her bass guitar.

*"Dum de dum, the song's in fifths. Dum de dum, she just can't quit, I'm dancing with the dame who got a letter from Frej."*

Her socks on the radiator are slowly steaming off the water from the changing room toilet. Her CD keeps spinning; Povel's voice takes over from Wenche. It is a good voice, a voice that sings only funny words with happy music.

# – CHAPTER 4 –

On her way to school she hears the music again. Perhaps she hears it just because her first class is biology. Perhaps it's just her imagination; music sometimes takes over her mind so that she's not always sure if she's remembering it or hearing it. But she sees that Alvar's window is slightly ajar and there's a fuzzy white shape that could be his head moving around inside the room. She pushes at the door to the retirement home and it opens.

Biology is hard enough as it is, but when Gunnel retired, they got a newly graduated substitute teacher who immediately figured out who were the most popular kids and did her best to keep them happy. Soon enough she was hired full-time. This new teacher was so adept at brownnosing that only Steffi seemed to notice. Steffi could see it in the way the teacher smiled whenever Karro called Steffi names and in the way she gestured whenever she talked about Darwin and the survival of the fittest. *Survival of the cunt,* Steffi thinks and stares at her textbook so that the new teacher, Camilla, can't look into her eyes and see that she's calling her a cunt. School is hard enough as it is. This month, they'll even have to endure Sexual Health.

Steffi tiptoes through the empty hallway of the retirement home like a burglar. Before she's reached Alvar's door, a nurse turns into the hallway from another corridor. Steffi stops abruptly and so does the woman.

"Well?" the nurse asks when Steffi doesn't say a word.

"Ah . . . ," Steffi says.

She can't think of anything more intelligible. But she does know all of Povel Ramel's lyrics on his first and second CDs; she could quote them at will.

"Who are you looking for?" the nurse asks. Her voice is harsh. Her hair is strictly combed back, slick and shining, and she does not smile.

"Alvar." Steffi exhales in relief.

Alvar breaks out into a wide clown smile when Steffi opens his door.

"Of course I know Steffi," he replies to the nurse's questioning if this girl really was coming to see him. "I've been waiting for Miss Steffi Herrera."

"So where were we?" he asks as the nurse closes the door behind her.

Steffi blurts out the entire riff by Wenche that she now knows by heart: *"Oh, my darling, there is only one like you, you, you, oh, every small detail of you is a miracle created by the gods, I worship your thin lean neck and the small wonder-filled dimples in your knees, every single golden hair on your amazing forearms, oh, I only dream of the next time I will embrace you, kiss you, hold you, oh!"*

It doesn't sound the way it does when she sings along with

Wenche, just more like a gush of words, but she knows them all. Alvar watches her recite and then wryly replies, "My thin lean neck has not been admired in a very long time."

Steffi blushes. "Oh, but . . . ," she says, and then sighs like Julia.

Julia's sighs, however, always seem to come from a deep, highly irritated place in her soul, while Steffi's sound more like embarrassed coughs.

"It's from 'Letter from Frej,'" she says.

Alvar is laughing so hard his mouth is wide open.

*"The small dimples in . . ."*

*"The small wonder-filled dimples in your knees."*

Alvar is sitting on his bed, still laughing heartily, but he's gazing at the ceiling, and then he says, "When it comes to the miracle of love, I'm afraid we really can't search for its explanation in our friend Povel."

Steffi ponders the idea of *the miracle of love* for a moment, but Alvar's gaze has moved from the ceiling to the carpet. Steffi really can't say she knows more about this subject than all the things Povel Ramel has sung.

"You can interpret this in many ways, of course," Alvar says. "One boring theory is that he did not know enough about love, himself, to sing about it very well, and another is that he knew it all too well and just decided to leave it be."

Alvar looks at her as if she understands what he is talking about. Grown-ups usually don't do that. Usually you have to listen to them, pretending you care about what they're saying, until finally they say something interesting. Usually they never do.

"Doing it his way, he could keep love for himself while the rest of us sit and debate about what he knew. I'm sure he'd appreciate our second way of looking at him."

Steffi throws herself into the armchair. She's supposed to be in biology class, but that was now the furthest thing from her mind. Alvar's room smells like soap and the musty gramophone. The scent of real thoughts.

"I know nothing at all about the miracle of love," she says.

Alvar draws in a deep breath before he replies. "Perhaps you have a mother or father who loves you."

"Yeah."

"Then you know the first half. The rest will come in its own time."

"Maybe."

"Absolutely. How old are you, Miss Steffi Herrera?"

"Fifteen."

"Fifteen years old. Yes, well, this age is as good as any to be surprised by love and its wonders. Have I told you about Anita?"

"Not really."

"I must have mentioned it. Surely I told you I went to Stockholm?"

"You just said that you went there and there was a woman named Anita."

"So I didn't give you the story in the right order."

"No."

"Well, then. Let me start from the beginning. I was just a boy when I took the train to Stockholm for the very first time. It was 1942. . . ."

Alvar was just a boy when he took the train to Stockholm. It was 1942; it was a death-defying gamble to take a train. His mother told him that trains transported war matériel and could explode at any time. Also the Germans could come pouring out of the freight cars and take over every unlucky traveler onboard: the wrong train at the wrong time. The more she talked about trains, the more they seemed to be erratic machines of murder. Alvar was more eager than ever to ride one. Stockholm drew him like a peg pulls its string into tune.

Alvar was already taller than his teacher and he'd played his father's guitar until it had fallen apart. He thought it was time to go.

"You don't have to go searching for trouble," his mother declared. "I forbid it."

So he went to his father. His father had good sense and could understand a solid argument.

"I've never even heard a real clarinet!" Alvar said.

His father grunted and scratched his chin.

"And what will happen to me if I stay here?" Alvar said, his voice shaking with passion. "Am I supposed to work in the forest hauling timber all my life, when I *know*, I really *know* that I could do more, be something big?"

Alvar's voice had cracked a bit as he said this, but that could be seen as a mark of his intensity and not his youthful immaturity. His father still scratched his chin. A good sign.

Alvar finally was able to leave Värmland because, first, Värmland was much too close to occupied Norway, from where the Germans could swarm just as easily as from the very next train. Second, his mother had an aunt who lived in Stockholm and who was having difficulty with her old legs. Third, Alvar was beginning to drum on every object in the house until even his normally even-tempered father could take it no more. Alvar had to promise that he would be quiet in his aunt's house and not beat up the furniture. He promised he would wear a muzzle and tie his hands together if that was what was needed. In the end, his mother gave in.

---

Alvar got his first look at the ways of Stockholm as soon as he climbed into the train car. People in fine hats passed below his window on their way to first- and second-class cars, but on the wooden bench across from him he found the most interesting people. A man with an odd-shaped case. A military man with an arm in a sling.

A blond girl his own age with a middle-aged woman who held tightly to the girl's hand. It looked like the older woman could barely contain her anger, and also that she hadn't had a great deal of practice doing just that. "Cry if you want to," she hissed from the side of her mouth. "But don't forget whose fault it is that we're here right now!" The girl bit her lip and didn't lift her gaze from the floor. Her tense shoulders and white knuckles gave witness to her unhappiness.

Alvar swallowed, tried to look away, but kept glancing back at that closed, delicate face. Was there anything he could do? But he had no talent for comforting unhappy girls. Unexpectedly she looked up at him and he caught his breath so abruptly he broke out into a coughing fit. He tried to draw attention away from this by drumming his fingers on his knees. He drummed with concentration, faster and faster, in time with the train's accelerating engine. He kept on until, from his left, a strong hand took hold of his and held it in the air until he calmed down. The passengers on the benches around them expressed their approval.

"You're not fully grown yet, are you?" the man across from him asked.

"I'm seventeen!"

He said this with emphasis so that the girl across from him could hear. Seventeen might not be so impressive, but it was still closer to being a man than a boy, right? The girl glanced at him quickly, but he couldn't tell what was going through her mind. Alvar made the great mistake of imagining what her legs might look like under her skirt and then couldn't keep up the facade of strutting masculinity. The man with the unusual case asked him where he was going, and Alvar's voice cracked when he stammered out, "Stockholm. I'm going to find a job and take care of my mother's older relative, but what I really want is . . ."

A few heads turned in his direction, and he avoided looking at the young girl to keep his voice steady.

"I'm really going to Stockholm to play swing music."

Someone snorted, but the man with the case grinned.

"So you like swing, do you? Some people go to Stockholm for a girl, for others it's a way to make a living, but you are one of the chosen few going there for music."

As the man said this, people around them snickered. Alvar laughed with them. What else could he do?

"I'm sure your latest tune is well known in . . . ," the man teased with a wink.

Alvar began to sing "How Do You Do, Mr. Swing?" in a wavering voice and heard a few other voices joining in.

The song petered out; nobody really knew the lyrics, but the fact that so many had enjoyed the song made Alvar feel good. He even managed to take another peek at the girl. The woman beside her had laid her arm over the girl's shoulders. Neither of them had been singing along.

The man with the odd case was still interested in Alvar. After a few kilometers of listening only to the train chugging along, he leaned forward to put his elbows on his knees. "You don't look like a jazz cat to me."

"Thank the good Lord for that," a woman sitting on Alvar's bench harrumphed.

*Jazz cat,* Alvar repeated to himself. He didn't know what cats had to do with it, but he was sure he'd find out when he got to Stockholm. He wasn't going to reveal such a gap in his knowledge in front of this beautiful blond girl.

"I'm just me," he replied. He hoped that would be good enough.

"And who *are* you, then?"

"Alvar Svensson from Björke." He held out his hand. Decided he would keep the name of his hometown to himself from now on.

"If you want to keep your good name, stay away from that swing music!" the woman to his right exclaimed.

"And what do you mean by that?" the man said, egging her on.

"I can tell by your case what you think," the woman replied with a snort. "But respectable people are forced to stand by while that horrible jazz music destroys an entire generation. No, my boy, you just make sure you find yourself a good job and take good care of your relative when you get to Stockholm. Make your parents proud of you!" The way her eyes drilled into him made it hard for Alvar to disagree.

Still, his curiosity about the man's case increased after her comment. It wasn't a suitcase, even though it resembled one. It was long and had a clasp. Alvar stared at it, his curiosity increasing moment to moment as the train chugged on. The man grinned slightly and then, without looking at Alvar, he opened his case. Alvar felt his pulse increase and knew everyone was watching as he craned his neck, but he couldn't help himself. The man began to lift out parts of a clarinet, taking his time, putting the reed to his mouth, checking to make sure each part fit properly. Then he slowly took the instrument apart again and set each section back in its place. He closed the lid and snapped the clasp shut. It was as if the doors to paradise were being slammed shut before Alvar's eyes. He tried to catch the man's eye, but he was now staring at the ceiling.

"Was that . . . was that a real clarinet?" Alvar finally had to ask, even though he already knew it had to be.

The man brought his gaze down. "Oh, that? Yes, that's the one I take when I'm on the road."

Alvar stared. A man who takes a clarinet on the road implied that he had another clarinet at home, and that meant that this man was a real musician. The other passengers had come to the same conclusion.

"Oh, please play something for us!" the blond girl asked, ignoring the stern look from her traveling companion.

The man laughed. "Oh, no, no, no." He seemed pleased, in spite of his protests, and finally gave in.

"So, just for the sake of the beautiful girl who requested it . . . ," he said, and managed to wink at everyone in the compartment.

Two of the women covered their mouths as they giggled.

The man quickly reassembled his clarinet as he said, "Give me a beat." He looked straight at Alvar. "Like this."

He clapped a simple beat, and it was entirely different from how all the folk musicians clapped in Björke. Something in the elbows, something much more exciting. Alvar tried to do that, too, until he could. Then the man put the clarinet to his lips.

Alvar didn't recognize the music. Perhaps it wasn't even a real tune, but an improvisation of melodies and rhythms like those that Alvar had heard only on the radio. This was jazz! Alvar found himself keeping time with the clarinet, his elbows moving in the same swing beat the man played, while the landscape of Sweden passed by outside the window. The blond girl across from him swayed her upper body to the music, her eyes fixed on the clarinet player, ignoring even the hard grip on her shoulder as the music took her away.

"So was that Anita?"

"Who?"

"The girl on the train."

"No, that was just a girl on a train."

"So why are you telling me about her then?"

"Well, it was terrible, what she was going through. She'd had to leave her newborn baby with relatives in Värmland to spare her family from gossip."

"You didn't mention that."

"We hadn't gotten to that point of the story. By the way, have *you* seen a real clarinet?"

Steffi nods. "Sure, we have one at school."

"Then you probably can't imagine how things were back then. I was seventeen and I never had. And to have one in school in those days . . . that would have been . . ."

Alvar begins to laugh instead of finishing his sentence. "Thank God times change! Your school can't be . . . you do go to school, don't you?"

Steffi nods. It's almost lunchtime. By now sex health class is over and any survivors had probably all gotten a condom to take home and study.

"We don't start until twelve thirty today," she lies.

At school, nobody had gotten any condoms. They seemed to have been divided into a boys' group and a girls' group. Next week they were supposed to discuss what is important in a good boyfriend or girlfriend. Steffi decides she'll skip that day, too.

After math class, she hurries into the music room.

Jake, her music teacher, often stays behind after school so that anyone who wants to can come in and try out an instrument. He's just putting away some percussion instruments.

"Can you hand me the maracas?" he asks Steffi.

She hands him both the maracas and the guiro.

Then she asks about the clarinet. Jake looks confused at first, but then takes it from the cupboard and says he can give her five minutes to look it over. *You take it up so well, your little clarinarinet.* Povel Ramel's voice in her head.

The clarinet is well worn and certainly had been used by kids to hit other kids on the head. How else could it have gotten so wrecked, with gaps where there should be connections? Still, she can imagine how it must have looked to a young boy traveling on a train in the forties.

She tries to blow it, but no sound comes out. Jake tells her to wet the mouthpiece first, then tense her lips and blow harder. She gets a sound. Yes! Not exactly Arne Domnérus, but it is a sound. *A wail between melodies,* she thinks. She tries pressing some of the pads on the keys. It sounds like a sick animal.

Jake is standing there, keys in hand. "Would you like to take it home?"

"May I?"

"Sure. Give me a security deposit but don't spread it around that I let you. OK?"

He winks at her. He lets her take instruments home now and again.

---

All the way home, she keeps her fingers crossed that nobody from school will see her with the clarinet. It would be hard to explain to Jake if it got broken, and she'd never be able to borrow an instrument again.

As she passes by the retirement home, she wonders if she should stop in and show it to Alvar. Then she reconsiders. It would be better if she learned to play something on it first.

# – CHAPTER 5 –

Steffi knows two things about the way she looks. She knows she's ugly and she knows she's pretty. The first is the truth agreed upon by everyone in school, and therefore everyone in the rest of the world. The second is the truth at Herrvägen Road, number 21, with the exception of a separate zone consisting of Julia's room. Julia thinks that Steffi is hopeless. Mamma thinks her "pretty just as you are" and Pappa calls her *linda,* which is Spanish for *beautiful,* not a Swedish girl's name. Edvin thinks she looks like a Muppet. Steffi has no idea at all. She finds her face a painting she's looked at for far too long. It's like a word repeated so often it's lost its meaning. Sometimes she's not even sure her face is really hers. "I'm just myself and me alone," she tells the face in the mirror and watches as the lips move. Since she's considered ugly in school, these words don't sound the way they did on a train to Stockholm in the forties. With one minute left of lunch break, she sneaks out of the bathroom to her class Civics and Society.

Bengt *assumes* they've all chosen the topic for their special project. He stares straight at each student in the room as he says this, and immediately, heads are put together to agree on some excuse for why their group doesn't have one yet. *Excuses, excuses,* Steffi jots on her piece of paper, and tries to find something that rhymes. *Induces, recluses, effuses.*

"Well," Bengt continues in his most tired tones, "you can't choose one on today's fashions. That's not a field of study."

"How do you know?" Sanja asks.

"Morgan and Linus, why don't you have a subject?"

"The thing is, we couldn't agree on math or physics. And Morgan's brother was going to be on TV," Linus explains.

*All these excuses,* Steffi writes. She hears music in her head. The same bass walking line as in the song "Klarinarrinetten," but with a different melody:

*Everything they taught you about duty*
*You forget the moment you see beauty.*

"What about you, Steffi?"

Steffi gasps and hides the piece of paper under her palm.

"I don't know," she says. She doesn't want anyone to think the lyrics she's just written are about her. "I can't think of anything."

Bengt turns and walks to his lectern.

"Anyone without a topic in either the field of social studies or science will choose from a list I have here. On Thursday, you will hand me your project thesis and your outlines. Do you remember what a thesis is?"

Steffi is given a choice between global warming, Sweden during the Second World War, and primates. Her choice is easy. Since they already call her slut, dyke, disgusting, there's no way she's going to add monkey to that list. She puts her name next to Sweden in the Second World War. She thinks about the last line of lyrics rounding out the verse:

*All these excuses you give*
*You're forgetting how to live.*

Drums sound a whirl in her head. She knows the refrain will come to her easily now.

She decides to show her lyrics to her bass teacher. Torkel is not really a bass teacher. He has a double bass that cost nine thousand Swedish crowns and a wife who keeps him in Björke against his will. After a lesson with him, Steffi knows more than anyone needs to know about his brown garden furniture, his unusual vision problems, and his aversion to green grapes, but not much more about playing the bass.

Torkel purses his lips as he reads her lyrics and he nods. "Excuses drive me crazy, too. Let's see . . . last week you were supposed to practice page thirty-four."

"As well as practice walking bass lines."

"Yes, sure, but right now we need to concentrate on your lesson. I don't imagine you of all people want to start making excuses, right?"

He winks at her, as if they shared an understanding of her lyrics. Steffi folds up the sheet of paper and opens her exercise book to page thirty-four.

By the time they've finished the lesson, there's only five more minutes to practice a walking bass line. She shows Torkel the transition from B to E that she's discovered, but he glances up at the clock and just says, "That's good."

She knows what he really means by that. She's not stupid. Read music or die.

---

These days, Alvar watches the pedestrian path outside his window more often than he used to. He finds he's somehow turned into one of the other pitiful old folks in this building whose happiest moments of the day come when they see a cat walking by or a child on a scooter. The main difference is that he knows exactly who he's looking for. The other day Steffi had come walking by with a clarinet case sticking out of the top of her backpack. For some reason, this made him extremely happy. Today Steffi had the case for her bass guitar strapped to her back.

Alvar opens his window slightly and turns up the music. Today he's not playing Povel Ramel, but he still thinks he can catch the girl's attention. He's pleased when Steffi stops abruptly in the middle of the path and turns her face toward him. He waves enthusiastically.

She stomps into his room like a near sighted buffalo, a bundle of teenager with bangs, but he can tell she feels more at home in his place than many other visitors. Herrera is a Spanish name, and she's probably South American, which would explain her black hair and eyes. She wriggles off the instrument straps and looks at him.

"Hi."

"I see you've brought some accompaniment."

She smiles slightly and gestures toward it. "My bass guitar."

He doesn't say anything and eventually she explains.

"I want to practice walking bass lines, but my teacher doesn't like them."

Alvar thinks that over and finds himself indignant.

"Nothing has changed in seventy years! So what does he want you to do instead of walking bass lines?"

"Practice. Learn how to read music."

An echo of her sullen voice hangs in the room. Alvar lifts an eyebrow.

"So?"

"So what?"

He nods toward the bass guitar in its case. "Well, then?"

It turns out that playing walking bass lines for Alvar is totally different than playing them for Torkel. Alvar grins with his clownish mouth and beats a rhythm with his forefinger against the arm of his chair.

"Then I wanted to go from E to A, and it just sounded stupid," she tells him, finding encouragement in the old man's rhythmically nodding head.

She shows him what she's tried and he pulls in his lower lip while he thinks. Then he suggests she go up the scale instead of down.

"You don't have to be afraid of going back and forth," he says, moving his hands as if he were the one fingering the guitar.

Steffi tries his suggestion. Much better. She is hit with an idea and tries it out, with the next-to-last note on B, and waits for Alvar's reaction.

"Oh yeah, you're swinging now. Try it again from the top."

"From the top?"

"From the beginning. When you play in a band, you say 'from the top.'"

Steffi listens to the beat he gives for a second and then starts from the beginning, from the top, and Alvar increases the tempo the second time around. It's a quick walking bass line that could fit into any jazz piece, though not an amplified one, since it could be heard only if the rest of the band were silent.

"You've got a bit," Alvar says.

"You mean a song?"

"The guys in the studio called it a 'bit.'" Alvar grins. There's a break in his warm Värmland dialect. "At first, it used to be they said a lot of things I didn't catch. It started with the man on the train calling me a jazz cat."

It started when the man on the train, smiling with practiced nonchalance, wearing a hat that shadowed his face just like a film star, called him a *jazz cat*.

During the rest of the trip to Stockholm, Alvar's vocabulary about swing music was so stuffed with new words he started having trouble remembering them all. The man with the clarinet seemed to be amused by his intensity, and he began to look at Alvar with deepening interest.

"So, hey, where're you going to crash? I'm sure you don't have enough cash to stay at a hotel."

Alvar pretended to think about that while he tried to figure out what *crash* meant here. It seemed logical enough, though the man started to smile at him and the blond girl had fastened admiring eyes on the clarinetist.

"*Cash*. That means money, you see. Better pick that word up before you roll into the big city. Somebody might ask you to loan him some cash, and you'll know enough to say 'not a chance.'"

"Not a chance," Alvar repeated.

The girl giggled. She'd spent a lot of time giggling on this train trip.

"Of course he will be staying with his aunt," the same old woman exclaimed. "And you should be ashamed of trying to get a decent young man involved in your . . . business."

The man lifted his eyebrows at her angry face. "What? There's nothing immoral with a bit of va-va-va-*voom*."

He sang the last bit like Alice Babs, with a wink to the girl. "And as far as my . . . ahem . . . business goes? I don't stick my nose into your business, so why do you care about mine? At least

I'm not shooting at an innocent Norwegian when I play my music."

Alvar took in a quick breath. His mother had always said you never know, you *never* know, who was listening when you talked about the war. Father never even called it the war, just *the unhappy events*. And here was this man with his clarinet who'd just suggested a fellow passenger sided with the Germans. In Sweden, now, both being a friend of the Germans or an enemy of the Germans could get you into trouble, depending on who was listening. Alvar was not the only one in the compartment who shifted uneasily in his seat.

The clarinetist continued without missing a beat. "In addition, I have not invited young Alvar here to join my band, or even to help out as a roadie. Just to get some insight into swing. If he wants more of that, he has to ask me himself."

Alvar's heart skipped. All he had to do now was ask! He braced himself against the unkind stares of the probably German-friendly passengers as well as the angry woman whose iron grip still held the young woman's shoulder. But how could he do it without looking ridiculous?

The train car began to creak and groan, slowing, as telephone wires appeared alongside the tracks. The passengers around him began to collect their belongings and their luggage. The clarinetist put on his overcoat and picked up his case without even glancing at Alvar. The moment had passed. The train groaned and shuddered to a stop.

A porter opened the door and the smells of Stockholm hit them all: oil and exhaust, horse manure, people, machines—along with the deafening sounds. The never-ending roar of motors, the screeching trains, people talking, calls of baggage handlers and of those asking for assistance, people saying goodbye or calling out a happy greeting to an arrival. Somewhere in this mass of humanity, his great-aunt Hilda waited and had to be found, but how he would recognize her was another question entirely.

The clarinet player was stepping down off the train, about to disappear with his precious swing music forever. Alvar grabbed up his belongings as fast as he could and stumbled off the train through the crowd until he caught sight of him. He rushed over to put a hand on his shoulder—and then did not know what to say. The man turned to look at him with that familiar raised eyebrow.

"And?"

"Umm . . . Umm . . ."

Alvar swallowed and blushed, as badly as if he were trying to talk to a girl. All the words he'd tried to formulate vanished into thin air. The man laughed.

"We rehearse at 140 Åsö Street. Do you think you can run errands and lift speakers?"

Alvar nodded.

"Well, then." The clarinet player reached out and heartily shook Alvar's hand. "I'm Erling."

Alvar could not hide his joy. His first day in Stockholm and Alvar was already a part of the swing music scene. Erling winked at him.

"But we don't have cash to spare, so you'll need to get your dough elsewhere."

# – CHAPTER 6 –

Why were you so eager to get into swing?" Steffi asks.

"Well, you see . . . as you know, they had *Gramophone Hour* on the radio—no, no, of course you don't know that. But they did. One hour of music every day, and everyone listened to that hour. Families would sit around their enormous radio sets to drink in the music they played."

"And it was all jazz."

Alvar laughs. "Some of it was jazz, but they had a great deal of classical music, too, not to mention accordion music! You'd have to suffer through Beethoven and Swedish dance music, like the schottische or the hambo, before you heard the opening notes of jitterbug. Then the grown-ups would sigh in dismay." Alvar sighs heavily to demonstrate how the adults had done it.

Steffi smiles at the wrinkled old man who is sitting in a swivel chair in a retirement home and talking about grown-ups.

"But why are *you* so interested in jazz music?" Alvar asks.

"I like Povel Ramel more than anyone else."

"Yes, he was as good as any of them."

"He died before I knew anything about him."

"Really?"

"I was seven and heard he'd died when my mother put on one of his records in his honor. And, well . . ."

"You were transfixed by jazz." Alvar couldn't help smiling.

"I liked his song about the coconut. But nowadays I like his songs 'Grass Widower Blues' and 'The Mischievous Trumpet' best." Steffi thinks for a minute. "My dad doesn't get it. He likes rock more than anything. Mamma gave me Povel's record as long as I only played it in my room. That was just fine. Later, they gave me a CD player of my own."

"I see," Alvar says, glancing at his gramophone in the corner of the room. "In my day, a person could call himself lucky if he had his own gramophone."

Steffi gets up and walks over to the gramophone. She thinks it looks really funny—just a big box with a large horn attached. She gently touches its shining surface and looks into the horn. It's dusty.

"So this is a gramophone?"

"Yes, indeed, one of the best. I didn't get it until later. In Björke, my family didn't own a gramophone. We just listened to the radio. And at my aunt Hilda's house, there seemed to be nothing but lace doilies everywhere."

At Aunt Hilda's house, there were lace doilies everywhere. Tiny, crocheted doilies greeted him the moment she opened the door to his new home. She hadn't been hard to find while he quietly repeated 140 Åsö Street to himself so as not to forget the address where the jazz band rehearsed. He found his aunt at the train station exit where she'd told him to meet her. Aunt Hilda was seventy-four years old. Walking with her from the station to her place took much longer than if he'd just tried to find it on his own. And once they'd arrived, all the lace doilies caught his eye. They had been placed on every empty flat surface—and not just one, but four, five, six of them. He looked around to realize there was no radio. He kept repeating 140 Åsö Street to himself. He wouldn't forgive himself if he forgot it.

"Aunt Hilda, do you know how to get to Åsö Street?"

Aunt Hilda stared at him as if he'd gotten the plague. Or was German.

"I'm sure you can't have any business there, my boy," she said firmly.

Since she was so adamant, Alvar decided to drop the subject. He would find his way there on his own. Instead he sat on the chair she indicated, declining her coffee substitute with the excuse that it made him nervous.

"But you do have a ration card for real coffee?"

"Pappa sent one for you, Aunt Hilda."

At this, Aunt Hilda's face lit up. The old woman's chair felt so much more comfortable to him when she smiled. "I'm glad to have you here, my boy. You seem to be a young man with a bit more common sense than most."

Alvar found it difficult to reply. He clasped his hands together to keep from drumming on the table.

"I hope I do, Aunt Hilda."

He was given an old-fashioned kitchen bench with a lid that lifted up to reveal a bed to sleep on. Aunt Hilda took away half a dozen doilies from the top of the lid and Alvar opened it. Aunt Hilda handed him bedclothes and he made up the bed. She realized now how tall a young man he was, but there was nothing to be done about a bench designed for short female kitchen help. He would have to make do.

"You could sleep with your knees up," Aunt Hilda said. "And as soon as you find work, I expect you to help with the rent."

Alvar reassured her, and she finally left him alone in the kitchen. The room fell silent. Still, nighttime was not as quiet as back home in Björke. The Stockholm night in this building was a cacophony of sound: creaking beds, crying children, footsteps running up and down the stairs, people coming home late from bars, garbagemen getting up early to go to work.

Alvar snuggled as deep into the blanket as he could with his knees bent. Only this morning he had woken up a child in his parents' home and tonight he was falling asleep as a young man in the big city, already an experienced train traveler, basically already a Stockholmer.

The thought made his heart swell and kept him from sleeping. *Jazz cat, place to crash, cash, dough* . . . all by itself his toe started to drum on the wooden side of the bed. The sounds outside had their own rhythm. It sounded like jazz.

When Steffi arrives home, everyone else has already eaten. She finds them all in front of the TV. Pappa wonders where she's been and she says she was visiting a friend.

Julia looks at her in disbelief. "No, you didn't."

"Yes, I did! What do you know?"

"Nothing and I don't care. Except I know you're lying!"

Mamma sighs. "Stop it. Steffi, there's food in the kitchen you can heat up. Julia, don't you have some laundry you need to fold?"

There's a celebrity dance competition on TV. Edvin is imitating them. He's stomping around, jerking up his knees and flailing his arms over his head. Steffi goes on into the kitchen and finds some spaghetti and meatballs to heat up.

Julia creeps in behind her like a shadow. "Why are you lying?"

"I *was* at a friend's house. I told you."

"All right, let's say you were. What's her name?"

Steffi turns her back on her sister and stares at the meat sauce bubbling in the microwave.

"Oh, it's a *he*!" Julia exclaims.

Steffi doesn't say anything, but Julia lets loose a high-pitched squeal. "A boy! I knew it! Or, actually, I *didn't*!"

Steffi takes her food out of the microwave and pours a glass of milk.

"All right," Julia says. "So you won't say. But we'll find out. We always find out. I bet it's some music nerd at school, right?"

Steffi decides that the warmed-over spaghetti and meatballs taste pretty good, even if the sauce has leaked onto the plate. Björke lies silent and deserted outside their kitchen window. Somewhere else, someone must be starting to play jazz. Someone in Stockholm. Maybe even someone a little closer to home, Karlstad maybe.

"You *know* I'll find out," Julia says, and she bounces out of the kitchen.

Mamma, Pappa, and Edvin are still in the living room in front of the TV. A member of the jury discusses the performance with a dance couple. A blond woman is smiling from ear to ear. Her partner is a soccer player Steffi recognizes.

"What impresses me is that you actually paused in the middle of a tango. Not everybody dares to stand still like that."

Edvin stands up on the sofa, his arms held stiffly to his sides. "Look at me! Look how still I can stand!"

Steffi goes past them into her room. She puts on the oldest Povel Ramel song she has. It's from 1942, the same year that Alvar traveled to Stockholm. Perhaps this very song had been played during *Gramophone Hour.* It's mostly a piano accompanying Povel's singing, but there's a clarinet near the end, and she can hear the bass walk in her head. She thinks about taking out her bass guitar but decides not to. Alvar didn't have any instrument to play when he lay in bed that first night in Stockholm and felt jazz move through his whole body. She lies down on her bed. Sometimes you just need to *feel* how much you really want to play something.

# – CHAPTER 7 –

Class 9B's homeroom teacher, Semlan, is standing in front of the class trying to explain the value of choosing the right *gymnasium* for their upper-level studies. Half of the class had already decided to attend a Karlstad vocational high school to learn vehicle technology, forestry, or day care. They spend the time in a not very quiet discussion of an Internet incident involving nude pictures and someone's older brother. The others are paying more than normal attention to Semlan, because their parents told them this was an important decision.

Steffi isn't like the rest of them, though. That becomes clear as Semlan is showing the class where to click on their computer screens to find a list of upper-level schools with nationwide acceptance plans.

"Do you know what this means?" she asks, and then answers her own question. "These schools will take students from throughout Sweden. You can apply to Gothenburg, Umeå, Stockholm. . . ."

Steffi realizes this is her way out, and so her choice of

*gymnasium* is more important than to most of the kids in class 9B. She feels the rush of blood to her head as she clicks on the site. Everyone else is clicking, too, even the ones who have already chosen their schools.

She clicks *Nationwide Acceptance.* Then *Liberal Arts.* In Stockholm, there are fourteen *gymnasier,* upper-level high schools, with nationwide acceptance that take music students. Fourteen! In Björke, there's just a single grocery and a hot dog stand.

Many of these schools have their own Web pages. Steffi clicks on one after another and opens many windows. One of the schools has mixed social sciences and the arts. It wants to form a *creative and positive climate.* Another school is called *the music gymnasium.* It's for students who want to become professional musicians. All of the pupils in their promotional photos look like kids who would be immediately bullied by Karro and Sonja. Steffi decides right away that this is where she wants to go. Stockholm is drawing her to it like the tuning peg pulls on its string, the way it pulled Alvar seventy years ago.

"I'm going to go to Stockholm," Steffi informs Alvar.

It's an hour later and they're listening to "Wonderful Doesn't Last." Alvar's record has only two songs, one on each side. Once the song is over, they play it from the beginning again. The record crackles like an old fire.

"So, when are you leaving?"

"I mean I *will* go to Stockholm. I want to study at the music school there."

"So in the bloom of your youth, you plan to move to Stockholm."

"Yep, in the middle of my youth."

Alvar nods as he considers this information. "Then you're going to go to Åsö Street."

"Like you did."

"Like I did, even though Aunt Hilda had strictly forbidden it."

Even though Aunt Hilda had strictly forbidden it, Alvar decided that the first thing he wanted to do was find 140 Åsö Street. Despite the ache in his legs from being curled up all night, it was the first thought he had the moment he opened his eyes on his first morning in Stockholm.

Aunt Hilda had already made him some porridge but told him not to get used to being pampered. She was just showing him the way she wanted it done so he'd know how to, in case he needed to make it for her someday. Alvar already realized how Aunt Hilda had imagined his days in Stockholm, but he decided not to protest.

"As I mentioned, I have my father's coffee ration coupons from Björke. Do you think they're valid here in Stockholm?"

He could almost picture the saliva collect in the old woman's mouth. She seemed to chew the air as she handled the ration coupons.

"Well, these come from the state and not the province of Värmland. Take them and go left once you leave the building. Walk past the first large gray building and you will arrive at Sankt Erik Street, where there is a grocer. If they don't take the coupons right away, just tell them your aunt Hilda sent you."

"Should I look for work right away, too?"

Aunt Hilda seemed to already taste real coffee, weighing the price of coffee against the amount of money she had. She nodded sternly. "Yes, I believe that would be best."

"I'll ask at all the shops. Maybe they need an errand boy. If one says no, I'll just go to the next."

"Make sure you stay on the north side of Stockholm, Vasastan or Östermalm."

Aunt Hilda then gave a short lecture on the loose morals, low education levels, and lack of culture south of the Old City in Södermalm. *Södermalm,* Alvar noted silently as he picked up his cap and scarf. Aunt Hilda inspected him before he left.

"Keep to the shops and make sure you pronounce everything properly and say the vowels like your teachers taught in school. You have to speak like people here in the capital if you want people to understand you. Be home in time for dinner and don't forget the coffee."

The grocer had named his shop after himself. *Åkesson's Grocery.*

Alvar was greeted by Åkesson himself, who studied Alvar's coffee coupons and ration card. "Björke is not exactly next door."

"It's in Värmland."

"Yes, I can tell by your accent. So they've run out of coffee in Värmland?"

Alvar was trying to tell if the man was joking or not. The grocer's gruff expression didn't change.

"No . . . no . . . you see, I just moved to Stockholm, so I brought the coupons with me."

He did his best to pronounce each word like a radio announcer but wasn't completely successful.

Åkesson smiled slightly and shook his head. "Just pulling your leg, my boy. Do you have a name?"

"Alvar Svensson."

"Of course, of course. Young Mr. Svensson, first name Alvar, you must be over twenty-one, I assume, and have your own ration card?"

"I'm also supposed to send greetings from my aunt, the widow Hilda on Torsgatan."

Åkesson now smiled widely for the first time and slipped one of the coupons into his box beneath the counter. "Give her my best, will you?" he said, handing Alvar the valuable package of 250 grams of coffee.

Alvar sighed in relief. "And there's one more thing."

"We don't have any chocolate."

"No, no, not that. I was just wondering if you . . . sir . . . need an errand boy."

"And you're putting yourself up for the job, are you?"

Alvar straightened to his full height. "Why not?"

"As far as I can tell, you've just gotten off the train from the middle of nowhere in Värmland. How could you be an errand boy if you don't know the city?"

"I learn fast."

A small bell jingled behind Alvar, and another customer walked in. Soon there'd be more and Åkesson would want him to move along.

"Think of one errand," Alvar said. "Just one. I'll show you how fast I can be. I'll check back tomorrow morning."

Åkesson laughed. "That's the spirit! Until tomorrow, then."

Alvar and Åkesson shook hands. Alvar hoped his handshake showed convincing strength.

"Until tomorrow. I won't disappoint you!"

Asking Åkesson where he could find 140 Åsö Street was out of the question. Instead, Alvar waved down the first pedestrian he saw on the street, a woman, who shook her head and kept walking as fast as she could. A few other people also ignored him until he met a young man, who seemed just a little younger than he was, who stopped his bike.

"Åsö Street? That's over in Söder. You'll have a long walk."

"You mean Södermalm?"

"You know any other Söder?" The boy gave him a long, somewhat confused, look before he jumped back on his bike and pedaled off.

All the boys seemed to have bikes like his, sturdy with large baskets attached to the handlebars. The longer Alvar walked through the enormous city, the more he began to understand what everyone needed the bikes for. After a while, he noticed a change in his surroundings. The buildings stood closer together and the people wore less expensive clothes. Only the wooden sidewalks had not changed. He stopped another errand boy—there were more of them here. The boy jeered when Alvar asked if he'd reached Södermalm.

"Does this look like Söder to you?"

"I wouldn't know. I just got here yesterday."

The boy put his hand behind his ear. "You said you were born yesterday?"

Alvar felt his spirits sink. He'd had no idea that people in Stockholm would be this unfriendly; he'd just assumed people said that about the city. He rubbed his fist across his forehead and wondered just how long his walk would be.

"Oh, just hop on," the boy said. "I'll take you part of the way. Then you won't keep looking like a lost sheep." He winked. Alvar felt his heart warm from the offer. Not everybody in Stockholm was mean. As he got up on the platform, the bike almost fell over from his weight. They both laughed at his further attempts.

"You better pedal and let me sit," the boy decided. "I'm

smaller. But make sure nothing happens to the bike, or you'll owe me a hundred fifty in cash."

Alvar was pretty sure the boy was talking about money. "You mean dough?"

The boy laughed out loud. He tried to imitate Alvar's Värmland pronunciation. "You're a good one, aren't you? Start pedaling and I'll tell you when to turn."

Riding a bike in the middle of Stockholm was really different from riding a bike in Björke. Alvar had thought all the straight streets and smooth pavements would make it easier, but he found he had to zigzag around huge carts of wood, other errand boys on bikes zooming along at full speed, not to mention being alert for the sound of vehicles coming out of side streets.

"There were more cars before the war," the boy yelled back to him from his seat on the platform. "Now they can't even buy wood gas. To the left! Now to the right!" Then he yelled, "STOP!"

Alvar had to brake to avoid crashing into a streetcar. They started over a bridge.

"We're in the Old Town now," the boy informed him. Then suddenly he leaped off the package holder so quickly that Alvar almost fell over.

"Here's my stop. Just keep walking along that way for a bit."

The boy took the handlebars and Alvar held out his hand.

"Thank you so much."

The boy grinned as he shook hands, as if there was something funny about Alvar's formality. Alvar realized that all he needed to say next time was *thanks*.

As he was crossing the bridge from the Old Town to Södermalm, Alvar felt it. The sun shone brightly on him and on the bridges all around, the streetlights, the melting snow, and he was now a part of it, part of the capital city. Nobody could tell, just by looking, that he'd arrived from the countryside yesterday. He stopped and waited casually for the streetcar to pass by, as if he'd been doing it all his life, even though the streetcar still scared him a bit. Then he entered Södermalm.

To his left was the water. Right in front of him was a huge contraption, an elevator? To his right, streetcars ran in both directions. He never imagined there could be so many. All the pedestrians walked among the tracks without a trace of fear. Alvar could not see what Aunt Hilda had been so afraid of, but then she was an old lady.

An unbelievably beautiful girl in a cape and hat walked past. Alvar stared at her, but could not say a word. Instead, in what had almost become routine, he stopped another errand boy, who pointed him in the right direction. Barely twenty minutes later, he was standing on Åsö Street.

# – CHAPTER 8 –

The buildings on Åsö Street were wonders of stone. People sure liked stone in Stockholm. But the street lacked both the detailed lion heads and extravagant entrances Alvar had seen on Tor Street and in the Old Town. As if to compensate for the lack of decoration in the architecture, the walls gave off the smell of beer, which, for many of the district's inhabitants, was very pleasant.

After hearing Aunt Hilda's condemnation of the people of Söder, Alvar was expecting to see ragged people and dirty beggar children, but the people he saw were surprisingly well dressed. Most people in Stockholm were well dressed, he realized. He was the only person wearing a knitted cap. Everyone else had hats that could hardly warm their ears. In the Old Town, he'd seen ladies with muffs.

Alvar thought about all this as he made his way to 140 Åsö Street, not an easy task, since not all of the buildings were numbered. When he found the right building, he realized that Erling the clarinet player had given him only an address. Not a time. Not his last name. In Björke that would have been good enough, but in Stockholm the buildings were fortresses. Alvar searched from window to window in the impenetrable stone wall above his head. When a loud voice called from the doorway, he jumped.

"Whaddaya want?"

A man, about fifty, with a fleshy lower lip so big Alvar couldn't help staring, even though he knew it was not polite.

"I . . . ," he stammered. He forced his eyes up from the man's lip to his eyes. "I . . . am looking for Mr. . . . Erling, who plays clarinet."

The man sucked in half his lower lip as he considered Alvar's statement.

"Mr. Erling," he said with irony. "So you're one of *them.*"

One of the musicians in Stockholm. Yes, he could say wholeheartedly that he was one of the jazz musicians in Stockholm.

"That's right."

The man took a step toward Alvar, who instinctively backed up.

"I don't know what devilish amusement you're looking for, or what small town you've crawled out of, but if you think I don't recognize those noisemakers from far off, you're dumber than you look. Now get lost!"

Alvar lost heart. He feared he might lose jazz music forever here in the big city. His eyes slid back to the man's monstrous lip in spite of himself. Then, in the middle of this tense situation, an angelic voice broke in.

"Now, Andersson!"

Right before Alvar's eyes a fascinating transformation took place. The man's lip changed from a piece of hanging flesh to a heartfelt smile.

"Oh, hello, miss!" His voice had a warmth that excluded the single young man from Värmland.

Alvar felt himself blushing even before he turned around.

The girl looked older than the sound of her voice. Twenty-one, maybe even twenty-five. Hard to tell, the voice sounded youthful, but her clothes were those of a young woman, a lady. Her eyes were gray. Alvar hadn't ever realized it before, but his favorite eye color in a young lady was definitely gray. He found that his favorite color in a young lady's hair was auburn, and his favorite nose was a button with a touch of red from the cold air. Alvar couldn't get a word out, but luckily he didn't need to.

"This snip of a boy says he's with the band."

The young lady looked Alvar up and down while his heart thumped ever faster. Single girls had never looked at him like that, and certainly no city girl with gray eyes and a real hat.

She smiled. "Yes, he is," she said, and she took his arm.

She took his arm! His own arm! It felt warm beneath hers, and she'd just saved him from Flabby Lip of Söder. He was just seventeen, perhaps even naïve, but he knew that his violently beating heart would belong to her for all time. Whatever her name was.

She led him down the basement stairs and through an iron door. Once his eyes had adjusted, he found paradise within.

"What was it?"

"What was what?"

"Paradise. What made that room paradise? You said paradise was behind the iron door and then you stopped talking."

"I found myself there, once again, just for a moment."

"So tell me!"

"It was the band. I mean, no players yet, because we were the first ones to show up, Anita and I."

"I *knew* it was going to be Anita!"

Alvar gives her a broad smile, his eyes turning as dreamy as a cherub's on a bookmark.

"Who else was it going to be?"

"So, what did it look like? Describe paradise!"

"There was a trombone. An upright bass. A piano and a few chairs. All in a rather cramped and chilly basement space."

Steffi could see it in her imagination. A room resembling the school's music room, but without the chill, of course. Yes, she could understand the music room as a warmer kind of paradise, at least when no other kids are there. The music had ended, so Steffi decides to play "What Wonderful Feels Like" again.

"So was that where Povel Ramel rehearsed?"

Alvar takes his thoughts away from paradise and focuses on Steffi.

"On Åsö Street? No, no, no, not there. He was already quite famous by then. This band was not Povel Ramel's band."

"But you told me Anita was there when Povel recorded?"

"Yes, but that was later."

"Did you meet him then?"

Alvar gets up from the plaid armchair. "Nothing against Povel Ramel, but he comes into the story later. Let me play something for you. . . ."

The song cuts off as Alvar gently lifts the needle from the disc. He holds the record by its edges, sliding it into its cardboard sleeve. He takes out another record from a different cardboard sleeve and puts it on the gramophone.

First there's just crackling and then the woodwinds kick in. Alvar's fingers begin to tap on the table and his thin body sways in time as the clarinet rises and falls in ever-wilder leaps. Steffi closes her eyes. Sitting next to seventeen-year-old Alvar and listening to an untamed clarinet on the radio while war rumbled through Europe and the cars in Stockholm had to use *wood gas,* whatever that was.

"Gösta Törner's Orchestra," Alvar says. Steffi opens her eyes. "Listen carefully!"

From the clarinet solo, the music merges into a jazz arrangement that in turn is broken, almost attacked, by a different, deeper solo instrument.

"It's like society," Steffi says.

"Like society?"

"Think about it. We do stuff together, like class or work, but it'll never amount to much unless we get to do our own solos, too. Or maybe I should say, it won't be anything special."

Alvar smiles and seems about to laugh. "Anita would have liked you."

"It's not going to amount to much unless we get to do our own solos," Steffi repeats, just to taste the sound of her sentence once more.

"You know, that's not a bad comparison. That's how it was. And that's why people liked jazz so much."

"Yeah," Steffi says as she keeps time to the music with her bass-player fingers.

The saxophone glides along in the middle of its solo. It's sighing. She wonders if she could do the same thing with a clarinet. If she ever learns how to play clarinet.

Once Steffi is back in her room, she realizes she can make all kinds of sounds with a clarinet. She just never thought about it before. Now she keeps time with her foot and listens to the rest of the band in her head as she whines, peeps, gasps with the clarinet and smiles each time she discovers something new so that air puffs from the sides of her mouth. She's still having trouble figuring out the notes, but she's starting to find them more easily.

The door is ripped open and Julia is staring at her. "What the hell, Steffi?"

"What's wrong?"

Julia rolls her eyes, tosses her hair back, and sighs as loud as she can as some kind of protest. Steffi watches her.

"What do you think you're *doing*! You sound like you're murdering animals in here!"

"I have to practice!"

"Practice? For what?" Julia furrows her brows and glares at her. She always has a great store of expressions to draw from.

"To get better!"

"OK, you're not getting better. Pappa is covering his ears back in the kitchen."

"No, he's not!"

Although Steffi is pretty sure nobody's holding their ears in pain back in the kitchen, she'd lost the thread of enthusiasm once Julia had left her room. It wasn't just Julia's declaration that Steffi would never be better. Julia doesn't know anything about music. She thinks Rihanna is the height of musical talent and she wouldn't even get it if Lucky Millinder stood in front of her in person with his entire band. Julia wouldn't hesitate to storm into Lucky Millinder's rehearsal hall and demand to know if he's murdering animals.

But Lucky would never feel any doubt and sadness inside while Julia glowered at him like that, saying he'd never be better. He wouldn't give a damn about what she thought.

After taking a few deep breaths, Steffi begins to feel like Lucky. If this was what was going to happen each time she tried out a new sound, she'd just have to find her own space to rehearse. She feels it all the way to her stomach—it feels like a basement stairway at 140 Åsö Street. She moves her fingers along all the silver pads of the clarinet, looking at her electric bass leaning against her blue desk, and then she stretches her neck so she can meet her own gaze in the mirror. She is Steffi and she needs a paradise.

# – CHAPTER 9 –

As if someone had heard Steffi's prayer for a paradise, Karro is absent the next day. Sanja says, in a loud voice so everyone can hear, that Karro has the stomach flu, and she adds that Karro probably caught it from Steffi's dandruff. Some of the kids giggle and Sanja smiles, pleased, but it seems more routine than anything else, just to keep the system in place, lacking the malevolence of what Karro would say.

It'll be an easy day. Steffi does her math problems. She eats potatoes and a beef patty just like everyone else. She almost feels like one of them.

During music class, two boys mumble their way through their reports on Johann Sebastian Bach and Claude Debussy. When Linus falls asleep, the rest of class 9B is roused to a pitch of cheerfulness that they manage, with some effort, to keep up for the rest of the period. Then school is out. The music room turns quiet as all the pushing, shoving, teasing, and giggling ebbs off into the hallway.

Jake looks at Steffi. "Do you want something?"

"Can I stay here for a while?"

"Stay here?"

"Just until you're ready to leave. I want to practice the bass."

Jake thinks that over and then says, "I'll lock you in. I'll be back in an hour. But you're responsible for everything in here."

As he walks past, he winks and whispers he's really not supposed to do this. She doesn't know what to reply, so she just plugs in her bass guitar and tries to look as grateful as possible.

A piano, a box of tambourines, and three guitars on the walls. The strong lights make the room look like a classroom, but it is not. On a whim, she turns off the lights. The instruments become shadows and a streetlamp outside turns into a soft spotlight. The bass makes the floor vibrate—Jake's amplifier is seven times more powerful than hers. She decides to play a walking bass line. She doesn't have Povel Ramel's music with her, so she follows it in her head. Then she tries a new line. From A to D. To E. Back to D. She hums along, even though it doesn't sound in tune. She keeps time with her foot and suddenly knows she's playing the blues. Steffi, a blues musician standing in the dark. She plays A—D—E—D and finds new ways to scale between them. She stops for syncopation, slides up to the highest A and then back down. A melody starts to emerge from all the darkness, and she puts down the bass and pulls the clarinet from her backpack. She almost gets the melody, even though it doesn't sound all that good.

She's about to return to bass playing when she hears Jake's key in the door. He laughs when he turns on the light and sees her standing there in the bright light.

"Still here, I see."

"I just wanted it dark."

"All right."

Her awkward words hang in the air. Steffi gestures vaguely toward the clarinet.

"Can I borrow it again?"

"You're teaching yourself to play it?"

"Yeah, kind of."

"You can keep it until May. Then I need it back for the eighth graders."

*Until May! That's forever!*

"Thanks!"

There's no good way to describe her feelings to Alvar. He's sitting in his armchair and is waving his fingers as he always does when he listens to Totty Wallén. His head has tremors like old people's bodies sometimes do, but if you look closely, you can see he's nodding in time to the music. Steffi is holding on to the feeling of playing her bass in the dark, but there really is no way to explain it. Unless Alvar had already felt it himself.

"Have you ever played in the dark?"

Alvar leans forward, as if this question is of the utmost importance. He rubs his chin.

"You know, now that you're asking, I don't know if I've ever played in the light."

He smiles, as if surprised at his own answer, and she has to smile back.

"It's better in the dark," she says.

"Your senses become sharper," Alvar says. "And things that seem clear in the daylight become . . ."

His voice disappears down into the carpet, but she knows exactly what he means.

". . . invisible," she says. "They might as well not even be there."

"Miss Steffi Herrera," Alvar says. He slowly gets out of his armchair to change the record. "Sometimes you hit the nail right on the head."

This new record crackles just like they all do, but then a guitar starts up, someone on drums, someone on bass, and someone is trilling up and down in a comfortable descant. Steffi closes her eyes and tries to follow the guitar's melody in her mind.

"It can be like that moment I followed Anita into the basement," Alvar says after a moment. "All I could see was her figure and the shine in her eyes."

The darkness of the basement space allowed Alvar to see only the contours of the girl's figure. He still didn't know her name. Her figure, the silhouette of an upright bass, and a piano—all of this—everything he'd hoped to find in Stockholm made visible. His clumsy movements, her high heels clicking on the stone floor—they resonated in the sound boxes of the various instruments—and only a misty ray of light from a gap in the blackout curtain reminded him vaguely of the world outside. The girl's smooth walk as she moved to the back of the room and turned on the light. A bare bulb revealed a trombone and a pair of chairs next to the piano. Alvar felt sure that it must also reveal his palpable fascination with the girl. He turned aside to pick up the trombone to minutely study all its parts and attachments. All he knew about brass and wind instruments was that they could be taken apart and some were called horns. But girls, for their part, knew nothing of instruments.

"Nice horn," he said. He used the same tone his father used to judge a piece of lumber.

"You think?"

"Well, nice is as nice does . . . a good instrument."

"The slide is broken. That's why it's just sitting there. You play anything?"

She was helping him save face by changing the subject. His own mother did that to save face for his father sometimes. This girl was understanding, and he was grateful.

"I play guitar."

"I didn't know they were going to take on a guitar player."

Alvar was saved from answering as Erling and a strange man clattered down the stairs and into the room.

Erling laughed in surprise when he saw Alvar. He clapped Alvar on the shoulder like a brother.

"Hey, Big Boy, we were just talking about you. And I see you've met Anita."

*Anita? Could there be a more beautiful name?* Alvar formed her name in his mouth without moving his lips. He was torn between wanting to be alone with Anita and relief that he was not.

The man sat down at the piano and played a chord. The instrument was not in tune, but with jazz that wasn't important. Exact pitch was out. The wild and untamed was in, and right now it was making itself at home in a basement with three musicians and a goddess. In five seconds Erling had his clarinet together and then he slid into the music with one of his wild glides. Nothing came from a page. It was just in the air.

The dim light made the corners of the basement dark and blurry like a photograph. Anita was watching the man's hands on the piano, so Alvar could devote himself wholeheartedly to watching her while the jazz music seeped into every part of his body. He observed Anita's hands, narrow except for the joint where the thumb was attached, with slightly pointed fingertips, and they were playing . . . yes, playing on her knee, as if she had an invisible piano. Alvar glanced down at his own hands and saw they were also playing. His left hand was pressing invisible guitar chords nobody could hear. Erling and his friend were the audible orchestra, Alvar thought, while he and Anita were the secret one.

The only indication of the passing time was the dimming light coming through the gap in the window. Alvar glanced up and realized it was dark. Erling had already played "Summertime," "I Got Rhythm," and a number of other bits and pieces. Time had gotten lost in some other place. Alvar realized he'd have to walk-run to make it back to Tor Street with a suitable lie to remain in Aunt Hilda's good graces. He couldn't keep anxiety from bubbling up as he reluctantly muttered that he had to head home right away.

Happily, Anita leaped up, too.

"Oh, my goodness!" she exclaimed, hurriedly gathering up her things. As if she were a normal person and not a goddess.

They ran through the streets of Stockholm—they flew. He wobbling like a reckless daddy longlegs, she with her scarf and coat fluttering behind her like butterfly wings. They ran side by side, panting and laughing, her eyes playful. But an anxious look came over her as she caught sight of a clock on the facade of a building. A moment later, she swung up onto one of those dangerous streetcars and she looked down at him commandingly.

"You can take this one as far as Central Station." She smiled.

She might have said the streetcar would take them all the way to Germany and he would not have hesitated. Without any money for a ticket, he found himself beside her among all the other Stockholmers who had places to go and they rolled through a blacked-out Stockholm.

"Hasse Kahn is playing at Nalen on Saturday," she whispered into his ear. "You going?"

He could only nod. To be on the safe side, he nodded a second time more energetically. She laughed.

"Great! Here's where you get off. Vasa Street is that way."

Alvar obediently stepped off with only a vague idea of where Anita had pointed, still feeling the breath from her words slowly evaporating from his skin. It was as he'd always believed: Stockholm was filled with miracles. First, no conductor had come to check for tickets. Second, he still had the package of 250 grams of coffee to placate his widowed Aunt Hilda so she wouldn't want to write home to his mother. And now all he had to do was find out what that Nalen could be and where it was.

"It was a nightclub, right?"

Steffi risks a guess, since she's read thousands of times that Povel Ramel had played at Nalen.

"You could call it that. It was much bigger than the jazz nightclubs you find around today."

"You don't find them in Björke."

"I tend to prefer . . . well, I can't really say I prefer the bigger or the smaller venues. It's hard to compare the two. It's . . ." Alvar makes a face and then shakes his head as he smiles. "But it's probably been at least fifteen years since I've been to one."

"Are there any jazz places in Värmland?"

Alvar stares right into her eyes and then he winks.

"One thing's for sure. Jazz is everywhere and it will never die. Now, I no longer know exactly where they are, because the nurses around here don't really care about jazz and wouldn't know but . . . I'm sure you could find some syncopated rhythm as close as Karlstad."

Steffi laughs and she's just about to tell Alvar about the walking bass line she'd been working on today when there's a knock on the door and a nurse peeks in.

"Time for supper," she says.

Alvar disappears toward what must be the cafeteria. He walks steadily, almost quickly, compared to many of the shuffling old ladies and the people in wheelchairs all around him. Steffi feels a little proud; her old guy is the best old guy in this place.

As she passes the door before the entrance, it opens and a gray-haired tiny woman peers out and stares at her with a hate-filled expression. "What are you doing here?"

Steffi gulps, startled, and she takes in a breath so quickly she has to cough it back out.

"Well, what do you have to say for yourself?"

"I . . . I'm visiting Alvar."

"You are not supposed to be here! Nobody wants you here!"

From the other end of the hallway, a nurse comes trotting up. "Svea!" she calls, forcing friendliness into her voice. "Svea, it's time for supper. This girl doesn't live here. She's only visiting. She's nice."

Svea stares at Steffi. "She is NOT nice."

"Yes, yes I am," Steffi whispers.

"She's a witch-spawn!" Svea hisses.

Steffi feels a lump in her throat. "I *am* nice," she whispers again.

"She's lying," Svea says slowly, sucking on each word.

The nurse takes Svea by the shoulders, but Svea angrily shakes her off.

Steffi backs toward the exit as the nurse gives her an apologetic look. Steffi tries to smile back, although her heart is racing. Once outside, she leans back against the outer door and stares up at the apple tree's net of snow-covered branches.

"I *am* nice," she says, half aloud.

Nobody answers. The snow doesn't move from the branches, the clouds are motionless in the sky, and nothing contradicts her as she stands on the wooden stairway of the retirement home. Perhaps this means she's right.

Her walking bass line comes back, and she thinks about it the whole way home. A—D—E—D with syncopation. You can't live without syncopation.

# – CHAPTER 10 –

She has a brilliant idea, but her Pappa doesn't get it. He's even pretty upset. Steffi hears it as his *v*'s turn to *b*'s and then sees his expression change. "What are you saying?" he exclaims, and his usual calm eyes have become fiery. "How did this man contact you?"

"He's my friend, even though he's really old."

"You may not talk to this man ever again! Do you hear me? Next time he tries to talk to you, just say no! Tell him your pappa refuses to let you meet him! Do you understand?"

Steffi is filled with rage and can feel irritating tears form. "Do YOU understand?" she asks, and is amazed at her loud voice.

"Going to Karlstad with a man is OUT OF THE QUESTION!"

It's impossible to have a discussion with Eduardo Herrera. Hard to believe he and she are even related, when she understands so much and he understands so little. Steffi wants to scream "OH, YOU!" like Julia does, but decides not to sink so low. Instead, she stamps into her room and slams the door behind her as hard as she can. She lies on her bed with her bass. A—D—E—D. Syncopates every other downbeat. A walking line with half notes at times, skips at other times. She needs to go to a jazz club. Anyone with ears could understand that. She needs to go with Alvar.

The door opens without a knock. Steffi shows her irritation over this invasion of her privacy by hitting the D string especially hard. She discovers, to her surprise, a *slap* bass.

"Pappa's really angry with you," Julia says, leaning on Steffi's wall. "Because you want to go to Karlstad with that guy."

Steffi sighs and hits the D string again to get that slap bass effect. It echoes through her room. "He's not a *guy*."

"I know. It's some disgusting old creep. That's what Pappa means by 'that man.'"

Julia imitates their father so perfectly it's a bit funny. Steffi can't help but smile.

"He's not a disgusting creep. He's just an old man."

"Of course it's disgusting. You shouldn't meet up with some strange old man. Do you know, my friend Fanny was almost raped by some old guy."

Steffi hadn't known that.

"Alvar is not like that."

"How do you know? Steffi, really, you don't know anything, even if you think you do."

"By old, I mean really old, even older than Grandma and Grandpa. He lives at Sunshine Retirement Home and he sits around listening to music on his gramophone. That's how I know he's all right."

Julia lifts an eyebrow in her typical skeptical manner that so few people can imitate. "You say he's at Sunshine Home?"

Steffi nods, closes her eyes, and ignores the fact she's revealed so much about Alvar to her crazy sister. Her crazy sister in turn laughs out loud and thinks it's hilarious that Steffi is hanging out at a retirement home visiting a really old man. When Julia goes away, Steffi keeps practicing slap bass. It sounds best on her E string, but she decides to practice on all four strings.

Two minutes later, there's a knock on the door. People never leave you alone in the Herrera family. Pappa comes in with a thoughtful look on his face.

"So that man," he begins. "Julia tells me he's retired?"

"Yep."

"Living at Sunshine Home? A really old, old man?"

Steffi silently moves her fingers over the fingerboard.

"He was seventeen in 1942."

Pappa nods and Steffi can tell he's counting in his head. He sits down beside her, and she claps the bass to her stomach.

"I misunderstood," he apologizes, and his normal, warm, fatherly voice is back. "But I don't understand how you came to visit Sunshine Home. Aren't you kind of young?" He winks.

He always makes these kinds of bad jokes. Only Edvin thinks they're funny.

"I was mature for my age, so they let me in," Steffi replies.

Pappa laughs and runs his hand across her hair.

"Stephanita, let me talk to him myself, and then we'll see about a trip to Karlstad."

She smiles as he gets up. She's already playing A—D—E—D. Before Pappa closes the door, he turns and says, "You can thank your sister."

But when Steffi and her father visit the retirement home, nobody opens Alvar's door. Steffi knocks again, a little louder. Perhaps Alvar is taking a nap. But the door stays closed and no jazz music is slipping out of the keyhole. Pappa looks at her.

"Should we ask a nurse?"

"That's a good idea," Steffi replies.

"There's one who's nice."

"Just one?"

"And watch out if we run into Svea. She's a little, you know, not right in the head."

She grimaces and Pappa nods.

"You know this place pretty well."

"A little bit."

They run into the strict nurse, but this time she smiles and reaches to shake hands with Pappa. When they ask about Alvar, she points to the cafeteria.

"He didn't tell us he was expecting visitors."

"Maybe he forgot," Pappa says.

"Forgetfulness is big around here," the nurse says and laughs. Pappa laughs with her.

They find Alvar in the corner of the cafeteria. He's at a table with a number of old ladies, but when he spots Steffi, he stands up courteously, as if she were a foreign dignitary. As someone takes them to a table for visitors, a gray huddle with their backs toward them turn around to look and one of them points a bony finger at Steffi.

"YOU!" she hisses, but Steffi doesn't get the shivers this time.

"That's Svea," she whispers to her father.

"You shouldn't be here!" Svea screams and two nurses try to distract her attention and calm her down.

That doesn't work until Alvar walks over and bends down to look her in the eyes.

"We don't scream here," he says gently.

Svea stares back a moment in defiance and confusion. Then she falls silent. "You're not my father," she says, but that's all.

They are escorted quickly to another room. In one corner

there's a closed piano with a vase of flowers on top. The piano looks untouched, as if it had become a sculpture instead of an instrument. The three sit down together. Steffi thinks that Alvar looks like Dopey in *Snow White and the Seven Dwarfs*. His ears are so big. She wonders if Pappa might think Alvar has dementia, even though he doesn't.

"Is this where you usually visit?" Pappa asks.

Steffi shakes her head. "No, we're usually in Alvar's room."

"I see. And what . . ." Pappa's question stops in the middle, but Alvar replies anyway.

"We listen to one record after another, just like candy, so to speak," Alvar says. He has a sly smile. "Bebop, swing, cool jazz . . . good times."

"Ragtime, even though it's not really jazz," Steffi says.

"It's a good base for further education," Alvar says, looking straight at Pappa. "Ragtime was the beginning of it all. So we can't ignore ragtime."

"No, of course not," Pappa says. He spreads his hands wide, as if he'd never even think of making fun of ragtime.

"And we talk about things that happened in 1942," Steffi says.

"Like what?"

"Like there were piles of wood in the streets of Stockholm back in those days," Steffi says.

"During the war," Alvar says. "We didn't have enough coal then."

"Even if Sweden wasn't in the war," Pappa remarks. "Same thing in Cuba. No matter who's fighting, the people are the ones who take the blows."

Alvar says it was probably worse for the Cubans during the Cuban missile crisis than for Swedes going without coffee during the Second World War.

Pappa nods but says it was probably the same. The lords start the wars; the people starve. They discuss war for a while. Alvar mentions the German soldiers in Värmland, and Pappa talks about his parents fleeing Cuba, and how he had to live with cousins until he was reunited with his parents in Sweden.

Steffi's heard it all before, but it's more interesting when he's telling it to someone outside the family. She herself has no war stories to tell, but she realizes she knows more about Pappa's than Alvar does and more about Alvar's than Pappa.

"The good thing back then was jazz," she says at last. "People got to play jazz even though it was wartime."

"That's right," Alvar says. "Although even back then, not everybody liked jazz."

Not everybody liked jazz, even back then. Aunt Hilda hated jazz music more than she hated the war.

"Jazz music is another kind of war," she said whenever the subject came up. "It's a war for the soul."

Alvar tried to tell her that jazz wasn't dangerous, but then she looked at him with such disbelief he was forced to change the subject and tell her that he had the opportunity to run an errand for Åkesson. Maybe he'd be good enough to become an errand boy. He'd soon be able to help out with the rent, if he got the job. "On Saturday," he said, and he turned his face away so she wouldn't catch him in the lie and see him blush. He told her he was supposed to inventory a load of potatoes arriving that evening. With this lie behind him, Alvar headed out to find Nalen for the first time.

Aunt Hilda had declared that the ultimate rat's nest of vice in Söder was found in Nalen. Thanks to her angry finger pointing to the ad in the newspaper, Alvar made out that the address was Regering Street 74, but once he got near and asked people, he realized that Nalen as a concept was better understood than the actual address. As he got closer, he found himself in the middle of a stream of perfumed people heading in the same direction like a school of fish. They were all dressed to the nines. The boys had tailored suits and ties, and if they had no hats, they'd slicked their hair back with some kind of grease, so they seemed like they'd just stepped out of the bath. Alvar touched his own hair, the same hair his mother had cut, and now it felt like hay sticking out in all directions. Perhaps they wouldn't even let him in.

There was no way he could even describe the girls. Alvar was right behind one of them, and the scent of her perfume drew him into her aura. Her skirt twitched and her high heels clicked against the sidewalk as she prettily stamped her feet in place to keep warm. The line to get in was long, and he was able to remain, admiringly, behind her for a long time. Of course, they weren't going to let him in. Looking back, he saw that the line was getting longer. The boy behind him wore a wide-brimmed hat, and he sounded just like Erling.

"He wasn't ready, but I didn't hesitate. I said I took care of your girl when you were away. It'll cost next to nothing, two bits."

The company around the boy laughed heartily. He caught sight of Alvar. "Well, hello, you look like something the cat dragged in. No offense."

"I'm Alvar Svensson." Alvar held out his hand.

The boy—or perhaps the man, they both shared that indeterminate age—shook it.

"Don't be mad, but you really stick out in this crowd."

"Yeah, I know."

"But you're here for Nalen? Or did you just get lost?"

His friends laughed, but he shushed them and then asked the question again.

"Yes, if they let me in," Alvar replied. "Because, you know, I do look a little different."

"But you're a musician, aren't you?" the boy said with a wink.

"How did you know?"

"So, hello, you *are* a musician! I mean, you could always tell them you're one. They do look pretty much like anybody. I can barely understand what you're saying, no offense. Where're you from?"

When the group got close to the door, they told the doorman that this was "the famous jazz guitarist from Värmland, Alvar Svensson." He paid his crown and was in.

He'd thought Nalen would be as big as a coffee shop, but it turned out to be twenty times bigger. Heat, sweat, music, and cigarette smoke embraced him as he walked into the hallway while young men and women swirled around him in all directions. He took off his woolen cap and leaned against the wall to ponder his chances of finding Anita in this crowd. They seemed minute. From the back, all of the girls looked like Anita, but from the front none did. Alvar decided to just follow the music, as he'd always done.

A twelve-piece band was playing the wonderful sounds Alvar had, up to that moment, heard only on the radio or the gramophone. Eight horns, one pianist, one drummer, one guitar player, one bass player—all live and focused on their work. The drummer's head nodded in time to the beat, the pianist sometimes frowned and sometimes smiled from ear to ear, and the horns stood up each time they had solos, so the band never seemed to be still for a moment. Alvar's body leaped. If jazz was in a war over human souls, he was already lost. He wanted to be up there, part of the band; no, he'd rather be out on the dance floor with a girl, a girl whose nearness didn't make his hands sweat. Some of the men were dancing so hard, their pomade was battling it out with their sweat and others did steps so intricate that Alvar despaired that he could never imitate them.

"Hey, you!" a familiar voice said in his ear. "Weren't you just thinking about asking me to dance?"

Anita's eyes were laughing as she took his huge hand in her own smaller one. All he could think was: *Please, hands, don't start sweating now! Stop it! Right now!* He could picture so much sweat dripping from his pores that it dropped through Anita's small-cupped palm, drowning the parquet wooden floor and turning it into a swimming pool.

"Thanks, that was an interesting story," Steffi's father says. "It must have been an exciting time."

Steffi wants to hit him. The story wasn't over—he'd interrupted right in the middle of all the hand sweat! She sees that Alvar has lost the thread. His gaze has returned to the table with its embroidered cloth and candlestick back in the middle of Björke.

"Yes, it was," Alvar says.

"We don't want to keep you too long," Pappa says. "It was very nice to meet you."

Steffi looks at him and then at Alvar. "Though we were going to ask—"

"We can talk about it later." Pappa interrupts her and gives her a meaningful look.

Then Pappa goes to speak with the nurses, as if Alvar were a minor who needed permission from the strict nurse, who would say Alvar is old but not suffering from dementia and he'd be able to handle a trip to Karlstad. Steffi could have told Pappa that if he'd listen to her.

She turns back to Alvar.

"Is he going to come with you from now on?" Alvar asks, glancing over at Pappa.

"He doesn't like jazz," Steffi replies. "He just wanted to check you out before we could go to Karlstad."

"You and me?"

"And Pappa. They're having a jazz afternoon at the library."

Alvar looks at her with one of his wry expressions and she wonders if he even knows he makes them. Maybe he was shocked to hear her plan. She hadn't exactly hinted at it before now.

"It's Annie Grahn's Quartet," she explains. "Next Sunday. With Peter Furubäck on the trumpet. That'll be good, right?"

"*Good*?" Alvar says. "More like greater than great. Hey, Ulla, did you hear that?" he says to a woman in a wheelchair not far from them. "I've been invited to a jazz party, though at a library, not like in our day but not bad, don't you think?"

Ulla looks up from her wheelchair and smiles. "You're talking funny again, Alvar, but you're sure something else. If I were only twenty . . . forty years younger."

When Pappa returns, he shakes hands with Alvar. Pappa has indeed made sure that Alvar would be up to the trip to Karlstad. As if they'd all be running a triathlon. Steffi feels she's in the gap between who Pappa thinks Alvar is, who Alvar really is, and the jazz musician he once was. The hallway smells like old people. Alvar's nodding his head. Sometimes he does this in seven-eight time because he takes pleasure in some of the experiments with rhythm in modular jazz. Only Steffi knows this.

# – CHAPTER 11 –

Semlan says that Steffi has been skipping class and it's an issue. "You're a smart girl," she says. "You have to understand that your future is at stake. You've been absent from gym and social studies sixty percent of the time this February, which means you aren't even passing."

She asks why Steffi cuts class so often. Steffi tries to explain.

"I can't concentrate because people talk about me. They're such idiots."

Semlan nods and swallows and mutters something about how hard it is to be young and that there's a counselor at the school. Then she repeats that Steffi is an intelligent girl. She has a good chance of getting into a good school if she just would make an effort these last few months. Semlan doesn't know that Steffi plans to be a jazz musician and therefore doesn't need a good grade in social studies. Steffi's not about to tell her that.

"Can we agree on this?" Semlan asks, her exasperated face barely creased by a smile. "Full attendance these last months, so you give yourself . . . you *give yourself* a chance for a good final grade."

"Except the fifteenth of March," Steffi says. "I'll be gone that day for an audition to see if I can get into a special *gymnasium.*"

"That sounds exciting," Semlan says. "Which one is it?"

"I don't remember."

The music school in Stockholm has real musicians as teachers, and both Robyn and Sarah Dawn Finer had attended it. It was founded in 1993. You can study ensemble and jazz history and you get there by taking the subway to a station named Mariatorget. But her homeroom teacher doesn't deserve to know all this. As Steffi goes out of the room, she notices Semlan pick up a trashy magazine and a piece of pastry.

Steffi doesn't have music today, but she heads for the music room as soon as her last class lets out. She has no trouble walking right through the building, because Karro is still out with the flu. For a while the hallways belong to everyone. Jake lets her in and lifts his hand a moment for a high five, but then he changes his mind and just winks. As soon as he leaves, Steffi turns off the lights.

She's already beginning to get nervous about the entrance audition. The fifteenth of March is not all that far in the future, and she still doesn't know what she's going to play. It has to be something special, because she's competing with kids from all over Sweden and some of them have been playing the bass since nursery school. When she thinks about this, she can't get a note out. She stands completely silent for at least fifteen minutes, turned to stone by the thought of all those other kids who play bass far better than she does.

Well, who did Alvar think *he* was when he got on the train to Stockholm? You have to think you're something in order to become something. She plays an open A. The lyrics to her song start to flow as she walks the bass up the scale.

*You've got to believe*
*To be somebody,*
*You've got to believe*
*To be the best*
*You've got to believe*
*The past can't hold you*
*You've got to believe*
*And keep on playing*
*You've got to believe*
*To be free.*

She does believe in the future, doesn't she? Even though she feels most at home back in the forties.

Her bass makes more squiggles. That's how she describes it to herself when the bass note is broken by slides on the E string by something that feels more and more her own. Having played it a few times, her fingers move on their own, and she can feel the rhythm in her legs. First she feels it on the downbeat but then she feels it in the downbeat syncopation instead until it goes through her stomach and her back like double pulses. When she turns up the volume, the whole room vibrates. She tries the slap bass on the walking bass line and then tries it again one octave higher. Goes back to slap on the syncopation and plays softly on the curlicues/squiggles/doodles. When she opens her eyes, three boys are standing between her and the door.

It's Kevin, Hannes, and Ville here in the music room. Jake hadn't locked the door. They had come into her darkness and they'll expose her now as the girl in 9B who plays the bass and hums to herself because she thinks she's somebody. The girl they all know as worthless, whose dreams are in their hands now like a fragile eggshell.

"Damn, you're good," Hannes says.

Steffi gasps out her surprise at not being immediately shot down. This is even more important. If she really *is* good on the bass, maybe she has a chance.

"I am?"

"What's the name of that song?"

She almost admits she's written it herself.

Instead, she says, "It's called 'Believe.' It's in English, but there's Swedish lyrics, too."

Hannes takes down an electric guitar from its hanger on the wall. Steffi can hardly believe she's standing there with Kevin, Hannes, and Ville in a dark room and they're talking while Hannes plugs the guitar into the amp system next to her own cable.

"I wanted to check if Jake was here because I wanted to show Kevin and Ville this thing on the guitar," Hannes explains.

Steffi starts to lift off her bass. She realizes it's time to wake up from this dream and go home. But Hannes stops her. "You can play along, right?"

Hannes's "thing" on the guitar is in D-minor. It's a riff between D and A, similar to many other riffs, and he plays it well. Steffi goes along by just playing the base note of the chord so she doesn't mess anything up for him, but Hannes smiles whenever she does a slide or an intermediate note and then she begins to add the same syncopation she was doing before they'd come in. This does make him mess up at first, but he soon understands what she's doing and he starts to imitate it on the guitar. They're playing in synch on the same amp and they're so loud the cymbals on the drum kit begin to vibrate on their own. Hannes nods in time so his bangs start swinging and he smiles at her when they happen upon the same note at the same time.

Then the lights are switched on.

It's Kevin who did it. He's laughing without a care in the world like he's a king, a king who never has to pretend he's anywhere else than where he is. "I thought the lights were broken," he says. "Didn't you ever think to turn them on?"

Ville and Hannes grin, but Steffi doesn't say anything.

"Wasn't that great?" Hannes says. "Let's try it with the drums, too. I'll show you what I'm doing."

Ville sits behind the drums and Kevin hangs another guitar over his shoulder. Kevin's the one who plays lead, he explains, while Hannes shows him how to walk between D and A. They've named their band the Lard Heroes and they've already booked two shows.

"Do you know what *lard* means?" Hannes grins. "It means 'fat.' "

"Grease," Ville corrects him.

"Grease is the same as fat."

"It's not."

"And of course you know the difference? Between grease and fat?"

"Yes."

Hannes looks teasingly at Ville, the way you look at a friend you've known since forever. "Tell me, then."

"*Grease* rhymes with *cheese*."

Kevin laughs at them and hits a high D on his guitar and tries to walk it down to A. "And *lard* rhymes with *fart*," he says.

Steffi casts a secret glance at Kevin. The corners of his mouth are turned down as he struggles with his finger placement. Not that she really cares how Karro and Sanja rank the boys, but she could never see herself being interested in this boy. Kevin was certainly not the one who had come up with the band's name. It was too cool.

"Lard Heroes!" she says to herself, amused, and Hannes turns toward her.

"Yeah, isn't it great?"

He'd heard her even though she'd barely spoken above a whisper.

Steffi realizes that saying Kevin plays lead guitar is more of a way to make him feel important rather than describe what he actually did.

Hannes had explained to him that the lead guitar carries the whole song while the second guitar just plays background melodies—without telling Kevin that those background melodies were actually solos. So Kevin, with great concentration showing in his eyes, plays between D-minor and A-minor while Hannes tries out new riffs on his guitar.

Steffi plays along with Hannes sometimes and at other times finds her own way, while behind them Ville does his best to find a steady rhythm on the drums.

When Kevin stops, the others stop, too, and Steffi dampens a bass note that had echoed for an embarrassingly long time. Hannes waves his hands in excitement.

"Damn! We sound really good with a bass!"

Ville agrees, and so does Kevin. They're looking at her, and she feels so horribly visible but she still finds she's feeling really happy. It hits her like electricity: *they're going to ask me to join their band!*

"Yeah, the bass gave us what we need, didn't it? Especially at the end. We can go places with a bass!"

Steffi's already blushing. What is she going to say when they ask her?

"All right, then," Hannes says. "So we'll have to find a bass player. But he's got to be really good!"

Her relief is, oddly, greater than her disappointment. Actually, her disappointment was more than minimal, but her relief was still bigger. It would have turned the world upside down if Steffi Herrera suddenly was playing in Kevin Storfors's band. It would have been absurd.

As she walks home, her old walking bass line comes back to her along with the lyrics that tell her she is somebody. As the snow crunches under her feet, the song repeats itself all around her. It manifests in the blue air and holds everything a fifteen-year-old could expect from the future. It feels like another life.

# – CHAPTER 12 –

It is a very well dressed man who meets them at the entrance to Sunshine Home exactly on time. His pinstriped suit is a bit roomy through the shoulders and long in the trousers. He wears a hat with a narrow, straight brim, and on his feet, his polished black shoes shine. Steffi's father looks almost shabby in comparison, even though he's put on his stylish black leather jacket.

In the car, Pappa and Alvar discuss a politician forced from office for some reason, and it is so boring Steffi doesn't need to pay attention. She doesn't understand why her father picked this topic—after all, they were heading to a jazz club!

She leans forward to Alvar. "Did all the men wear hats like those at Nalen?"

"Not inside! No, no, then we'd have died of heat exhaustion. And our hats would have come flying off while we danced. Have you ever seen people dancing the jitterbug?"

"Isn't that the one where you throw yourself around?"

Steffi had Googled jitterbug, Nalen, modular jazz, and "neat." And once she'd even typed "Anita and Nalen" in the search engine, but only people who'd been really famous in the old days showed up.

"Did you do throw Anita around?"

"What? Throw Anita up in the air with my trembling deer legs? I told you I had sweaty palms, didn't I? I had to discreetly wipe them off before I even tried to dance."

Alvar tried to discreetly wipe the sweat from his palms on the cloth of Anita's tailored dress but became ashamed when he saw a dark spot spread on her innocent back. So he took a moment to shove his hands into his pockets to absorb the wetness there, but this just made new waves of sweat pour from his palms, as if he were engaged in a matter of life and death. If he was going to dance as wildly as the other boys on the floor, his partner would eventually simply fly unhappily out of his hands, over the dance floor, and into the band.

These visions filled his mind while Anita led him directly to the middle of the dance floor. Without any warning, she simply began to move her body. He watched her as if hypnotized. The band was playing "Jazz Me Blues." Anita's body made the music real. Alvar had once read in a music magazine that jazz was the music of the flesh. Anita's arms and legs moved to an internal rhythm and her eyes glittered as she looked at him and laughed.

"I had no idea you couldn't dance."

Her disappointment could be heard above the band and all that glittering throng. Alvar shook his head and swallowed as he readied to prove his manhood. "I *can*!"

"What did you say?"

He shook his head and looked aside to see if he could catch the steps from some other men. He tried throwing one foot forward, lifting his arms and trying to mimic the swing others around him had in their elbows. He failed dramatically. Anita was laughing even more and he caught looks from at least ten other worldly, swing-dancing girls—perhaps from the entire room. His face burned and his eyes stung as if he, a seventeen-year-old who had traveled on a train, was about to burst into tears because he couldn't dance.

Anita laid a hand on his shoulder. She let it rest there. From her fingers calm spread bit by bit throughout his tense body until he was completely still in a wild, dancing sea of "Jazz Me Blues."

"Right foot first," she said, tilting her head down without looking away from his eyes. "And don't think about the music."

Alvar did as she said.

"And back. Once more."

He concentrated on doing the step again.

"Now your other foot. Forward, back, forward back. Good!"

Her praise sounded like a mother's when her child is being potty trained. But he still listened eagerly. The second round went better and he was moving in time. Even though his feet were not sliding like the others, he was now one of them. By the time they'd done the steps for the fifth time, he could feel the music. Anita laughed again and he could tell she laughed because she was happy.

She took one of his hands and he was no longer worrying about sweaty palms—they were stepping in time to the same dance. Her head nodded like his. From his perspective, they seemed to be still together while the rest of the room was whirling around them. Her eyes during the "Jazz Me Blues" became the Stockholm of his dreams—and a moment later she was gone.

Erling had grabbed Anita's free hand and simply twirled her away into a pirouette and then lifted her high into the air. This was real jitterbug. Alvar was filled with admiration, desire, and shame thinking he'd actually attempted this dance.

"Hey, Big Boy!" Erling grinned at him. "So the boy from Värmland found his way here!"

Erling had slicked his hair in a wave and then toward the back like all the other men at Nalen. Alvar wondered what they used on their hair to get it to look like that; he'd probably have to ask somebody, a daunting task.

Erling grabbed his shoulders and turned him toward the band. "There!" he said. "I'm going to be up there one day!"

"Doing a solo?"

Erling laughed and slung his arm around Alvar's shoulder.

"Naturally, Big Boy."

"Weren't you angry when Erling began to dance with Anita?"

Alvar's smile lifts one corner of his mouth, but he doesn't say anything.

"I would have been mad," Steffi continues. "If I'd just begun to dance with her and then Erling butts in . . . I'm not so sure I like this Erling guy."

Her father gives her an inscrutable look. Why? Because she didn't like clarinetists who think they're big shots?

"You'd probably have liked him if you'd met him." Alvar laughs. "Erling had a real effect on young ladies. Older ones, too, for that matter."

Steffi thinks about that girl magnet Kevin, who rhymes *lard* with *fart*.

"He wouldn't on me."

Pappa looks back at her via the rearview mirror while Alvar laughs again.

"You would have been a very special and resistant young lady! Oh, look, here we are!"

The library has come into view and they drive past it to look for a parking spot. Then they all walk back, three across. Alvar's excitement can no longer be hidden. His old man legs, once shaky, now have a spring to them and he laughs at everything.

They find their way to the small room at the library, where a handful of people have gathered to listen to jazz. A few older guys. A blond girl with lipstick and a colorful scarf. A woman wearing a French beret. Two men with beards. And a couple dressed alike in black clothes who'd be identical if it weren't for the man being a foot taller. The library's chairs are arranged in neat rows. Alvar quietly makes a quip about what a nice change it is to sit on library chairs instead of retirement home chairs all day. They find places far in the back, with Steffi in the middle.

Annie Grahn's Quartet has been around since 2008, when some jazz-loving souls found each other on a trip to Harlem and began to jam together on the plane, the representative of Karlstad Jazz Club informs them, before the quartet is allowed to take its place. The announcer adds that the quartet had been influenced by early Harlem as well as by later big stars like Norah Jones and Diana Krall, although eventually they developed their own style. *This guy sure likes to talk,* Steffi thinks. After giving them the Web site for the Karlstad Jazz Club and all the upcoming events, he finally beckons the musicians onstage. The quartet consists of the blond woman in the scarf, the two men with beards as well as one of the old men. This decreases the audience by almost a third.

During the first measures of the first verse, Steffi is struck by three thoughts. *I'm never going to learn how to play like this! Damn! I* have *to learn to play like this!* Then she glances at Alvar. His eyes are lit up and his head nods to the beat. He avidly follows the pianist's keys and the singer's dark wailing, the bassist's quick fingers and the trumpet solo. This room should be completely filled with admiring people, with, perhaps, even a dance floor. She realizes her own head is nodding to the beat just like Alvar's. He's taken off his hat, and she sees he's slicked all his remaining hair into a wave and back. She smiles, plucks up his hat, and pops it on her own head. He doesn't notice then, but in the break between the first and second songs, he glances sideways at her and gasps, but she can't tell if he's just playing.

"Well, what a Nat hepcat!" He grins, speaking in the Stockholm accent he sometimes uses.

She wears the hat for the rest of the concert.

Steffi? Steffi who? Oh, *her*, Nalen hepcat!

The quartet pauses before playing their last song when something makes them stop. The old trumpet player waves to the man from the jazz club. They whisper together, shaking their heads and nodding. They call over the blond woman and another old man up from the audience. Something's going on. The jazz club man then walks back through the audience, right over to them. He stops by Pappa, but he isn't looking at him, or Steffi either.

"Are you Alvar Svensson?"

Alvar lifts his bushy white eyebrows. "In the flesh. Do we know each other?"

The man looks amazed, almost as if in religious wonder.

"Ladies and gentlemen!" he announces in a loud voice, as if everybody wasn't already focused on them to find out what's going on. "I have the great honor to inform you that in our audience today we have none other than the legendary jazz guitarist and bass player Alvar 'Big Boy' Svensson."

All fourteen people break out in cheers. Alvar laughs nervously, elegantly bows, and Steffi could clearly see how he must have blushed as a seventeen-year-old boy in the big city. They escort him to the stage and diffidently ask if he would be so kind as to play something on the string bass for them. "It would mean so much for the club," the representative says breathlessly, and the thirteen remaining members of the audience cheer in agreement.

Alvar laughs and lets himself be led up onto the stage. He's already flexing his fingers before he even touches the instrument. *They ought to be stiff; fingers get stiff in old age, right?* Steffi thinks. Alvar's don't seem to be and Steffi holds her breath as he tunes the bass to a chord from the piano. Alvar's stooping body moves in time as he makes music on this enormous upright bass; his foot taps as his fingers walk up and down the huge fingerboard, drawing out more emotion than Steffi believed was possible. He plays a whole piece through, verse and refrain, before he laughs and hands the bass back to its owner. He's out of breath.

As he comes to sit back down next to Steffi, he says he'd once been better—he'd once had full control without having to fake it like he did today. But the jubilation among the library's audience doesn't end, and the jazz club representative says they're going to put this event on the first page of their Web site and then asks to have his picture taken with Alvar.

Steffi has a proud lump in her throat. Her old guy.

After the concert, Alvar doesn't want to go home. It's been years since he's been in Karlstad, he says, and they must get a souvenir of the day. Pappa says he'd promised the nurses to drive him right back to Sunshine Home after the concert. And after his wonderful playing, he must be tired, right? Steffi smiles when she hears Pappa call Alvar's playing wonderful. Pappa says they must go straight back as soon as Alvar finds his souvenir.

"It's a hat, of course," Alvar says. "For Steffi, who is going to be the next star in the jazz sky."

It takes them a while to find a hat store open on a Sunday. Pappa sighs deeply at least three times, but only Steffi hears him. After three streets, Alvar is walking more slowly and Pappa suggests again that they just head home. But then they see *the* hat. Both Alvar and Steffi. It seems to leap to their attention from the display window and both their heads turn to it at once.

"Were you really that famous?" Steffi asks as she tries on what would soon become her very own new hat.

Alvar laughs in embarrassment. "Well, maybe." He adjusts the hat on her head. "Look, it fits as if made just for you."

"Do I look like a Nat hepcat?"

"An honest-to-goodness Nat hepcat. Of course, girls wore different clothes in those days. Swing dresses, they were called."

Steffi looks at herself in the mirror. The hat gives her a different air, like Steffi with extra spice.

"Dresses are not my thing. But this hat, I like it. Were the girls also called Nat hepcats?"

"No, but Anita was a really jazz crazy girl."

Steffi smiles at all the names. Pappa looks at his watch.

"But what was it like, being famous?" Steffi asks. "How did it happen?"

"I'll tell you when we reach that part of the story," Alvar says. "But let's make your father, Eduardo, happy and go get in the car. The hat's my gift."

It is eleven thirty at night and Steffi is looking at herself in her bedroom mirror. She's already taken thirty-four selfies on her cell phone. With the night-light shining down from above, all you can see is the hat, a deep shadow, and the corner of her chin. In coal-black profile, she's become someone else.

Still wearing her hat, she sits at her computer, blinks at the bright shine of the screen, and logs in to The Place. "Hi, whore!" Karro has written in her guestbook. Steffi stares at the phrase and realizes Karro must really miss her if she's still online to talk to Steffi even with the stomach flu. She wonders if she should write something back, but doesn't. This is a game she can't win.

She logs out from The Place, from the parties she's not invited to and the chitchat she can't be part of like everybody else. She still wears her hat as she stares at The Place home page. Then she clicks the log-in button and creates a new user.

# – CHAPTER 13 –

Create a new user. If only it were that easy in the real world.

In the real world, all the students at Björke School have to eat breaded fish. It should be good, but the breading was so disgusting that they figure the lunch ladies made it especially to torture them, so it was called "Punishment Fish" by everybody.

In the real world, Karro has come back to school. "Have you made yourself extra disgusting today or did I just forget how ugly you are?" Karro sneers in a normal conversational tone while they stand in the lunch line.

Sanja, Morgan, Linus, Jenny, and another student from class 9A are all listening. Jenny and Sanja giggle as Karro scrapes the breading from her fish and dumps it onto Steffi's plate.

"Yours, too." Karro gestures at Sanja's and then Morgan's plates.

Linus has already taken his food away. Perhaps he doesn't want to play along; perhaps he actually likes Punishment Fish. Everyone else's breading turns into a huge gray pile on Steffi's plate.

"You sit here so we can make sure you eat properly."

The question is, why is *she* the one who has to sit and eat three people's collected fish breading? It is no longer a desperate question and now has become more of a philosophical one: How did these people decide that she was disgusting? How can a person be disgusting? Can a person's genetic composition be disgusting via some unknown quality? Sometimes she feels so disgusting that she hates herself, and sometimes she hates them instead. Her best moments come when she thinks they are the disgusting ones.

Someday Steffi will figure out how to explain it all. Until then, she has to force herself, bit by bit, to eat the spongy breading as everyone looks on. It's the only way to avoid a tougher punishment in the locker room or the bathroom later. Somebody snorts that one of the lunch ladies is actually a man and that he puts his sperm into the breading. That would explain a lot. They laugh so loud they're howling.

But a second later, Karro silences them with one look, and everyone's attention turns to her. "Some guy in Karlstad has been on my Web page."

"Mine, too! But he didn't write anything!"

"He didn't write anything to me, either! What if it's the same guy? What was his name again?"

*Hepcat,* Steffi thinks. *His name is Hepcat.*

"Is he cute?"

Of course they can't tell if he's cute or not. Steffi's picture is a black profile with her hat over most of her face.

"Of course! He's hot! And mysterious! Perhaps like a guy in Stockholm or New York. Not like the guys around here!"

"I don't know why he didn't write anything. No boys visit my site without writing something! Isn't that true, Karro?"

Karro doesn't understand and neither does Jenny. This mysterious guy is self-confident, that's for sure, they think. They'd all checked his page. He'd written a description of himself and some girl he'd dumped. But in rhyme! He's definitely complex, they agree, their eyes shining. A difficult guy in Karlstad.

Alvar is sleeping when she comes to visit. It's not like him. He puts it down to the excitement of their adventure yesterday, but when she asks if it would be better if she left, he gets up quickly. "Oh, no, this old man still has some song in his heart." He uses both eyes to wink at her. "Or I should say, song in his fingers."

"You were really good yesterday," Steffi says honestly.

"Do you want to play for me now?" Alvar says.

"Yep." She pulls out her bass guitar and they sit down like they usually do, she on the chair and he in his armchair, close enough to hear the notes without an amplifier.

"I thought I'd show them I know stuff. I thought I'd play something written down, like Torkel forces me to play, and then something I've written myself—or that I'm still writing, I should say. I'm not finished yet."

"Let me hear."

"I've written lyrics, too." She blushes as she says this. She's not sure she really wants to sing aloud.

"I'm looking forward to hearing them," Alvar says.

"OK."

She sings her song for Alvar. She plays her bass with syncopation on the downbeat and sings the song about believing you're somebody, and the song and the bass notes weave around each other until she feels exactly what she meant when she first wrote it:

> *"You have to believe you can to do it.*
> *You have to believe in your smarts to get through it."*

Alvar nods in time, looking first at her and then up at the ceiling. When she finishes, he seems deep in thought.

"You did something very nice in the bridge there," he says at last. "You should repeat that and make it stronger in the refrain."

"Make it stronger?"

"You could take it and make it the base of the entire refrain. Perhaps in another key."

"Maybe in F."

She looks at him to see if he caught her joke. He has.

"Yes, why make things too easy?" he snorts.

He's silent for a moment. He's thinking about something.

She's thinking about something, too. "Alvar."

"Yes?"

"Do you think I can get really good?"

"Yes, I believe so."

"Do you think I'll get into the music school in Stockholm?"

"I'm absolutely sure you will."

He says nothing more. He just seems to mean exactly what he says. She's not so sure, but she thinks about her lyrics one more time and decides to believe she is somebody.

"Are you going to tell me how you got so famous?"

Alvar is silent for a long time, but Steffi can wait him out.

"It's hard to say where things begin and end. But one of the first times I started to think I could become good was in that basement space at Åsö Street. Erling had had an argument with his bass player, Sigge."

The bass player in Erling's three-piece band was named Sigge. He was big as well as tall, almost a foot taller than Erling, and he hit the bass strings with convincing power. But one day he'd let a shop melt one of Erling's records. At least, that was Erling's version of events. Sigge's was that Erling had given him the record long before so he had the right to let it be melted down. Such desecration could happen because record shops had demanded old records in exchange for new ones, due to the lack of shellac during the miserable war. So you could blame the war when Erling said that Sigge was a German lackey, so cuttingly effective, since Sigge resembled a certain German soldier from the First World War more than he resembled the small man he called father. The hateful words flew across the rehearsal space because of a melted-down Louis Armstrong record, and finally Sigge simply strapped his bass onto his back and left.

Alvar silently watched the whole thing. Anita tried to speak up, but they told her this was between men. The result was that Erling's three-man band became a duo. Ingmar on the piano and Erling on the clarinet.

"Go tell him you're sorry and maybe he'll come back," Anita said.

"I know you like tall men, but what should I be sorry about? Beg forgiveness because he melted my record?"

Alvar found himself stretching to his full height. Was it true that Anita liked tall men, or was Erling just teasing her?

Anita turned to stare at him. "How about Alvar?"

"What about Alvar?"

Alvar became nervous hearing his name spoken aloud twice. His body shrank back down and he turned red without even knowing why.

"Well, he plays guitar, and they're tuned similarly as far as I know . . . at least he can pluck strings and he certainly has finger strength."

Erling lifted an eyebrow. "You know we're a serious jazz orchestra."

"Just give him a chance."

Erling looked at Ingmar, who shrugged. Then he looked over at Alvar. Three pairs of eyes focused on him and he felt his legs begin to tremble until he stiffly clutched his knees.

"If you can find a bass, you can play with us. I'll give you a trial, say for two . . . no, one month."

"Don't be stupid," Anita protested. "Where's he supposed to find a string bass? And what sort of a chance is that—just one month's time?"

Alvar suddenly heard his own voice. Yes, he was speaking and he felt himself opening his mouth and the words just coming out. "I'll do it."

The quest for a string bass would color Alvar's entire first summer in Stockholm. Without Anita's help, he wouldn't have found one. She knew someone who knew someone who needed help with his garden more than he needed his string bass over the summer. Why Anita had helped him was a question Alvar pondered often at night in his kitchen bed. The consequences of the deal she'd magically managed to bring about kept Alvar hurtling from one end of Stockholm to the other all those summer days and even a few nights. He pedaled the cargo bicycle he was working to pay off from Åkesson. First and foremost, he had to make deliveries for Åkesson's grocery. Then he had to bike around on errands for Erling's trio. Then, finally, he had to transport soil and flowers to the gentleman on Djurgården, whose string bass he was allowed to use and guard with his young life. Aunt Hilda asked him once what he was doing all day long but was content to hear how he was working off his payments on the bicycle so that he could help Aunt Hilda with the rent as soon as possible. She didn't really seem all that unhappy that he was gone so much. Alvar was worn out when evening came, but he was content with his work—where some people had no job, he had three. He was becoming a *self-made man.*

The first time he tried to play the upright bass, he was surprised. He had not realized that, in contrast to a guitar, the instrument had no frets, making it more difficult to find the notes on the fingerboard. In addition, there was no way to comfortably sit when he tried to reach the fingerboard with one hand and the strings with the other. Erling would laugh at him, not in a mean-spirited way, but it didn't make things better.

Anita glared at Erling. "Will you help him or make it worse?"

Alvar counted another finger against his palm. Seven times she'd stood up for him since he'd started keeping track, and that meant something, didn't it? By now he knew that she was twenty-two years old. He was seventeen. Seventeen, twenty-two. Twenty-two, seventeen. If he kept saying the words, they soon lost any meaning.

He finally found help at Nalen. He still could not work up the courage to talk to any of the girls. When Anita was all dressed up, it was even hard to talk to her. But men were just men. The worst they could do was brush him off. All that Wednesday evening he studied the bass player in one of the jazz bands performing that night, and when they finished their set, he walked over and took a slight bow.

"I'm Alvar Svensson."

The bass player grinned. "Well, hello, then."

"I would like to compliment you on your fine playing this evening."

He thought he'd managed a precise Stockholm accent, but the man laughed.

"If you've come all the way from Värmland just to compliment my playing, I feel honored!"

"I'm trying to learn the bass, too."

"You are?"

"Yes, and I'm just wondering if you could give me some tips . . . things I really should learn. First of all, how I should stand."

The bass player seemed flattered by this request to teach a boy from Värmland how to play. Privately, Alvar decided to stop trying to emulate the Söder slang, which often gave him problems.

The bass player showed him how to press the bass against his body and let it rest against his hip to relieve any stress on his shoulders and back and allow a free range of motion and as much strength as possible in his arms and fingers, especially for pizzicato.

"There you go!" he exclaimed as Alvar had almost gotten it. "Soon I can hire you to play for me and I'll be able to retire!"

Alvar laughed. Then he heard Erling's laughter echoing behind him.

"Thanks so much for sharing some techniques to our Big Boy. We're trying to teach him a thing or two ourselves. Erling Karlsson's the name and I run the Erling Trio."

The bass player didn't seem impressed. That was often how it went with the men who met Erling. They were not taken in by his charm the way women often were. Alvar wondered if this was due to jealousy. He had to admit that he could get jealous of Erling.

"Erling is a good clarinetist," Alvar said. "He's played at Edermann's and everything."

"I'm not surprised," the bass player said, wooden-faced.

Erling frowned at Alvar, as if Alvar had said something wrong. Alvar had no idea what that could be.

"Alvar here will be a hot item," the bassist said over the sound of the next jazz band starting up in a fox-trot. "I'm looking forward to hearing your trio."

The bassist disappeared into the crowd.

Erling snorted. "He thinks he's so great."

Alvar laughs as he repeats this last remark. His laugh soon turns into a yawn.

"But if you only played string bass in those days, what did you say for my kind of bass?"

"That problem was not yet in existence."

"There weren't any electric bass guitars at all?"

"No, not a one. The electric bass guitar was invented in the fifties."

"Oh."

Steffi runs through all the records from the forties she carries about inside her head. Nope. Not a single electric bass in all those songs she's tried to play. And she hadn't even considered that they'd all been uprights.

"But you had electricity," she protests.

"Of course."

"Because otherwise you couldn't turn on the lights."

"You haven't missed a trick."

Steffi laughs, although she is feeling a little stupid. "Why weren't you supposed to say Erling played at . . . what's the place again?"

"Edermann's. It was a hole-in-the-wall where untested bands

could come and play. Anyone could play. He'd impressed me, but not Hasse Kahn's bassist."

He smiles to himself. His small smile becomes a third huge yawn. It was time to let Alvar Big Boy Svensson go back to his nap.

# – CHAPTER 14 –

HEPCAT'S LOG, March 10

I never listen to their shit. My future will be completely different, and once I leave, all that shit will drop and you'll be able to see that it was just hanging in the air and none of it stuck to me. I know. We've all felt small. Some people stay small the rest of their lives.

"He's got to be a bad boy," Sanja suggests. "It must be the principal . . . and the police . . . who are on his case. They don't get it."

Karro shakes her head. "It must be all the adults. They want him to be a doctor or lawyer or something, but he's not letting them tell him what to do. He's going his own way."

Karro has visited Hepcat's page five times at least. He hasn't visited her page at all since that first time and she can't understand why. She's changed her photo and everything; she took her picture from slightly above while pressing her breasts together and after having put on mascara like fashion blogger Luna in her video.

She would never start a conversation with a guy. That would be like writing *desperate* on her forehead. But—she's thinking a forbidden thought—if she decided to write to him, what would she say? Nothing too common. Hepcat is deep; she could tell.

Her thoughts are disturbed by Ugly Steffi brushing past in her nauseating manner to get a sheet of graph paper from the teacher. The paper isn't gross until Steffi's hands touch it. It's sick how some people can walk around being so disgusting that it rubs off on everything they touch.

"I have to throw up!" she whispers to Sanja, loud enough so Steffi can hear. "I can smell her from here!"

Sanja smiles and agrees with her. Karro can always trust Sanja's loyalty. Nothing will ever come between them. But sometimes Sanja disgusts Karro, too. She'd tell these secret thoughts to Hepcat, if he ever decided to write to her.

Steffi isn't listening and she's trying not to hear what they're saying. She knows she doesn't smell. She takes a shower every morning and uses the perfume-free deodorant from the drugstore. *I can't hear you,* she thinks. *I can't hear you, so why would I fear you?*

The words don't fit into a ragtime or bebop, but they fit a slow jazz song, like Monica Zetterlund used to sing. She'll write them down.

In the afternoon, something completely unexpected happens. It's almost invisible. Steffi is at her locker and Karro is walking toward hers. She's turning in from the other hallway and heading to the bathroom, and they happen to find themselves in the same small space at the same time. Karro opens her mouth and her smeared lip gloss moves in slow motion as she starts to say "Disgu . . ." before Hannes appears and says something totally different. "Have you worked more on your song?"

"My song?"

Steffi hadn't told them it was hers.

"Yeah, the one you called 'Believe.' "

"Well, yeah, it was mine."

Karro is staring at them. The shifts in her expression could be photographed one by one.

"It was cool. I knew you had to be writing it yourself, because you hadn't figured out a refrain yet."

"Right . . . that's right. But I have one now. I tried to emphasize the motif in the transition and made it the basis of the entire refrain, and I changed the key, too."

Hannes nods. He doesn't ask her if she wants to be the bass player in Lard Heroes, but he does say: "Cool."

Then he heads into the bathroom, as if he hadn't done anything special at all, and Karro and Steffi are left standing there in an unclear universe.

"How the hell do you know Hannes?"

Steffi doesn't answer.

Karro puts her face back into place. "I never thought he'd sleep with whores."

Steffi thinks about this the whole way to Alvar's place. It doesn't matter what Karro said. She'd panicked when Steffi talked to Hannes. Because Hannes is cute and Steffi is Steffi. She goes through the conversation again and again, listening to the tones of the voices, plays back Karro's expressions and how they changed from one to the next. The warmth she'd felt when Hannes said: *Cool.*

Does this mean she's in love? Is there anyone who could answer that question?

"All that between boys and girls," Alvar says after she'd asked him. "I can't say I ever understood it."

She shakes her head. "Me neither."

"Really?"

"'Letter from Frej' doesn't speak to me anymore," she says, and she catches a smile from Alvar. He doesn't say anything, so she sits up in her chair. "There's a kind . . . of pecking order," she says. "It's determined by the girls the boys want to have and the boys the girls want to have. You never think about it. I mean, you *have to* think about it, but you never ask yourself why it is the way it is."

Alvar thought he was going to tell her about Anita and his burning desire for her, but there's something in the girl's voice, something in her reality. *What is she really trying to tell him?* "So what does this pecking order look like?"

She presses her lips together as she thinks.

"Some are at the top and some are on the bottom. Some have everything."

"And others have nothing."

"Others have no significance whatsoever."

Her voice is crisp and to the point, but it squeaks like a violin when a player demands too much from it. This dark-haired girl sitting in his chair takes a deep breath.

"People can't handle it if you don't stay in your place. It's that important."

Alvar is not sure what Steffi needs, but he knows he can help her with a little white lie. "I wasn't a popular kid before I left Björke."

"You weren't?"

"At least the girls didn't think so. In that pecking order you're talking about, I would have been on the bottom rung."

Now he is telling the truth. The only girls who had crushes on him in Björke were little kids, and he wasn't afraid of them.

"And when I got to Stockholm, I didn't understand a thing about girls."

That much was absolutely true.

Alvar didn't understand a thing about girls. He didn't understand how some guys could make them giggle, what the girls liked and didn't like, and why Ingmar always had a girl on his arm and Erling always had three at a time while Alvar was just dreaming rose-colored dreams about Anita. To win her, he'd have to figure out the secret. Which he found in Bonde Street, high up in an apartment not much bigger than a pantry with a kitchen nook.

This was the second time he had come. The building was packed with families. Their large-eyed children would follow him up the stairs. When he talked to them, they just stared back. It was a bit unnerving, actually. An excited face met him at the door.

"I snagged some new records!"

Erling gestured to him to close the door. The staring children disappeared. When the door was shut, he could hear them laugh and yell like normal kids, and he breathed a sigh of relief. Erling headed to the other side of the apartment.

"Artie Shaw," he said as he dropped the needle of his gramophone.

It was always magical to listen to new music. Any record could bring a new emotion, a new way to feel a note or a new melody he'd want to imitate as soon as he could. The best records came by boat—they brought not just new rhythms and melodies, but also America. For Alvar, feelings welled up in his body and his hands wanted to move.

"That was hep," he said. "That spot where he went up the scale. Did you hear the bass?"

"It cost me two bits and a half," Erling said. "But it was worth it. One day I'm going to be playing the clarinet for three crowns a record, count on it."

They sat in silence, their heads bobbing to the music. Alvar was beating the rhythm with his fingers as Erling swung his elbows with a pleased smile on his lips.

When the needle began to scratch at the end of the record, Erling got up and took off the record, placing it gently into its sleeve. Grinned. "So you want to know how to pick up chicks? Get the girl? Have a fling with some swing?"

Was Erling making up these phrases on the spot? Alvar tried to memorize them, just to be on the safe side.

"Yeah, that's right."

Erling gestured for Alvar to follow him across the floor.

"The first thing you need can be found in this cupboard."

Alvar opened the door to his cupboard with the same devotion as if it held the Eucharist. At the bottom of the cupboard, he spied a jumbled heap of what must be handkerchiefs. The cupboard had just one shelf. A red tube with a screw-on cap lay beside a brown comb. Erling was waiting for a reaction, so Alvar reached out for the tube. Erling grabbed his hand. "Careful, buddy. This, Big Boy, is the stuff of dreams . . ." Erling paused for dramatic effect. "This is Brylcreem."

Brylcreem was a snuff-colored jelly that you pressed out onto your palm. Once Erling was reassured that Alvar respected his Brylcreem, Alvar was allowed to rub some into his hair according to Erling's strict instructions. The inside of the cupboard had a mirror speckled with black spots.

Alvar watched himself transform into someone else. A young man, an elegant gentleman, his reddish blond hair shiny and just slightly wavy in the tight grip of the jelly. He looked at Erling in surprise.

"Well, well, well, what a hepcat we have here! I see I have some competition!" Erling winked and Alvar blushed.

Erling insisted that Brylcreem alone would not make the girls run after him. Girls liked three things in a man, and they all had to be in one and the same man.

"Brylcreem, adventure, and nonchalance. It's a golden triangle. If you have adventure and Brylcreem, but no nonchalance, they don't think the adventure is exciting enough. If you just have Brylcreem and nonchalance, they think you're just dull, and they figure that out pretty fast."

"But if I have adventure and nonchalance?"

"Not going to work without the Brylcreem. Got it?"

Alvar didn't exactly get it, but he had to give in. How do you look adventurous? How do you look nonchalant, especially if nonchalance was not part of your nature?

Erling was a generous man, however.

"I'm going to give you three, no four, pickup lines. But you have to say them the right way."

Alvar wrote them down in the notebook Åkesson had given him for shopping. The three qualities. The four pickup lines. Rules for how long it would take before calling a girl on the phone, rules for taking your time. Three days. A hard-and-fast rule. Then an address where Alvar could buy Brylcreem, even if you could get some at every other barbershop.

"Come on," Erling said before Alvar had to leave. "Just listen to this one. It's Barney Bigard."

Alvar stopped dreaming of Anita's soft hands and stopped running through bass lines in his head. Instead, he repeated the pickup lines over and over until he fell asleep dreaming of an insinuating intonation. It had to sound natural.

—

Alvar decided to attempt to seduce Anita on a wonderful June day.

Erling's trio had a gig at Solis. It would be Alvar's first attempt at being a bass player in public. They had to play schottisches and fox-trots, but the owner had decided to let them play "I Got Rhythm" as well. "You know how the young people are," Erling had said, with a confidence-inspiring smile. "They're crazy about Gershwin."

Alvar was now a real musician in Stockholm. The words seemed too big to fit and he had to keep repeating them inside his head to make sure they were true. He was still repeating them as he took his spot on Solis's tiny stage, holding tightly to his borrowed bass. Erling took the spotlight in front. Ingmar sat down at the piano in a completely self-assured manner.

Alvar couldn't remember much of their performance afterward. He remembered he'd made a mistake during "I Got Rhythm," but he'd found his place right away, so quickly that maybe nobody noticed.

Or maybe everyone noticed. Ingmar told him he'd played well. He couldn't see Anita. Maybe she'd gone home? Erling walked over, holding two bottles of pilsner, one for Alvar. "Wonderful! Absolutely wonderful! Don't you think so?"

Erling was saying this to Ingmar, who nodded. Where was Anita? Alvar gripped his pilsner, and he couldn't decide whether to drink it (as Erling would want) or not (as his mother would want).

"You recovered nicely in that piece," Anita's voice whispered in his ear.

He almost dropped the bottle.

---

The trouble with trying to seduce Anita was that she made him feel everything but nonchalant.

"Are you all right?" she asked, putting a hand on his shoulder.

This did not help him feel more nonchalant.

"*Ijustwanttotakeawalk,*" he forced out while trying to keep a deep voice. "*Gottacheckthebass.*" He walked through the restaurant and stopped in front of the stage.

At a table beside him, two guests were arguing about whose turn it was to pay the next round. Not his concern. He was now a musician, a musician in Stockholm.

A voice came through the cigarette smoke.

"You played very well," said the owner's wife, a tall woman of around forty.

He looked at her and wondered if she made him feel nonchalant. He squinted like Erling had shown him and smirked. "If the ladies were pleased, I'm pleased, too," he said, without blinking.

He was ready.

He was not ready. His hands, though they'd become steadier as he'd been learning to swing and do the Charleston, were now just as shaky and sweaty as they'd been the first time he'd gone to Nalen. Still, it was now or never. The guests at Solis had been going home, two by two or in groups, and now just the owners and Erling's trio were on the terrace. Erling had a girl on his knee, and Ingmar was talking to the owners about the war.

The United States had just declared war on Hungary, Bulgaria, and Romania. It seemed as if Germany and the Axis were losing ground.

"I think the Axis are losing, and for Norway's sake, I sure hope so," Ingmar declared. "Still, keep in mind that the Germans are strong. I don't think they'll be scared by an attack. Things might escalate further."

People would talk about the war all the time, in spite of the government's urging that "a Swede keeps quiet." The war was always present in all the rationing affecting daily life, and as time went by, it was on everyone's mind. The war was like a bear in the woods: people assumed Sweden would not be attacked, but the possibility kept them on edge.

Except for this moment, on a terrace after a successful gig. Alvar's thoughts were far from the war and Ingmar's comments on the state of the conflict in Europe seemed almost meaningless compared to the immediacy of this summer night.

The sun had made an attempt to set, but it was June, where it would not be gone for long, so it just floated along the horizon, making the sky around it blush.

"It's so pretty," Anita said with a sigh.

Was she speaking to herself or to him?

"So *purdy,*" Alvar repeated. Then he realized this was not romantic. He could have hit himself.

But Anita giggled.

Alvar swallowed. He had nothing to swallow, unfortunately, as his mouth was as dry as his palms were damp, but at least he managed not to cough. He took a deep breath as quietly as he could. "Shall we look at the sunset from over here?"

He pointed at a spot farther along the iron fence. The June air brushed past the sweat on his upper lip. Anita got up, leaped up, as if she'd been waiting for this.

"I liked the way you played this evening," she said as they reached the fence.

She wasn't looking at him but at the clouds meeting the setting sun, turning orange and pink. She looked like a girl ready for romance. She was with him.

He launched into a line. "Was that cannon fire, or is my heart pounding?"

Anita turned away from the horizon and stared at him in confusion.

Alvar's heart skipped a beat. What had he done wrong? Erling had told him that nothing could go wrong, not if you said it the right way! Complete *idiots* could use Erling's pickup lines! He grinned involuntarily, but he hoped it looked charming. He ran his hand through his hair the way Erling had shown him and peeked at Anita nervously.

Anita burst out laughing. She couldn't stop. She grabbed the iron railing so as not to fall over. The entire Stockholm night was tinged with her mirth.

Alvar was crestfallen.

"Erling!" she called out. "Erling! Did you teach Alvar this line? My heart is pounding like . . . no, wait, how did it go?"

Alvar had a choice. He could stand there in his humiliation or he could smile. He chose to smile. He turned toward the others on the terrace, laughed with Anita, laughed with Erling, who repeated his pickup line with a grin and made them all laugh, even the owners. Alvar laughed until his cheeks ached, and only the setting sun saw how he suffered inside. In the distance, it dipped below the horizon, leaving only its halo to light up the night air.

# – CHAPTER 15 –

Mamma is standing next to Steffi, but Steffi pretends she's by herself, just her and the train, and not just for two days but for an eternity. The skies are gray in Björke. Mamma is carrying the bag with the linens and Steffi is carrying the most important things: her bass and a plastic bag.

She keeps the plastic bag shut as long as they're taking the local train. They pass one small town after another with station names on lacquered wooden signs. At some stations, the stop sign has been lowered and a few people get on. At other stations, the platforms pass by as gray and fleeting as the clouds.

Mamma says she's happy she could get a few days off and accompany Steffi. She's sad that she's not home as much as Pappa is, and already Julia and Steffi are so big. "Soon you'll be all grown up," she says. "It goes so fast."

Steffi is just listening with one ear. She's not sure time goes by all that fast. "For you, maybe," she says when her mother stops speaking and looks at her. "You're forty-six and one year is one forty-sixth of your life. One year for me is like three for you. Imagine three years!"

Mamma looks at her with a half smile. "If you decide to quit music, you can always be a mathematician," she says.

Steffi replies immediately. "I will never quit music."

"I only meant *if*."

"Do you want me to quit? Just because I'm not like Julia?"

It comes out too fast for her to stop it. She didn't mean to sound so spiteful. She really didn't.

Her mother looks puzzled. "Julia? How could she ever be a mathematician?"

Steffi laughs. Of course, Julia would never be a mathematician.

Mamma laughs, too, and seems relieved. "Well, she could be if she wanted," she says a few seconds later. "I mean, she's not . . . she just has other interests, is all I'm saying."

"Boys and makeup."

Mamma smiles in agreement and keeps smiling until she starts thinking of something else and her smile fades. "And what about you?"

"Me?"

"Yes, I mean . . . boys and makeup . . . and . . . well . . ."

Steffi doesn't understand the question. Her mother is starting to blush. "What are you getting at?"

"Well, you . . . it . . . you know, of course, you can talk to me and Pappa about anything you need to know, right?"

It's not a bad theory. Steffi likes it. She nods and looks out the window. The station house at Kil is a colossus in red brick. There's one more station before they reach Karlstad.

They have seats eighteen and twenty-two, across from each other, and they are no longer on the local train. The rails vibrate beneath them. Mamma asks if she wants to play cards, but Steffi shakes her head. She takes out her mp3 player and then Mamma takes out a book. She lifts one of Steffi's headphones.

"Just tell me if you need anything."

Steffi nods.

Arne Domnérus is wailing on the saxophone. She'd thought yesterday that his music would fit her trip to Stockholm. She plays air bass guitar, finding a nice bass walking line that would fit.

Red and brown houses. Fields. Trees. Barns falling apart. Forest. She sees her own face in the window when they pass the dark green forests, and it disappears in the white spaces between the forests.

After a while, she bends down and takes out her hat from the plastic bag. She's tired of playing air bass. Mamma is deep inside her book. It has a blackish brown background, red letters and blood on the cover.

Steffi thinks that her mother doesn't see as she puts her round hat on her head and watches her reflection go past. Her reflection shows a brilliant musician. A jazz-crazy girl of her own unique kind, one nobody at Björke School had ever met. She breathes on the window and then traces letters: S. H. H.

For Steffi. Herrera. *Hepcat.*

They're staying with one of her grandfather's army pals while in Stockholm. He's a seventy-year-old man with a fifty-year-old wife and a dog. Both the wife and the dog are blond and fluffy. The man is bald and his first name is Göran. Steffi had met them once before when Mamma had turned forty and they'd had a big party. Steffi had been a little kid. She knows the first thing they'll mention is how much she's grown.

"Oh, Stephanie, look at you! A real young lady!" the wife says.

Steffi bites back a sarcastic reply and just says hello instead. She answers Göran's question about being almost done with ninth grade and choosing a *gymnasium*. She says she feels fine about it. They have coffee and sandwiches and, afterward, Steffi asks to be excused so she can make a few calls.

Alvar answers at once.

"I suppose you haven't had time to look up 140 Åsö Street yet," he says.

"Not yet."

"It doesn't matter," he says, laughing. "It's just an address, when you get right down to it."

"If I get a chance, I'll make sure to go past it. And I'll take a picture, like I promised."

"The most important thing is that your audition goes well. How are you getting ready for it?"

"Playing the piece through. Thinking of the emotion behind it. Like you said."

"And?"

"And trying to think of something else."

"It's not the easiest thing, but it's the best thing to do. Did I tell you when Thore Ehrling came to listen to our trio?"

"Just a bit."

"It was 1943 and I had been practicing for twenty-four hours straight."

It was 1943 and Alvar had been practicing for twenty-four hours straight. He'd told Aunt Hilda that he was going to get a load of coffee from America for Åkesson. Sometimes he wondered if she had figured out that he did more than just run errands for the grocer, but as long as he was generously helping out with the rent, Aunt Hilda didn't say anything. And she didn't seem to suspect that his activities outside the Vasa Stan quarter could be in any way connected to jazz music. She would certainly have reacted if she had.

"Wait a minute . . . weren't you going to tell me what happened with Anita?"

"What do you mean?"

"What happened after you were all standing on the terrace and she was laughing at you while the sun set?"

"Yes, well, she was a part of everything that happened, even in 1943. Once the sun set, it had set and everything was the way it always had been. Erling set me to rights, though. He told me all the stuff he'd taught me, the Brylcreem and the pickup lines, they were for normal girls, simple, young girls. A girl like Anita was beyond me. I would never get her, so I shouldn't even try."

"Just as I told you. There's a pecking order."

"So I decided to lick my wounds and be a real expert on the bass. So now we've come to that day when Erling's trio was going to play at the Avalon."

"It was 1943 and you'd just been practicing for twenty-four hours in a row."

"That's right."

It was 1943 and although Alvar had practiced for the past twenty-four hours, he had a bad feeling about it. Erling's Trio was going to play at the Avalon. Thore Ehrling was looking for new talent, and this was the chance of a lifetime. He kept telling himself this, but it didn't sink in, and their turn was coming closer and closer.

Erling and Ingmar talked easily about a topic that had been important to all of them that spring: taking care of shoes. Erling was saying that the best way to take care of them was to take Brylcreem and regular shoe polish, half and half, and rub it into the entire shoe, including the sole. Ingmar had run across a kind of galoshes that were thinner and better looking than earlier models, so they could work for a wider range of occasions. The entire conversation—shoe rationing and the unpopular wooden soles—made Alvar think that both Erling and Ingmar were convinced everything would go well.

Alvar kept running his bass lines through his head over and over again, tried to find the right emotion, press through. When his turn came, the walking bass wound around his legs and whirled through his head into a mixture of unclear rhythms and melodies without any meaning.

And then: Thore Ehrling.

There were some names that came up more often than others when you tried to count who really mattered. Topsy, of course, the owner of Nalen, with his crazy ideas and dangerous flair. Gösta Törner, Lulle Ellboj, Seymour Österwall—all excellent musicians with bands at Nalen, Gröna Lund, The Winter Palace. Thore Ehrling. His name had been thrown about in Erling's jazz quarter on Bonde Street, always with great respect.

Thore Ehrling was now the orchestra conductor at Skansen, the large park at the eastern end of the city. Now here he was, in person, standing at the back of the hall. He was younger than Alvar had imagined, but advanced in musician years.

Alvar couldn't for the life of him remember how "Indiana" began. It came back as soon as the pianist hit the first chord. *Concentrate, Alvar! You've done this all night long! Just come in on the right note, on the F.*

Thore Ehrling was watching him from the other side of the hall. Alvar could sense it. Thore Ehrling was watching *him*. Not Erling, not Ingmar. He had this.

Alvar made his entrance on G, even though he knew it was supposed to be F. Then the whole thing was off, even though he was able to save some of it, but whenever he felt happy it was going well, he lost the feeling and hit the wrong note again. He never had played so badly in his entire life.

Thore Ehrling stopped him at the entrance. He was kind, but fair, like a god. Alvar's cheeks burned.

"I imagine you usually play better than that."

Alvar nodded unhappily. "I came in on the wrong note."

"Have you ever studied music? Learned harmony?"

"No, I'm self-taught."

"Good for you. You have talent. You're young. Don't be so hard on yourself because you messed up this round."

Alvar knew that he missed his one and only chance. It would never come around again.

"You're talented, all right, but you will have to learn that if you want to play in a good band, you have to come in on the right note every single time. Get some tips from someone with more experience."

The words floated past Alvar and faded away. Just like his chance of a lifetime.

"I might as well give up now," he told Anita a few hours later.

He'd ridden his bike across town with some letters from the former bassist on Djurgården—part of his way to earn his bass—and he'd exchanged ration coupons for syrup at Åkesson's supplier in Norrmalm. He no longer cared if they laughed at his

Värmland dialect. By now, he knew the streets of Stockholm better than most.

"Don't be stupid."

"I'm sure of it. He said I didn't have a chance."

"Did he really say that?"

She had a way of bending her head and looking at him from below, catching his eyes in hers and smiling slightly. He couldn't resist it—his heart lightened every time.

"No. All he said was I had to get it right every time I played."

"And?"

"And that I'm talented." He said this with extra surliness just to see her smile.

She laughed. "What can I do to cheer you up?"

Was there a glimmer in her eye, the kind girls gave to boys? It almost seemed so. He was eighteen now.

"Do you want to do something you've never done before?"

"What?"

"Come home with me."

Anita lived in the most exclusive part of Stockholm: Östermalm. This district had elegant columned entrances and immense apartments; ladies in fur coats and shiny new cars. He had never understood how Anita fit in. Now she was leading him up a stone staircase toward a huge entrance with a gold nameplate. She greeted the doorman, who was dressed in a stuffy uniform. She pulled open the grate of a small elevator. Now he was standing just inches from her all the way up to the fifth floor.

"Mattias won't tell on us," she said, her mouth close to his shoulder. "The doorman, that is. He's always nice to me."

"Won't tell what?"

"Won't mention you to my parents."

"But your parents are home, aren't they?"

She shook her head and took out her key, put it in the lock, and turned. There was another gold nameplate on the door.

"Not for another week."

He didn't know where to look. Crystals glittered in the electric chandelier, which lit up when Anita hit the switch. Heavy curtains with classic patterns in a modern style hung from the windows. New armchairs in leather stood between finely decorated china cabinets from the eighteenth century. The floor was some kind of smooth stone. Everything seemed to breathe money. Anita made sure to hang up their coats in the closet.

She walked through the apartment, smiled at him to encourage him to follow her, and then sat down at the stuffed piano stool that flanked an enormous white piano. On the music rack there was a Handel prelude. Anita swung one foot and looked content.

"Can you play that?" Alvar gestured toward the sheet music.

"How do you know I play the piano?"

"I don't know. That's why I'm asking. But you often . . ."

He intended to say that she often moved her fingers as if she were playing, but it would sound strange.

"I often do what?"

"You like music so much. So I thought maybe you played piano, that's all."

Anita lifted her feet and half-spun on the piano stool. First she just plunked a few notes, giggled to herself, and hit some chords at random. He pulled up a chair and sat as close to her as he could, so he almost touched her. Even though she wasn't playing a melody, it sounded absolutely beautiful. He had no idea a piano could sound so different depending on who was playing it.

When she stopped, he said, "Keep playing."

Anita breathed easily.

The air was theirs and theirs alone up on the fifth floor. Alvar felt her breath like vibrations. Then she laid her left hand on the keyboard. Her right hand began to play a descant. She was playing swing music.

He wasn't surprised, not perplexed, not shocked. He was happy deep down in his soul. Anita played swing, her emotions were in both the rhythm and the melody and she was improvising, just like the big names. He began to stamp his feet in time and hummed a bass part, which then turned into some kind of trumpet solo, and she began to hum, too, at a much higher pitch. Neither of them had the best singing voices, but it didn't mean a thing. Swing music was being played in Östermalm, and Alvar and Anita sang their solos to the crystal chandeliers and were mixed with the cuckoo-cuckoo of the clock's chime on the hour.

They drank tea in a room Anita called the "dining room." In Aunt Hilda's apartment, it would have corresponded to the few feet of space in the kitchen where the table was crowded by the kitchen bench. Aunt Hilda would say "When I used to live in Östermalm . . ." with such bitterness that Alvar wondered if Anita would be just as bitter if she were forced to move away from an apartment like this one. He had the feeling that a swing band bass player would never be able to afford an apartment in the district.

"I only play when I'm home alone," Anita said. "Or on Åsö Street, if nobody else is there."

"Why? You're really good!"

Anita laughed, and her cheeks turned rosy. "Thank you. But I'm not that good. Not as good as Ingmar. He studied at the music conservatory, you know. Or did you know?"

"Erling didn't go to music school. Lots of people don't go to music school. I didn't." He blushed. He hadn't meant to put himself on the same level as Erling and a number of other anonymous musicians who were really good. "I mean, it doesn't mean much one way or the other," he added, quickly.

"You're better than Erling."

"What?"

"You're more talented. He knows more than you do right now, but you will be a better musician in the long run. He's too sloppy."

Alvar didn't know what to say. It was an incomprehensible compliment. He peeked at Anita, her soft face and her blunt nose and the lively contours of her eyes. Her hand almost touched his on the keyboard. Should he take it?

"And, as far as that goes . . . ," Anita was saying in a slow voice. "I can never be a jazz pianist. My parents won't allow me to go see jazz music. They'd never accept it as a career for me, even if I was good."

Alvar looked at her in surprise. "But you go to Nalen every week!"

Anita sipped her tea. She sipped with finesse, not slurping like everyone did at home. Or the way people did in Södermalm.

"As far as my parents know, I'm at the riding club. And that's what you'll say, too, if they ask."

He stared at her to see if she smiled mischievously about her deceit. She didn't.

"Aunt Hilda thinks I'm out delivering things day and night," he said.

"I know."

"It's . . . it's ridiculous that we have to pretend."

She imitated his Värmland vowels. "Ridiculous." She smiled. "And there's another thing on my mind," she said.

She leaned closer to him, her lips just a breath away. Alvar had never kissed a girl and he was not sure how people did it, but he did know that the boy was supposed to take the initiative.

Anita looked into his eyes. Her lips parted slightly, she smiled. “I’m in love, you see. I’m in love with Ingmar.”

# – CHAPTER 16 –

Her bass is in its case on her back, her hepcat hat on her head. Mamma asks her if she's nervous, if she likes riding the subway, whether she would remember the way if she had to ride it by herself. Steffi grunts as an answer to the first two questions, and to the third she says to her mother that she has to concentrate. "Sorry," Mamma says. Her mother sounds almost as nervous as she feels.

She's someone else now. The bullying victim stayed behind in Björke. It is Hepcat taking the subway through its tunnels and stopping at Karlaplan Station, Östermalm Square Station, Central Station, Old Town Station. *You are who you want to be,* Alvar had told her yesterday evening on the phone. *Changing into, and out of,* Steffi thinks. It's not that hard to make herself into Hepcat. She just has to let her fingers fly and be the future hope of Sweden when it comes to playing her bass. Alvar had told her: *You reach a breaking point when you are tired of having to be the person your surroundings want you to be.*

---

His breaking point came after Anita had disclosed her love for Ingmar. For five days, he sat listlessly on the kitchen bench, so listless that Aunt Hilda finally asked him if he shouldn't leave the apartment. Then he spent a second day pounding various fences with his fists in a vain attempt to rip Anita's soft gaze and lively piano-playing fingers from his mind. On the seventh day, he went to the barber. Using some of the money he'd saved, he bought a better quality used suit and a tie in the latest style. He polished his shoes, ran Brylcreem through his freshly cut hair, made his most serious face in Aunt Hilda's mirror, became a man.

"You aren't going to be getting into trouble, young man?" Aunt Hilda asked.

"A meeting on procuring supplies at the store," Alvar replied, and Aunt Hilda decided not to press him on the matter, even though it was late in the evening.

He walked with confidence to Nalen. While in line, he practiced his poses—no, he was becoming them. He was turning into the new Alvar, reflecting all the other men in the long line in front of Nalen, and he didn't look away from the girls' glances. For a second, he thought he saw a girl he recognized. Was it the sad girl from the train? The one with the angry aunt? She didn't seem to recognize him—perhaps it was someone who looked like her.

On the dance floor, he got the reaction he'd hoped for. Erling took a leap backward and exclaimed, "I hardly recognized you!" Large, ugly old Ingmar clapped him on the shoulder and Alvar let him, didn't let anyone see behind his serious expression that he'd practiced so well. A girl smiled at him and he smiled and said, "Hey, good-looking, wanna swing tonight?"

Anita laughed so hard when she heard him that it would have hurt his feelings if he hadn't changed into a different person.

"So Hepcat is out tonight?" she said.

"Well, ma'am, please excuse me. There are some girls who are demanding my attention."

*Still, Alvar changed because he was angry,* Steffi thought. *I'm not changing; I'm becoming more myself. The ugly, disgusting Steffi was someone* THEY *thought up, not me. They'll see. They'll* ALL *see. While they will never make it, I will.* Steffi and her mother are walking down a long hill and are soon in a canyon of enormous brick buildings. Perhaps Alvar had walked down this same hill. Or perhaps one of the other streets they'd been walking along.

"Don't forget that we are going to Åsö Street later."

"I won't forget," Mamma replies. "But aren't these buildings impressive?"

One of the brick buildings has the form of a tower and the others are ten stories high with ornate windows and archways. Three young people are walking over the courtyard. One has hair dyed red and another is carrying a guitar case. They're laughing at a joke Steffi cannot hear, sparring with each other, owning the courtyard.

She turns toward her mother, as she suddenly feels very small. "Is this it?"

Mamma looks at her phone. "Yes, we're here. We just have to find the entrance."

In the elevator, they're crowded together with a boy and his mother and another girl on her own. The parents start to chat about the auditions, nod and smile nervously. Steffi glances at the boy and the girl. Neither of them have instruments. The boy is chewing the inside of his cheek. The girl looks as bored as if she's on her way to the grocery store.

"Are you nervous?" the boy's mother asks them and Steffi makes an unclear sound as a reply. The other girl says she's not nervous at all, as she's gone to auditions since she was seven. Steffi's mouth goes dry. She's been playing bass for only three years.

The hallways have wall-to-wall carpeting. It's the first difference from Björke School that Steffi notices. The lockers bear stickers, hearts, strawberries, notes: *"At Ensemble until 4 p.m. Wait for me!"*; *"Couldn't get Fri, took Sat at 11"*; *"Jossan, I effing LOVE you!"*

There's a waiting room at the end of the hallway. There are some sofas. Steffi sees through a glass window a room with a number of electronic keyboards, and everywhere else there are fifteen-year-olds with dreams of getting into music school. It's easy to tell them apart from the ones that actually attend. Their eyes show blank, lost looks and subtle fear. They all are trying to focus. Some have parents with them and others are alone with their instruments. Steffi sits down along the same wall as the girl who wasn't nervous. They don't know each other, but at least they shared an elevator. On the other side, there are two guys with basses and at least eight with guitars.

"Perhaps this means it'll be easier to get in if you play bass," Steffi whispers to her mother.

"Maybe so." Her mother squeezes her hand.

"Hey there." One of the boys speaks up. "You're the only girl trying out on bass."

"OK." Steffi can't think of anything else to say.

"They'll let you in just for that."

The girl next to him giggles. "Why would they just let her in? If she's good, she'll get in, if not, no."

It's the first time in three years that someone her age has gone to bat for her. She secretly hopes that the boy is right and being a girl gives her an edge.

"Could be the opposite," the boy next to him says. "Could be they won't think she's good just because she's a girl."

The boy next to Steffi looks at the other three, who are discussing Steffi's future based on her sex. He's wearing a beret and looks like a stereotype of a French artist, except for the fact that he's also wearing a denim vest.

"They're professionals, you idiots," he says. "They couldn't care less what's between your legs."

Steffi feels she ought to speak up. She's Hepcat, of course. In Stockholm, she's not going to be a victim before she even opens her mouth. "They have a girl bass player on their Web page," she says. It may have been an idiotic thing to say, but at least she was speaking up.

The boy in the beret says, "The first girl bassist who studied here was murdered."

Nobody says a thing after that. Steffi wonders how he knows this.

He adds, "Not because she was a bassist, though."

They start to discuss the musicians who have influenced them. Nikki Sixx, Craig Adams, Lee Rocker. Steffi hasn't heard of any of them. Then everyone looks at her. "What about you?"

She knows it's a test.

Her mother is sending her nervous signals, as if she also knows.

But Hepcat always tells the truth.

"I haven't listened to many modern bass players, but I like Ray Brown, Slam Stewart, Jimmy Blanton, Gunnar 'The Duck' Almstedt . . . Alvar Svensson." She smiles as she says Alvar's name.

The fifteen-year-olds across from her look impressed, or at least not scornful. One of the boys nods. "You from Gothenburg or what?"

"Can't you hear she's from Värmland?" the other boy says and turns to Steffi. "My stepmom is from Värmland, so I hear that accent every day."

The boy with the beret says, "If you like jazz bassists, you must love Avishai Cohen."

He's peering at her with an intensive look. She peers back, wishing she had known the person he was talking about. "He plays . . . like, not really experimental in a difficult manner, but a new way. A little more ethnic. Avishai Cohen, here, I'll write down his name for you. Who were the other ones, besides Ray Brown and Jimmy Blanton?"

Mamma is relaxing—Steffi can tell. The beret boy is looking into her eyes in a way that makes her stomach flip.

"Stephanie," an authoritative voice says from behind the magic door. "Stephanie Herrera?"

# — CHAPTER 17 —

Afterward, she can't remember how she played. Her mind goes blank after she damps down the last note. All she remembers is feeling good once she was halfway through with the song "Have to, Want To."

A real bassist and another teacher were observing her. The bassist begins to smile. "Let me guess. The first song was one you were forced to learn and the second one was one you wanted to learn, am I right?"

Steffi cautiously smiles back. Perhaps it's not so good if he can hear which one she liked to play and which one she didn't.

"I wrote the second one," she admits. "It has lyrics, but . . ."

She falls silent as she feels her heart pounding, as if she's just run a marathon. Both teachers give her encouraging smiles.

"We like that in a student, don't we?" one teacher said.

"It's cool to write your own stuff." The bassist nods.

She wants to ask if she's going to get in, but that's not possible.

They ask her the music she prefers and she tells them jazz and blues. They ask how long she's been playing and she says three years. She can't read their faces. Finally they ask her about her grades. Her regular grades, like math and English. She's on the spot.

"Well, they're . . . they're all right, I guess. I mean, I can't get in if I have bad grades?"

"Not if they're especially bad, or if you have incompletes," the bass teacher replies.

"All subjects are important," the other teacher says. "We don't want people who botch it once they get here."

She doesn't hear what they say after that. She goes cold. How much has she skipped social studies? And the weeks of Sexual Health and Relationships? Not to mention English! She remembered how Semlan had tried to drill the importance of attendance into her just a few weeks ago. Now she feels what Semlan was trying to make her feel back then. What can she do about it now?

"If you don't have any more questions, I believe we're done now."

She has tons of questions but can't squeak out a single one.

Both teachers shake her hand before she leaves the room where her fate has been decided. A preliminary letter can be expected in May.

So that was that.

Steffi feels empty as she leaves the old Brewery housing the music school with her mother. They walk up the hill and past a hot dog stand and a large collection of buildings. They take the escalator deep into the underworld. She is suffering a strong feeling of having lost her only chance.

"Chin up," Mamma says. "You don't know for sure how it went."

Steffi is looking at herself in the dark windows of the subway car. She's remembering the boy with the beret.

"I like your hat," he'd said to her right before she was called into the audition room. When she'd finished, he was gone, just as she felt her chances of getting into music school had disappeared. Now she's absolutely convinced that she'd messed it up.

"Do you still want to see Åsö Street? Or should we just head back to Göran and Annelie's place?"

Steffi decides to ignore her increasingly pessimistic thoughts about her audition. Alvar didn't get into Skansen's Dance Orchestra, and he became a famous bass player nonetheless.

"Let's go to Åsö Street."

*I will find a way to get to Stockholm,* Steffi decides as they exit the subway station at Medborgarplatsen. *Karlstad will just be a stepping-stone on my path if I don't get into the school here. But it won't keep me from Stockholm.*

The web of streets and tall buildings is bigger than she'd imagined, almost infinite, but if she gets a bike, she'll be able to figure out how to get around.

She notices two tall Africans with dreadlocks standing around the station entrance. Another man, pushing a baby carriage, is heading off to the left while a woman with her hair dyed red and a hat heads off to the right. A few young men are laughing so loud they're almost screaming. They're all Asian or South American. One of them has tattoos all the way up his neck. Only two people look like they'd belong in Björke. Hundreds look like anything but.

140 Åsö Street is a yellow building with a rough stone facade. They needed to ask only one person where it was. Compared to Alvar's difficult journey seventy plus years ago, the trip was noth-

ing. Steffi stops to look at the entrance. It is arched and somewhat sunken into the building. Two stairways, one on each side, lead up to it. So that's where Alvar walked inside and was met by an angry doorman with a fleshy lower lip before he entered paradise with its blackout shades. None of this can be seen, but Steffi feels his devotion. She takes out her camera and photographs the entrance, the facade, the windows all the way up, and the basement doors with their locks hanging outside. She walks up to the building and touches its walls. Then she asks her mother to take a picture of her standing in front of it. She studies the picture after her mother has taken it, nods, and says, "We can go now."

Her mother doesn't ask anything for a while, but as they are heading down the escalator back into the subway, she can't hold back any longer.

"Is there something special about that particular address?"

"Yes."

Mamma smiles, nudges her shoulder. "What's so special about it?"

They're walking through the gate, showing their tickets to the attendant. Real Stockholmers have cards they swipe in machines on their way through.

"Alvar used to talk about that address."

Part of her wants to tell her mother all about Alvar, even if she wouldn't understand it all. Her mother would never understand how it *felt* to walk down a staircase and find jazz music in the middle of the darkness in the middle of a war. Steffi decides to keep the story for herself.

"Are we taking the Green Line this time?" she asks instead.

She's already figured out what the different subway lines are called.

—

The fifty-year-old wife of Steffi's grandfather's army pal gives Steffi a conspiratorial wink when Steffi decides to go speak on her phone instead of watching an episode of *Dancing with the Stars*.

"I can understand how important it is to talk to your boyfriend," she says with a laugh.

"He's not my boyfriend," Steffi says and blushes.

She can still hear the woman laughing at her own imagination concerning Steffi's wild teenage life as she waits for the call to go through. Four rings and nobody picks up, but then she hears Alvar's sleepy voice.

"Were you sleeping again?"

"It's been a long time since ladies called me at this hour, so I'm not used to being up. So tell me, how did it go?"

"Terribly."

"I see. What went wrong?"

"Nothing. I'm just sure it was terrible."

"What did the panel say?"

"That it was terrible."

"Did they really say that?"

"No, well, they said it was *good* I wrote my own stuff. But I *know* it went all wrong."

Silence on the other end of the line.

Then Alvar says, "Sometimes things go wrong, but then they go better again. As long as you don't give up."

"Did things get better for you?"

"After Anita had unburdened her love for Ingmar to me?"

"No, right after you failed to get the chance to play at Skansen."

"Well, yes and no. The funny thing about goals is that you have to be aware of when to modify them, you see."

---

Alvar had realized one thing about goals: you have to be aware of when to modify them. *Goal: to be Anita's guy and reason for living* had now changed to *Goal: make a living with music and be kissed by a girl.* Alvar was a new man, with emphasis on *man* and not *boy.* With the one glaring exception that he had never kissed a girl.

With Brylcreem in his hair, possibly a bit too much, he looked like someone who'd kissed girls. In his suit and hat, he looked like he might already have gone so far as to touch a girl's breasts or even more. Just the thought sent a shiver through him. He cleared his throat.

"The thing is, see, I can only let one girl in without a ticket."

The girl in front of him in line turned slightly so she could see him. She looked puzzled. This was normal, just as Erling described how it would go. They were in the long line to get into Nalen. She wasn't going anywhere.

"What are you talking about?"

"Oh, I'm sorry, I thought I heard you ask if you could come on Thursday."

"Where on Thursday?"

The girl's friend had also turned toward him. She cocked her head and her eyelashes fluttered like exotic fans. Alvar repeated to himself what Erling had told him—girls got nervous, too. It was difficult when they were standing so close he could smell their perfume.

"My swing band, Erling's Trio. We're jamming at the Monk. But as I said, it's going to be full, so I can only get one girl a free ticket. Two max. But I've already promised one ticket to . . ."

He scratched his stiff hair to distract them from his blush. It really was not a lie, he told himself. Anita was a girl and she'd promised to come, even if he wasn't the one who'd asked. And they were playing at the Monk.

"But if it's your band . . . ," the second girl said.

She spun her body like a fashion model and peered at him with an entire amusement park of promise in her eyes. At him—Alvar from Björke! He was exhilarated and had to cough so as not to break out in laughter from sheer exuberance. He made his eyebrows sink in furrowed worry. Erling had told him it was important to keep cool. The slightest sign of weakness and he'd be lost. He measured them with his eyes and tried to ignore all the softness behind their blouses, their mouths, their white hips and thighs, and that perfume. . . .

"Let me see what I can do," he said. "But I need your names."

Alvar leaned against the wall at Nalen and contemplated his life. The huge crowd no longer frightened him. All of these people were now a backdrop to the most exciting evenings of his life. He knew many of the guys and they'd nod to each other and could toss comments back and forth in the Söder slang he now understood, though Aunt Hilda did not. He'd danced with many of the girls. He'd grabbed them by the waist and could throw the bravest ones into the air in a jitterbug he'd now mastered. He was eighteen years old, he had a good suit, he played in a band, and he had just shown he could chat up girls.

One girl peeped "Erling!" right beside him, but soon they'd be calling "Alvar!" in that same twittering voice.

He felt his hair and made sure it was still in the stiff wave demanded of every hepcat at Nalen. He drew his finger over his chin to check his shave. It was hard on his self-image that the hair on his chin was still more like peach fuzz and wouldn't leave a manly stubble, but it was better to shave than to leave it and have people think he was just fourteen.

He glanced over to the band, raised high on the platform

over the jitterbugs. He felt the longing in his stomach to be up there—he watched the bass player and followed his fingers.

"Erling!"

Someone touched his arm. The scent of perfume from earlier this evening intruded. It was the girl with the eyelashes, and she was laughing. "What are you dreaming about? Dancing a jitterbug?"

Perhaps because he'd been philosophizing about his own life and how grown-up he now had become, or perhaps because she'd called him Erling and he *became* Erling for a moment—something made him not feel nervous in the least.

"One day I'm going to be up there," he said and nodded toward the band.

She giggled. "Wouldn't you rather be on the dance floor?"

He was still watching the bass player. The man behind the upright bass was the foundation of all the music and the reason everyone could dance.

"No."

"Not even if you could dance with me?"

His gaze moved from the band to the girl in front of him. She touched her hair—why do girls always touch their hair and why does this make it hard for him to breathe—and she smiled with her rosy velvet lips.

What would Erling do?

"For you, then, let's go."

This dance was unlike any previous dance at Nalen. He felt it in her hand as she gripped his; he saw it in her look and that made his legs ready to leap. Her wide eyes made him want to tell her things, secret things, like this was the first time he'd danced with a girl he'd actually spoken to first.

"By the way, my name isn't Erling," he said as a swing brought her close.

She was panting, her cheeks red, her dark hair flying even though it had been set with hair spray.

"What is your name, then?"

"Alvar."

"What did you say?"

The music had reached the middle bridge and the horns were blaring, so it was hard to hear.

"Alvar."

"What?"

He yelled at the top of his voice at the moment the trumpets stopped. "ALVAR!"

Four or five pairs of dancers glanced at them and Alvar felt the blood rush to his face. The girl laughed and sneaked closer to him. He was sweaty. She had dimples. She let her body press into his as she said:

"And my name is Inga-Lill."

As the band switched to a fox-trot, they kept standing on the dance floor. She stood on her toes and whispered into his ear that he was a good dancer. Her breath against his cheek had a different feel from the sweat. Her breath was for him alone. If he just moved his head slightly, his lips would meet hers. Just the thought made it hard for him to breathe: he finally would kiss a girl for the first time. In reality. Not in a dream with a vague image of Anita. He decided to do it.

Alvar kissed Inga-Lill as they stood on the large dance floor of Nalen.

Inga-Lill's lips were thin, soft, and warm.

She was breathing quickly through her nose; she'd closed her eyes.

Her cheek was so soft that Alvar's felt stubbly, in spite of his lack of thick beard growth.

The band was playing "A String of Pearls."

Her lips parted slightly and the tip of her tongue met his. It was wet and rough. He had no idea it would feel like this.

He was holding her back and she turned up toward him and that feeling of her bending waist called him back to reality. She giggled at him and he started to giggle, but then he laughed a real, rough man's laugh. He twirled her around so he could have the chance to compose himself. He was determined never to ask if she could tell it was the first kiss he'd ever given.

Inga-Lill. Her name was as sweet as a piano solo. He said it out loud every time he went to buy a drink or go to the bathroom. Each time he left, she was still there when he returned. She took his hand whenever he held out his own. Her hands were streamlined, with narrow fingertips, and she liked to use them to touch his face. Whenever they reached his neck, he shivered, swallowed, laughed, and he took her out to dance another jitterbug and then another fox-trot that ended with their mouths touching.

"So, do you think I'll get in on Thursday?" Inga-Lill asked with a smile.

Behind her, coming inside Nalen's entrance, another girl was walking with steps so familiar they could belong to only one person. She was taking off her hat with a sweeping gesture and her laugh could be seen but not heard over the music. Next to her, Ingmar clumsily draped his arm around Anita's shoulders.

"Hello? Are you in there?" Inga-Lill was waving her streamlined hand. His gaze went back to her, the girl whose lips he'd kissed in reality.

"Excuse me?"

"Thursday, silly! When your band plays at the Monk!"

Her laugh was simple and the way her lips moved as she called him silly—they were real, warm lips.

"Of course," Alvar said. He stood as tall as his eighteen-year-old body would let him. "Trust Big Boy—I'll make sure you get in."

She closed her eyes and she kissed him. He closed his eyes as well.

# – CHAPTER 18 –

The entire way home, Mamma keeps asking her strange questions. Steffi doesn't really notice until after the train has passed Simrishamn Station. "What about the boys at music school?"

"What about them?"

"Well, you haven't mentioned them, though I guess that's not strange."

"I only met them for, like, five minutes! The same thing with the girls, too, by the way. What are you talking about?"

"I mean, yes, well, I thought . . . it's not so strange, I guess."

"What? WHAT? Mamma!"

"You weren't noticing them because you were focusing on your audition."

"What do you want me to say about them?"

"What would you say about them?"

"WHAT?"

"Or the girls. If that's what . . . I mean . . ."

Steffi stares at her mother, who seems to have gone off her rocker. Steffi will soon have to put her into the Sunshine Home with all the other dementia patients. She says this, too, which makes her mother laugh.

"I was just wondering," Mamma says.

"I get it, but what are you wondering about?"

"If there's anyone . . . in particular . . . that you like. Your own age, I mean. Not the man at the retirement home."

"Oh." She thinks for a moment about the boy with the beret at the music school, the one who liked her hat, the one who said that she wouldn't be murdered even if she were a bass player. She thinks about Kevin and about Hannes, who likes how she plays bass. She shakes her head. "No, there's nobody in particular."

Not like she'd tell her mother if there was. If she *was* interested in the boy with the beret, she was not about to mention it. It would be her business, not her mother's.

"Even if I did like someone," she added, "it's not like I'm going to tell you first thing."

Mamma looks down at her book, keeping her eyes still.

"It's not like teenagers go running to their mothers about stuff like that," Steffi tries to clarify.

The tension between them starts to ease, and her mother starts to read her book for real.

The atmosphere at home is also strange. Something odd has come over the entire Herrera family, and now her father is looking at her the same way her mother had while they were on the train. Julia is not looking at her at all. After five minutes at the dinner table, Julia asks to be excused and heads off to talk to her friends. The only normal member of the family is Edvin. He's trying to figure out if gold is just a metal or if gold is also a color or if gold is both a metal and a color. He finally stops talking only to ask why everyone else is silent. Steffi tells him that gold is also a color. Then Pappa asks how everything went at the audition, and finally things start to seem almost normal again. Except for that incomprehensible stuff.

After dinner, it's too late to head over to the Sunshine Home, so Steffi sits down at her computer. She opens Word and writes a list.

1. MAKE SURE TO PASS ALL CLASSES. UTMOST IMPORTANCE!
2. Check out Avishai Cohen, Lee Rocker, other bassists.
3. Ask Alvar if he's ever played bass guitar. Does he have any tips?

She can't think of any more tasks to add to her list, so she decides to surf the Web. Stephanie Herrera is long gone. She has another life and is not ever going to return. She logs in as Hepcat. Immediately there's a message.

From: Karro N
To: Hepcat

You're quiet. What r you doing? ;)

A winking smiley from Karro is so far from Steffi's reality that it's absurd. If Karro knew that she was winking at Steffi, she'd explode. She'd burst from shame, because Karro's world is Björke School and nothing else. Steffi is still in Stockholm. She's walking down the streets where Hepcat has been preparing the way for her for decades already.

From: Hepcat
To: Karro N

I'm thinking about the world. It's like fog, you can only see what is directly around you and as soon as you take a single step to the side you are somewhere else, and there's so much more than you thought. I'm going to get out of here as soon as I can, believe me.

She hits the send button, and releases it from her mind. Then her father knocks on the door.

Pappa is holding a sheet of paper. He's looking at Steffi as if she were a baby bird he shouldn't scare. He sits down on the bed and smiles at her. He unfolds the sheet of paper as if it weren't all that important, almost nothing at all. But his trembling hand gives it all away. "Do you recognize this?" he asks as he waves it.

"How would I know? Can you hold still so I can read it?"

She sits down next to him and reads. It's a printout from a Web forum. The title says: *Am I a Lesbian?* The questioner calls herself: *Little Me*. The writer says she's trying to feel something for her boyfriend, but she finds she's always fantasizing about the girls she sees in the shower. Ten people have written back to tell her to wait and see. Others say she should sleep with a girl and see what it's like. Others say she shouldn't bother to define herself as a lesbian before trying sex with a boy other than her boyfriend. A few write to say they have the same problem.

"I wasn't meaning to pry," Pappa says. "Julia found this lying on the floor and we thought that maybe you wanted us to read it. Julia didn't want us to ask you about it, but I just don't want you to feel afraid."

Steffi looks at him, confused. "Why would I be afraid?"

"You know we love you, just as you are."

Steffi's mind leaps into overtime. What is he talking about?

She reads the sheet of paper again and sees the rescuer of frightened birds in her father's eyes.

"What . . . ," she says slowly. "What do you think I am?"

Pappa puts his arm around her. It's like a bear's, always warm and easy to cry against when you need to.

"We don't have to talk about it if you don't want to. I just wanted you . . . yes . . . well . . . it doesn't matter to me or to your mother who you like. You will always be our Steffita."

Steffi nods. "I know, Papito."

"Your papers are your business, of course."

He leaves the printout on her bed. She can't figure it out.

She picks up her bass, her eyes still on the answers to the question posed on the Web site. They're all badly written. She's pretty sure she's never read them before. Could she have printed out something without realizing it? Like when she thinks she's put her plate in the dishwasher, but really didn't? Is this her subconscious? Or did someone just hit print while they were reading the newspaper online?

She hums as she reads:

*Why not relax and let it all work out?*

She finds herself rhyming to a ragtime bass:

*You know it's your life to live.*
*Whoever you love, it's your love to give.*

She thinks she could start a radio talk show, giving advice on relationships based on jazz music. She shifts to a walking line and keeps thinking. There are so many things she could do. Errand boys probably no longer exist in Stockholm, but she could probably get some other kind of job until she got a spot in a band.

If the Monk and the Number One were still around, maybe she'd be able to play there. If not, there must be other places. She thinks about this sleeping-with-a-girl business, like one of the answers to *Little Me.* Probably not. Right now she has no interest in any of the guys she knows, either.

She hits a wrong note. She shivers, tries the note again. She's already figured this out. If it sounds wrong, just keep playing until it sounds right. Or play it wrong with confidence, so you could feel it all the way in your stomach. Alvar tells her she has what it takes.

Steffi never prays. There's not much God in the lives of the Herrera family, except when Pappa says "Good Lord!" in Swedish or Spanish. This evening, however, she felt she had to figure out how to open a line to the One Upstairs.

"Dear God," she whispers from beneath her blanket. "You know, if You are up there, that I'm really having a tough time down here. If You can, do what it takes so I can get into music school and move to Stockholm. Otherwise, my parents aren't going to let me go, even though there aren't any Germans in Norway like there were in Alvar's days. You know Alvar, the old man at the Sunshine Home."

It seems strange to be talking out loud to Someone who could already read your thoughts, so she doesn't bother with *Amen.* If He exists, He knows that she's finished.

She thinks about God for one more minute and then turns her thoughts to her mother's strange behavior on the train. Her parents must have found that sheet of paper before they got on the train that morning, she thinks. That explains all those strange questions. God doesn't say anything in response to her prayer, but she imagines He agrees with her request. If her request was the right thing to ask for, that is. God probably wouldn't agree if it were the wrong thing, just to remain friends. She realizes she knows next to nothing about God. Then she falls asleep.

# – CHAPTER 19 –

It's a much different thing to go to school when you know your future depends on it. Steffi manages to be early to social studies.

Karro's early, too. "Dyke slut," she says.

Steffi swallows the impulse to say "Good morning to you, too." Instead she just looks at the floor.

But Karro's eyes are bright as she tries to catch Steffi's attention. "I've heard it's official!"

Steffi doesn't say a word and doesn't give a damn about what Karro is making up. She doesn't give a damn because she'll be out of here in three months.

"You're a dyke slut. The whole Web is full of your sluttiness," Karro continues.

"What, what?" Sanja walks in, her eyes shining in excitement.

They were two dying queen bees in a hive that would soon be torn down. They just don't realize it yet.

"She's been surfing all kinds of lesbian sites. Her dad found out. I'm not making this up," Karro tells Sanja.

"What's that?" a third voice chimes in until the whole classroom is buzzing with Steffi's supposed lesbianism.

The rumor will fly through all the other classrooms like the smell of cooking food. It will get into all the lockers through all the gaps and be breathed from mouth to mouth in bathroom lines and jokes across the Ping-Pong table. The nasty kids will say "dyke slut" to her face and the nicer ones will just say "lezzie" because rumors are like drugs in Björke School. But that's not what ties Steffi's stomach in a knot. It's the fact that Karro knows what Steffi's father has talked about with Steffi behind a closed door at their house on 21 Herrvägen Road. She wants to tell Bengt that she can't stay in class today, because she feels like she's going to vomit. But if she leaves, she won't get a good grade.

Bengt bores his gaze into her, but she can't breathe. Steffi's still thinking about how Karro knew what was going on in her family. Was she spying? Did she use a webcam? Did Julia tell Fanny, who then spread the story around? Steffi feels like she's going to throw up any second.

Bengt is asking her how her project is going.

Steffi focuses. "Yes, right," she says. "It's that . . . it's on . . ." She can't even remember the topic she's chosen. It makes it so hard to lie about her progress.

"In my notes, I see you've chosen Sweden during the Second World War."

Steffi nods. Bengt raises an eyebrow.

"It looks to me as if you have no idea what your topic is. If you haven't even started, you have a great deal of work to do in the next two weeks."

Steffi nods again, convinced. "I have started. I'm sorry, I was just thinking about something else."

*Second World War,* Steffi thinks desperately. *Second World War, Second World War.* Time stops. She sees Alvar, his wild hair as he bikes through the strange new world of Stockholm.

"My topic . . . I'm writing about the Second World War and music."

"And?" Bengt's eyebrow heads up again.

"How things were for jazz musicians in Stockholm."

"In Stockholm?"

"Yes, not in Björke, because people didn't want to listen to jazz here when the *Gramophone Hour* came on the radio. They just wanted to listen to Beethoven, schottische, and hambo."

"It sounds to me as if you've started your research."

"I've been talking to an old guy . . . an elderly man who knows all about it. That's why I haven't been here the past few days."

She takes a peek up at Bengt. As she's saying this, she finds her voice is serious and even ambitious. Perhaps he's also thinking along those lines.

"It is completely unacceptable to be absent, even to do research, without informing me first. You ought to know that."

"I know."

He nods strictly and measures her with his gaze, and she breathes out a sigh of relief because he's calling her visits with Alvar research.

"I still think your main focus should still be on Sweden during the Second World War. If you want to write about jazz musicians, you should make a clear connection to the war. Make sure that you use quotation marks, and you need to clearly identify which source you are citing for which passage. You will also have to find written material to verify and complement your oral source."

"OK."

He smiles. He rarely smiles. "I'm looking forward to reading it."

It seems as if it's been a whole year since she has seen Alvar. He's playing "Jazz Me Blues" on his gramophone and he's directing the music with one hand, and as she walks into his room, he asks her if she's had the chance to get the pictures developed yet.

"I'm fifteen," she says. "I don't know what 'develop the pictures' even means."

She feels extremely young as she says this. As if she's no different from Karro, Kevin, and all the other idiot kids who are busy calling her lezzie these days. She pulls out her phone.

"Here's the music school," she says, and holds the phone to Alvar.

He peers at the tiny screen.

"I'll print it out in a bigger size," she reassures him.

"It's so small, but I recognize the old München Brewery," he says.

"That's where the music school is these days," Steffi says, smiling as she realizes his pronunciation shifts as soon as he looks at a picture from Stockholm.

She swipes through a few photos. "Do you recognize this place?"

He bends closer to the screen. His clown smile appears.

"Isn't that Åsö Street?"

"Number one forty!"

His bushy eyebrows knit. He inhales the pixels, his eyes narrowing.

"No, no. That doesn't look like Åsö Street. No, it can't be. Not at all."

Steffi's heart sinks. She wants Alvar's memory to be crystal clear. She wants everything he tells her to be true. She wants her *oral history source* to be *verifiable with written material.*

"Sure it is. The number's on the building."

She zooms in on the number with two fingers.

"I see it," Alvar says. "But there's something wrong here. Look at those hatches . . . they'd lead to the furnace, and that would make it too hot to play swing music down there."

Steffi searchingly looks into the old man's face. "Maybe you got the number wrong."

Alvar shakes his head, as if to get his memories back into place.

"No, no," he says. "No . . . perhaps . . . it was so long ago. But no."

He sinks into his own thoughts concerning the street number. It seems to distress him. Steffi observes him. She sees the brown flecks on his cheeks. Bushy white hair grows from his ears. It looks like a tuft of cotton.

"Everyone in school thinks I'm a lesbian," she says.

Alvar looks up from the screen at Steffi. "They do?"

"But I'm not."

"I see."

He says this in a way as if he's not sure about how to talk with a teenager about sexual orientation. But he's a hepcat, so Steffi's not worried.

"But I don't like any of the boys in my school. Kevin and the other boys all the girls like. So, maybe I am?"

"There were two girls at Nalen," Alvar says. His eyes get that gleam. "They only would dance with each other. La . . . no . . . Lena. Lena and . . . Well, I forget the name of the other one. One girl would call herself the gentleman, I recall. People had a certain kind of respect for them."

Steffi stretches out on his bed with the Sunshine Home covers that smell of laundry soap.

“Then you were more civilized seventy years ago than the kids at Björke School in the twenty-first century. If you had respect.”

Alvar knocks at the cell phone, which has gone out. It doesn’t come back on. Steffi tells him to press the green button.

“Well, I was in the entertainment business,” Alvar said. “You learn all kinds of things about people. I realized that some people were like that fairly early on. You can’t force people to feel things they don’t feel. Otherwise you’re just stomping on them.”

She understands. Björke School was nothing but stomping on people.

“And that’s what was going on between me and Inga-Lill,” Alvar says. He sets the phone on his nightstand.

The thing with Inga-Lill, she had narrow fingertips and warm, soft lips. The first three weeks, he sang their praises from his kitchen bench bed. Quietly, of course, but Aunt Hilda’s hearing had been declining lately, so Alvar could go around humming to himself while in her doily-covered apartment. The first three weeks, his tunes had swing. After a month, swing turned to blues.

He noticed the change because he’d started to compare them.

Erling’s Trio had been busy rigging the stage before an important dance at the Zanzibar. Inga-Lill burst out that Alvar looked so elegant as he bent down to play lower on the strings.

Anita looked at Inga-Lill in amusement. “So you think he should always play in that position, no matter what pitch the notes are? Just because he looks good? By the way, the strings aren't going lower the farther down you play, they're going up. You don't even know how string instruments are played."

Inga-Lill looked back in defiance. "We girls don't notice things like that and we don't care what you boys call them!"

This was the second time that evening that Inga-Lill had included Anita with the boys. Alvar wasn't sure what was going on, but it seemed Anita's knowledge about musical instruments was part of the problem.

Anita raised an eyebrow, but Ingmar was the one who spoke up. He laughed as he wrapped an arm around Anita's shoulder. "I can guarantee that Anita is a real woman, through and through!"

Those words rang in Alvar's ears right through the entire concert. He took out his irritation on his string bass. He banged the strings as if they were spreading rumors. Ingmar had basically said that he'd embraced Anita all . . . well . . . been . . . well . . . seen her naked. Totally naked, with all buttons undone, and her panties . . . people aren't supposed to talk like that about respectable girls. Not surprising that a certain bass player got upset.

Playing the Zanzibar was a definite step up for Erling's Trio. Not just the bigger audience but also the walls themselves, covered with the signatures of visiting jazz players from the days when the papers still condemned jazz as "jungle music" and called Louis Armstrong "a primitive ape." Alvar could feel how Armstrong roared, forcing jazz from his solar plexus and spreading it all over Sweden, all the way to Värmland via the radio. Now, ten years later, he himself was experiencing, no, living this world, hanging on the syncopations and half notes vibrating through Zanzibar's floor and making Anita move her shoulders and hips as if she couldn't help herself. Not to mention Inga-Lill, of course. Alvar Svensson, by day an errand boy, by night a jazz musician, thumping on his bass and breathing in sweat and cigarette smoke as if it were a part of him. At the start of the evening, there'd been three couples on the dance floor, but now it was full.

Ingmar didn't like it that Anita could play the piano. Nothing had provoked it, but Ingmar said it, right after finishing his solo after the third riff. "Girls shouldn't play instruments, and certainly not in public," he said. "They'll never play as well as men."

"What about Alice Babs?" asked Alvar.

Both Ingmar and Erling laughed. "It must have been some trick they used when they filmed her."

After that, Alvar could never admit that he'd heard Anita play and he thought she was good. But he also couldn't get angry with Ingmar on her behalf. He couldn't say right out that Ingmar didn't really love Anita if he didn't let her do what she loved the most. It was none of his business.

The smoky dance hall was filled with laughter and talk as soon as Erling had played the last note on his clarinet. Excited voices, flirting, angry, sad. At the Zanzibar, as opposed to Nalen, you could drink as much as you wanted. Alvar lugged his bass along the wall toward the door, where cold air met overheated bodies. He needed some lungfuls of fresh air. His bass was somewhat secure in its case, but a shove from a jitterbugging knee or a flailing elbow could jostle it and knock the bridge loose, so Alvar had to protect it at the same time he was moving it. With his back to the dance floor, he couldn't identify a man's voice behind him.

"That was an unusual waltz. What do you call it?"

In the short second it took for Alvar to turn around he was able to make out three things. Ingmar had his arm around

Anita's waist, with his hand on her hip. Erling was staring at Alvar from the other side of the hall and was opening his mouth to say words that Alvar couldn't hear. And the man making the comment had a uniform and a mustache.

"Your trio played well today," he added.

He spoke with an exaggerated roll to his *r*'s and finished with a short, controlled laugh. He was at least twenty years older than most of the Zanzibar audience and really didn't fit in at all. His mother had always warned him to beware of military men. "Especially if they have a German accent!" The man held out his hand.

Alvar knew the man hadn't spoken with a German accent, but he saw the seriousness in the man's face, perhaps even war experience. Terror-struck, he shook hands.

"Sten Persson's the name."

"Al . . . Alvar Svensson."

"What do your friends call you?"

Alvar looked right into the man's eyes. He heard his mother's warning: "They want to know everything!" Suddenly his mother felt very far away. Sten Persson had truth serum in his gaze. "Erling calls me Big Boy."

The man smiled. It did not make the seriousness in his face disappear.

"So, Alvar Big Boy Svensson, how close are you to your band?"

They wanted to take him, stuff him in a uniform, and make him shoot at innocent Norwegians fleeing the Germans. He'd have to salute and hold a rifle instead of play a nice walking bass line in a dance hall. That black mustache . . . His heart pounded in a way that made his brain think of thudding march rhythms.

"I . . . I . . ."

"Here's what I think," the man said, and Alvar's heart started to calm down.

"You're starting to get a reputation. Arthur Österwall can't make it in to Stockholm this weekend and he told me to go listen to Erling's Trio."

Alvar couldn't believe what he was hearing. Arthur Österwall? *The* Arthur Österwall?

"I'd like you to meet Seymour and Charles on Friday and try out for us. I imagine that will work for you?"

Seymour? Charles? Alvar could hear his heart pounding for an entirely different reason. Arthur Österwall, Seymour, Charles, put them together and they spelled *Nalen*! He tried to catch Erling's eye, but Erling was gone. So was Ingmar. He was probably trying to get beneath Anita's skirts.

"Just . . . just me?"

"No disrespect to your friends, but we're looking for a bass player."

Then he was gone.

Alvar found himself standing there with a slip of paper in his hand, an address and a time, and watched the man with the black mustache, who turned out not to be Hitler after all, walk away. His other arm was still clutching his lady companion, his string bass, and all around him, people were laughing and talking as if nothing special had just happened.

"Alvar! Big Boy!" Erling was right next to him. "Do you know who that was?"

Alvar turned his head to the excited clarinet player. His words came out, relaxed and easy. "It was Sten Persson. He asked me if I wanted to play Nalen."

*"You?"* Erling's disbelieving eyes and the suspicion in his voice, the slip of paper in his own hand, and the relief of not being shanghaied into the German army made him laugh out loud.

"Yes, me!"

---

The gramophone playing "A Sailboat in the Moonlight" is slowing down and the pitch of music drops as it comes almost to a standstill. Steffi gets up and lifts the needle. She puts it to the side as she winds up the gramophone.

"I would hardly believe my ears if I heard I was going to play Nalen," she says as she drops the needle onto the track.

Alice Babs begins to sing again, from a groove in a disk of shellac.

"Probability goes up with each attempt," Alvar says.

"As long as you're not trying to do something impossible," Steffi replies. "Like . . . trying to eat up an entire tree."

Alvar snorts. "Who would ever want to eat a tree?"

Steffi shrugs and laughs. "Anything that's completely impossible, I mean."

"On the other hand," Alvar says, "who has the better chance of succeeding at eating the tree? The one who starts or the one who never tries?"

Steffi understands what he's getting at. The more times you try out to play at Nalen, the more likely you will finally find yourself playing Nalen.

Alvar snorts again. "A tree! Where in the world did you come up with that!"

"I was thinking of the record. It's a 78. You said it has 78 revolutions. For some reason, that made me think of trees, or rather tree stumps. Now I always think about trees when I change the record."

Alvar can't help smiling at her reply. He reaches for a pen and a memo pad. "You're going to get this gramophone from me, I've decided. So I have to make sure I have your name spelled correctly."

She looks at him. "You're dying?"

"Not today. Or at least I hope not. But I will. And then you'll get the gramophone and all the records, too."

Steffi doesn't say what she thinks, because she knows it's not logical. But this is what she feels: old people have always been around, and they've always been old for a long, long time. Therefore, they ought to know how to continue to be around for a long, long time. She doesn't want to say it out loud, because she knows it sounds stupid. She just wants to hold on to that feeling.

"Not for a long time," she says at last.

Alvar is handing her the memo block and the pen.

"The sound you're hearing, you can't get it on your CDs and your mp3s and all the modern digital stuff. We wind it up by our own hand and there's not a single electron involved. Just human knowledge of sound."

She doesn't like the way he didn't reassure her he'd be around a long, long time.

It scares her.

# – CHAPTER 20 –

Steffi has made an important decision. She's going to stop taking lessons from Torkel. Or, rather, if Torkel doesn't take her interest in jazz music seriously, she will quit. He's getting one more chance, but he doesn't know it yet. She's going to ask him some well-chosen questions about his knowledge of jazz bass, and if he gives the wrong answer, she's going to ask her mother to give Alvar money for lessons instead. Torkel will have to cram classic bass into the head of some other poor middle school student instead of hers. She has to concentrate on her own future now.

As soon as she opens her locker, she sees something's wrong. At first she can't take it in—the arrangements, the forms of everything inside—her books, her jacket, her bass, it's all wrong. As she grabs her bass, she feels it come apart inside its case.

It's like trying to hug a human being whose head has just been cut off. That's the first image that comes to her, complete with the same anguish, which now pushes down her throat and into her stomach. The neck of the bass is in her hand while the rest has fallen against the bottom of the case. Further down the hall, Karro and Sanja are sitting with their entourage. They keep glancing at her and waiting. Karro laughs, as if someone, most probably herself, has just said something funny.

Steffi grabs the case by the handle and rushes off in the opposite direction. The severed neck of the bass droops beyond the handle like that of a dead giraffe. She doesn't open her case until she's inside the music school where she takes lessons from Torkel. She sits on a bench, takes a deep breath, and zips it open. The body is still nicely fastened by its Velcro straps, but at the first fret, the neck has been sawed from the body, and then, the neck itself has been sawed into many pieces.

Steffi takes each one out. She presses her middle finger on the part where the D string should be and her index finger where the E string should be. She feels nothing at all, not even deep down inside, and she can barely breathe. Sends a thought to the eighteen-year-old Alvar who is about to play at Nalen, thinks: *my bass is dead.*

As Torkel comes down the hallway toward her, she quickly puts the pieces back and zips the case shut. Torkel has never understood her bass. Why should he see it die?

As he walks nearer, she gets up and looks at him, not right in the eye but at least chest level. "I'm not going to play today."

"Why not?"

"I'm quitting the bass."

Torkel scratches his head. "So, um . . . have you lost interest in it?"

Steffi thinks about playing a walking line, stamping her foot, stopping at a blue note, syncopating with Hannes on guitar, feeling the rhythm in her stomach. She thinks about practicing

Torkel's lessons, playing scales and using his guitar to accompany his Bellman songs.

"Yeah."

"Sorry to hear that. But I imagine you have a great deal to do in the ninth grade."

"Yes."

She cradles her bass in her arms. At first she doesn't want to go to Alvar's apartment, but she sees his white hand waving to her in the window and so she goes on in.

"What's happened to your instrument?"

He asks that before she can even take off her jacket. She doesn't answer but just sits down on his bed with the case on her knees. Breathes in the scent of soap, feels the broken instrument inside the nylon cloth. She has felt nothing all the way from school, but now she feels pain, as if her stomach was going to burst open. It is as if . . .

"Anita would have offered you a cup of coffee," Alvar says as he walks to the shelf with his records. "But I don't have any here. So all I have to offer is 'How High the Moon.' "

"It's as if they understood," Steffi says.

Alvar turns toward her, still holding the record in its cardboard sleeve. "Who?"

"Karro and all the other mental cases."

Alvar sits down in his armchair, still holding the record. "What have they understood?"

"That I don't give a damn about what they say to me. That they call me slut and all the rest. That I don't give a damn."

Her voice breaks as she pronounces the word *slut*.

Alvar furrows his bushy brows and leans sharply forward, his elbows on his knees, as if he were suddenly a younger man.

His eyes seem filled with anger, though not at her. "They called you that?"

He speaks as if she were an angel, and his warm Värmland accent stresses the word *you.*

"But," Steffi says, and she has trouble speaking around the lump growing in her throat. "But now . . . I mean . . . I don't know how . . ."

She hates that she's crying. She hates that her nose is running, making her sniff loudly and that she can't stop. She's sitting on Alvar's bed like a three-year-old and not a fifteen-year-old. She hates that in one second they'd managed to cut through her extra layers of thick skin.

In a way, she also hates that Alvar is so kind, too, because it means she can't make herself stop. Now he's come to sit next to her. He puts a hand on her bass case. He looks down at it, his neck bent and his eyes as sharp as a hawk's.

"This," he says. "This is the work of someone who does not know how to handle things in the proper way."

Steffi sniffs snot back into her nose loudly. "That's one way to put it."

She doesn't want to be here. Since only Alvar is listening, she says so out loud. "I just want to blink my eyes and when I open them, I'm in Stockholm at the music school and I have a bass that's not broken."

She takes the record from Alvar's hands and walks over to the gramophone because if she sits still any longer, she's going to break into pieces. She winds the gramophone, sets the record in place, and sets down the needle.

"When I was in Stockholm, it felt like all of Björke was just a dream. But when I'm here, Stockholm is just a dream, too."

"Yes, that's how it feels," Alvar says, his eyes looking far away. "Yes, indeed, that's just how it feels."

Steffi comes back to sit down on the bed again. She takes out the pieces of her bass and lays them out in order on the crocheted bedcover. "How High the Moon" fills the room.

She glances up at Alvar. "Tell me how it went at Nalen."

"Do you really want to hear about it now?"

"Yes."

"We can talk about what's going on at school instead."

"No, right now I'd prefer hearing about what happened at Nalen."

"At Nalen . . . it was just as advertised . . . full of people . . . a wonderful atmosphere . . ."

Nalen's advertisements were legendary. Topsy Lindblom was irreverent in every way, from his typography to his spelling and, if his goal was to annoy all the Swedish teachers in Stockholm, he was certainly successful.

*Saturday 8–1,* said the ad that Alvar was to keep for the rest of his life. *Kick up your Heels to our FAMOUS ROOF. This Sat ONLY with Alvar Big Boy Svensson. Promising player from the HEART of Värmland.*

Erling had found the ad, and it was with both delight and ill-concealed jealousy that he showed it and in the same breath added that he should get a royalty because he was the one who had first encouraged Alvar's talent and had come up with the nickname Big Boy. "Now we have a foot in the door," he kept repeating at least four or five times that evening.

Being in Nalen's orchestra was totally different from being in the audience. Alvar was not religious, but before Nalen opened, walking across the empty stage to tune his upright bass, he felt something spiritual in the house, something divine that had brought him to that moment, right there on Nalen's stage floor creaking beneath his feet. It felt as real as Charles Norman giving him an A from the piano.

When the first people trotted in from the line outside, he shivered from his toes all the way up to the top of his head. Once he, too, had been down there on that dance floor, too nervous to dance the jitterbug but too excited to be able to sit down.

Someone came up to him and slapped him on the back so that he hiccupped. "I heard you were going to play tonight!" Most of them, though, had no idea who he was—the anonymous bass player in the middle of everything.

Erling walked up. "Want to come?"

That meant that they'd leave the dance hall and take the stairs down to the restaurant for a couple of pilsners, and then return to Nalen, where alcohol was strictly forbidden, and pass the guards, who were there to make sure no alcohol came in, while keeping their mouths shut and holding their gaze steady.

"Are you nuts? I'm going on in half an hour!"

Erling grinned a grin that was hard to interpret. "Aren't you the prima donna already!"

Alvar didn't allow himself to think of the names of the other musicians. If he thought about them, he wouldn't be able to play a single note. Just like when he'd met Thore Ehrling. His hero worship would get in the way of his playing. Instead of their names, he focused on their heads and their hands. Swing was all that mattered, not the men who played it.

Everyone was dancing. Every single person in the hall was spinning, bouncing, their feet moving back and forth, side to side, their shoulders and legs carefree and swinging. From Alvar's position, they were a sea of bobbing heads: shiny with pomade, and curls from curlers or by secret methods. After their first set, he got a thumbs-up from Seymour Österwall.

"He gave me a thumbs-up!" Alvar exclaimed to Erling, and

his voice cracked into a falsetto. "I'll never forget that thumbs-up as long as I live!"

Erling laughed and thumped him on the back. "You made us all proud, Big Boy! Even if you missed a note here and there. Typical beginner mistakes."

Alvar couldn't remember dropping a note, but on the other hand, he was so excited he wouldn't have noticed if the ceiling had caved in.

"You were perfect," Anita said when she'd found them in the bar. "You were absolutely wonderful!"

Inga-Lill came up from behind and hugged her arms tightly around him. Then she swung around and kissed him on the mouth. "My man!" she said loudly. "You were so elegant up there with the orchestra!"

Alvar wiggled loose. *Elegant! Why couldn't she ever come up with a word besides* elegant*?*

"Time for the next set. Now you will really get the chance to dance!"

He knew it wasn't right to look at Anita while he said this. Because Inga-Lill was his girl, of course. He felt a little prick of conscience during the first measures of the next set, but then the swing music caught him like a whirlwind spinning through his body. Nalen was pulsing and Alvar's eager fingers were getting everyone to move.

Once the dance was over, girls flocked around him. Tall ones, short ones—all in swing skirts, all with smooth skin and lips that smiled, smiled, smiled. For a second, Alvar remembered himself as the shy seventeen-year-old waiting in the line to get into Nalen and frightened to death of just these girls. Now he was able to laugh.

"No, I don't think I'll be a band member. Arthur is back tomorrow."

"Alvar plays in Erling's Trio." This came from Erling, who was standing behind the most eager girls.

"Oh, that's right! I saw you at the Zanzibar!" one of them exclaimed.

"That's right," Erling answered, even though the girl wasn't looking at him.

"How old are you?" another girl asked Alvar with a glint in her eye.

"So you want to know if he's legal?" said another girl to her, even more forthright.

Alvar blushed, but laughed it off. "Any other questions?"

"Yes, I have one," a quiet voice came from behind him. "Are you planning to go home to Björke anytime soon?"

It was the blond girl from the train.

She was thinner now and he could see some crow's-feet around her eyes that hadn't been there before. But when they were sitting at the Gramophone Café over cups of coffee, he remembered her voice as if it came straight from his childhood.

"I've watched you a few times," she said. "But I didn't want to . . . oh, I didn't know if I should talk to you. Or if you would even remember me."

She was staring at him intently, but he couldn't figure out why. But he made his voice sound low and reassuring. "Yes, I remember that train ride like it was yesterday."

"Why haven't you gone home?"

The question hit him hard, just as it had done outside Nalen. He remembered his mother hugging him and warning him about Germans. She'd just baked bread and she'd told him to call as soon as he reached Aunt Hilda. She smelled like kitchen and children.

"There was no reason to."

"Not even for Christmas?"

Two Christmases had gone by since he'd left Björke. Every Christmas he'd regretted his decision to stay in Stockholm, but that feeling lasted only a few days.

The girl looked at him with something like desperation in her eyes. He didn't understand what she wanted from him. At least he was being honest. "I came here to play jazz music. You see, there are a lot of musicians already here who are much better than I am. They've been playing a long time. Some even studied at the conservatory . . . but at least I have the will."

"And the talent."

"So I took every chance that came my way. I'm still working off the debt on my bass and I learn everything anybody has to teach me. And it's . . . it's what I have to do. Do you understand?"

She nodded but added, "Still, you must think about your mother now and then."

"We write letters."

It came out more harshly than he'd intended, but he didn't want to go into details with this girl, whom he really didn't know that well. Sometimes when he thought of his mother, tears came to his eyes. Sometimes that happened even when he thought of his father.

The girl stirred her coffee. She didn't say anything. He started to speak, but then the images of his parents were mixed with his brothers and his neighbors and he couldn't open his mouth.

"Anyway, I was wondering," the girl said at last. "If . . . when . . . you go to Björke . . ." Her voice was choking, as if she were holding back tears. "If you could . . . go see my little baby."

---

"So did you?"

Steffi has a different kind of lump in her throat. Even if her bass was not a child, she could understand that sad girl.

"Did I visit? We haven't gotten to that part of the story yet."

"Was the baby here? In Björke?"

"Oh, yes, up in the forest hills by Knut Storfors. Elna Storfors was her . . . aunt, I think. They should have been taking care of the child."

"What do you mean by 'should have been'?"

Alvar looks thoughtful and puts his hand on his clown lips, pinching them. He's looking down toward the floor.

"One of the kids in my school is a Storfors," Steffi informs him. "Kevin Storfors."

Alvar looks at her.

"In little Björke," he said, "it would be more strange if there *wasn't* a Storfors at your school."

Steffi walks through the hallway of the retirement home. The case drags on the ground, since the neck of the instrument can't hold it straight. She's pulling it along like a sledge. She's thinking about what Alvar said. Storfors, Isaksson, Svensson, and Berntsson—they'd always been in Björke. No Herrera, of course, Steffi thinks, but Mamma was an Isaksson before she met Pappa.

A woman with a walker meets her in the hallway. She has a vacant smile, but it's friendly. She says today's sermon was nice.

Steffi usually just agrees and keeps going, but this time she stops. "Today's Wednesday," she says.

She really shouldn't do that. Alvar has told her that it's most important to keep the people here in a good mood and not question what's going through their addled brains.

The woman wrinkles her forehead and worries. She starts to mutter: "Sunday, Monday, Tuesday . . . Sunday . . ."

"But it was a really nice sermon," Steffi says and the white-haired lady brightens up.

"Yes, it was, wasn't it?"

Her gray eyes are suddenly clear and bright, as if they'd gotten their focus back. Steffi could see that she'd once been beautiful and had not always been shuffling around in the community nursing home.

Then she sees Steffi's bass case. Her smile disappears. "But, dear child, what has happened to . . . your dog?"

"It was . . . somebody hurt it."

The woman shakes her head and her breathing is agitated. "It wasn't our little Svea, was it?"

"Oh, no, it wasn't her. And we're going right to the vet's, so I'm sure he'll be fine."

The woman looks at her with worry.

Steffi reassures her. "He's going to be just fine."

"That's good to know," the woman says, looking relieved.

For the sake of the woman's peace of mind, Steffi picks up her bass and hugs it in her arms as she leaves the retirement home. Between Björke School and Sunshine Home, she thinks, the Sunshine Home is her favorite madhouse.

## – CHAPTER 21 –

She's avoided talking about her bass. She knows what would happen if she did: Pappa would talk to Karro's parents, Karro would promise to be nicer, and then she'd hide her even more nasty nastiness better. Or else they'd be forced to have "friend days" at school. She already had been through those. Karro would look her in the eye and say "You're good at math" in an appreciation exercise. Karro would then whisper *slut!* so that the teacher couldn't hear her. That's the only thing Steffi remembers from Björke School's first attempt to "improve the atmosphere." *You're good at math, slut!* So she never brought up Karro's bullying again, not since fifth grade. That's why she doesn't know what to do now about her bass. Until she figures that out, she'll just keep busy with the clarinet.

It's hard to make the music sound happy when she feels so exhausted and broken. She can't lie down on the bed while she plays it, either, like she could with her bass guitar. She sits on the edge of the bed and lets the clarinet run down a minor scale. It's playing what her heart feels. Some notes are nothing more than squeaks. Nothing makes her feel better. After half an hour, she puts the clarinet aside and sits at her computer.

She's put on her hat before she logs into The Place. It feels better that way, as if Hepcat is really alive somewhere inside her. When she sees Karro's name in the in-box, at first she wants to delete it right away, but she doesn't. "I hate you," she says, in the same quiet way Karro had whispered *slut* when Steffi was eleven years old. She opens the message.

From: Karro N
To: Hepcat

I feel like U. I just want to get away from here. But U already live in Karlstad. I live in a shithole with the world's craziest people. I can't explain like U cause UR so deep and all, not writing, but sometimes I think really weird stuff. Anyway, I can't stand it here. I really can't!

While Steffi is still reading, there's a *bing!* from her speaker. A new message has arrived. She opens it, too.

From: Karro N
To: Hepcat

Hope you don't think I'm really weird. I don't write emotional stuff to people I don't know most of the time but I feel I can say anything to you. Anyway, hope you reply.

Steffi leans back in her chair. She considers this message from a distance. She thinks about who she really is. A girl Karro is desperate to destroy. And a boy Karro desperately wants to get to know. Steffi thinks about erasing the message and letting Karro disappear from Hepcat's life, but that would mean that the girl who would be destroyed would be left all alone. She hits reply.

From: Hepcat
To: Karro N

What kind of weird things are you thinking about? Why can't you stand it anymore?

I'm feeling blue myself. Feeling blue, that's English for feeling like giving up, feeling like you have to keep putting up with stuff. With people who want to destroy you. But only cowards try to destroy other people. Strong people, well, they keep focusing on the future.

She doesn't know if she's writing this for someone else or for herself. She doesn't really care what Karro thinks. There's a certain pleasure in calling Karro a coward without Karro realizing it. Steffi hits send and logs out before Karro has a chance to reply.

*Strong people look toward the future,* she thinks the next day as she walks toward Sunshine Home. It's nothing written by Povel Ramel. It's something written by Steffi.

*When outside it's storming, strong people keep still*
*When others are fighting, strong people are chill*
*When space allows, strong people fill it*
*When a door opens, strong people walk through it*

She decides to sing the lyrics for Alvar, but he's not in his room. His door is locked. There's no jazz music coming through his keyhole.

Alvar is not in the visitors' room, either, and not in the dining room. An emotion starts to sneak up on her, the same one she didn't want to feel when Alvar asked her to write down her name so he could put it in his will. *You're not finished yet,* pounds through her brain. *You still have to tell me about when you played with Povel Ramel and what happened to the baby and everything with Anita, and we haven't gotten there yet, that's what you said!*

"My dear child." It's a small, hunchbacked woman whose pink scalp can be seen through her white hair. She stares at Steffi. Her blue eyes bulge. "What's going on with you?"

Steffi gives her an irritated look, feeling a panic-filled prayer go up to avoid being caught in a rambling conversation right now, but the old lady doesn't give up. "See, you can tell me and then you'll feel better."

Steffi shakes her head. "Where's Alvar?"

The lady laughs, for Steffi's shoulder reaches, and with a warm hand turns her halfway around. "He's outside enjoying the sunshine. It's such a pleasant day. The first day of spring, if you want to be generous."

Steffi wants to correct the old lady and say that it can't be spring yet, but then she realizes how warm the sunshine felt as she'd walked here. Through a French door, she catches sight of Alvar's enormous ear and his bushy hair and his knotty hand waving, explaining something.

She turns back to the wrinkled angel beside her. "Thanks so much."

The lady smiles a friendly, empty smile.

"You're welcome, child."

Steffi expects to find him at the center of all the attention from all the ladies, but this time it's the white-haired lady with the gray eyes who is entertaining everyone with a story about when her father couldn't figure out a newfangled toilet. Her story is unconnected in certain parts, but everyone seems to have heard it before, and they fill in the gaps when the story falls apart.

Steffi stands and listens for a while. She glances at Alvar, who is also listening attentively and who laughs when she reaches the end of the story. She thinks about what he'd been like as a seventeen-year-old, and she can almost see it. She looks at the others. The lady in the corner with her mouth hanging open. The white-haired, gray-eyed lady telling her story for the thousandth time. Svea, who's quiet for once. All of these people had been teenagers once upon a time.

"Steffi!"

Alvar sees her, and this sets off a chain reaction. The first thing that happens is Svea pounding her fist on the table.

"Whore! Bastard child! Get out of here! Go away!"

Three of the ladies at her table shrink back and look around helplessly. Everyone wants to avoid listening to her nasty words.

Alvar turns toward Svea. "Now, now, she's a good girl. She's a nice girl."

Svea hisses. "None of you are nice! You're all bastard children! Whooooore children!"

Two of the old ladies hasten out as best they can with their walkers.

The storyteller takes Svea's hand and begins to stroke it. "Now, now, Svea. Now, now."

Svea calms down, little by little. Steffi watches as a miracle happens. Svea's hateful stare softens and she almost seems peaceful.

Alvar relaxes and looks at the white-haired lady. "So, is there any more to your story?"

"My story?"

"The one about the newfangled toilet?"

The woman looks at him in confusion.

Steffi recognizes the empty look, the smile that is friendly but void of context. "Toilet?"

Alvar nods and pats her on the cheek. "That's all right. It's all right."

"You can understand," Alvar says later. "You can understand why I appreciate your visits. First, because I like jazz, and second, because I don't forget what I'm saying in the middle of saying it."

"That's right."

They're sitting on a bench behind the Sunshine Home buildings and they each have a blanket over their knees because the April sun doesn't yet have a lot of warming power.

"Can I record some of your stories? I have a special project I have to do for school. I have to get started on it soon."

He laughs. "My first professional vocal recording! It's about time!"

"You can tell me about the Second World War. If there's anything you can say. I'm supposed to write about the Second World War in Sweden."

"*If* there's anything I can say? Oh my, well, then. For most of us, it was just rationing, lack of coffee, and blackout paper covering the windows. In spite of the anxiety in the air, the news coverage, and the children from Finland who were taken in as refugees from the war, people were still mostly concerned with the mundane issues of daily life. But there was that one day when bombs fell on Stockholm. It was in February."

On the twenty-second of February in 1944, bombs fell on Stockholm. The first explosion was heard throughout the city. In Södermalm, it was so loud that people thought the end had come.

In Vasa Stan, it was more like a puff, like the way the gas burners go out when the token's time had finished. Aunt Hilda didn't even notice because her hearing was now at such a comfortable level that it let her keep on sleeping while Alvar was able to drum on tables and chairs whenever he felt like it.

When the explosion came, Alvar startled awake and got up to look out the kitchen window. He stared in all directions but couldn't see anything, so he went back to sleep. He slept well for the rest of the night.

The next day, the twenty-third of February, the headlines filled the papers.

**BOMBS FALL ON STOCKHOLM!**
**RUSSIAN BOMBERS OVER STOCKHOLM!**

Just like everyone else, Alvar bought a morning paper and tried to comprehend the unfathomable. The papers said it was clear that the Russians were behind it. Nobody could say why. Nobody could say if they were going to do it again. The papers said the bombs had hit Södermalm. Alvar didn't finish reading before he leaped on his bike. If his mother had been there, she would have told him not to bike to a place where the Russians had just dropped a bomb. But his mother didn't know Erling.

Alvar calmed down when he saw that Erling's city block was unscathed. He was panting, and let his head hang over the handlebars until his breathing was back to normal. He was suddenly able to hear the people around him. Many people had rushed to Södermalm just as he had so they could see things with their own eyes. Others had rushed away from the block that was hardest hit. Those windows had all been shattered by the blast. Many people were crying. Others were afraid. "Now the war has come to Sweden!" The sentence was breathed throughout the city that morning. Perhaps even Anita was afraid.

First he took his bike to Eriksdal Theater. There was nothing remaining but a crater. Police inspectors were wandering back and forth without clear instructions. A crowd of people had gathered to see the damage. They were all very quiet as they tried to comprehend what had happened.

"If it had just hit a few meters in this direction . . . ," one of the other errand boys said and didn't finish his sentence. Alvar stared at the gaping hole that had once been a theater building. The stone walls lay in heaps and the trees surrounding it were broken off like sticks. *This*, he thought to himself, *this is what a bomb does*. This realization was uncomfortable. He saw now what war could do right at his feet. When he couldn't stand it any longer, he got on his bike and headed toward Östermalm.

This was the second time in his life that he had visited Anita's home. He hadn't been invited this time, but he reasoned that in time of war, all the rules were suspended. Two elegant ladies with fur muffs were standing by the entrance, speaking quickly and quietly to each other. Alvar could make out only the word *war*. The doorman did not recognize him.

"Message for the Bergners."

On the elevator he had time to think. Should he pretend to be there with a message and give Anita a secret sign? What message could he give, and how would a lie like that help him to marry Anita one day?

Alvar's plan to marry Anita had just spilled out one evening with Inga-Lill—which effectively ended their relationship. Erling had told him that the key was in making a girl feel like she's the only one in the whole wide world. Alvar could see how he'd messed up on that point.

The elevator stopped and he still had not found a good way

to meet whichever parent would probably answer the door. He stopped thinking and simply rang the doorbell.

The woman who opened it was about forty years old and looked exhausted. Any resemblance to Anita would have to have been only in the body shape. She smiled questioningly at him. "Yes?"

Alvar took off his cap. He'd understood immediately that Södermalm slang would not be acceptable in Östermalm. So he said in as formal a manner as possible, "Good day, Mrs. Bergner. I would like to see An . . . Miss Anita."

The woman smiled again and shook his trembling hand, but explained that she was not Mrs. Bergner. She said she would bring Anita to him.

"Rather . . . Anita . . . in that case," Alvar stammered, blushing, but the domestic was already walking back into the apartment.

The real Mrs. Bergner had dark hair and gray, searching eyes. Alvar wanted to say that she resembled her daughter, but didn't know how people took compliments here in Östermalm. Mrs. Bergner did not take her eyes from him, even when she lifted the teacups from the sideboard. The domestic watched them with curiosity until Mrs. Bergner said, "Thank you, Edna," with such clear dismissal that she was forced to leave the room.

Anita was seated on the other side of the table. The last time Alvar was here, Anita was walking around and showing him the furniture arrangements and the portraits. Now she looked scared to death.

Mrs. Bergner started the conversation with a question. "Where do you live, Alvar?"

"In Vasa Stan."

"But you don't come from there."

"I'm from Björke in Värmland. I'm staying at Mamma's . . .

my mother's aunt's place. My aunt is the widow of a major in the army . . . Mrs. Hilda af Uhr."

He could see a slight upward tick at the corner of Anita's mouth as he said his aunt's entire name. The "af" in a name was the kind of thing people in Östermalm appreciated. He was well aware of this.

"And your parents?"

He swallowed. "Svensson, just like me. I'm Alvar Svensson. Af Björke."

He laughed a bit at his own joke, although he didn't know if it would be appreciated or even acceptable in a house where family background was important. But Anita's mother smiled and he saw she had an appreciative glint in her eye. He hung tightly to that thought.

"Svensson af Björke," Anita repeated with a nervous laugh.

If her mother hadn't been there, she would have laughed out loud.

"And your father? What does he do?"

Alvar realized he should have discussed all this with Anita before he'd come here. His hands were sweating so hard they were leaving spots on his trousers. Any lie about his parents would bring no honor to anyone.

"He works in forestry."

"In what way?"

Alvar looked down at the table so as not to see Mrs. Bergner's puzzlement. How many ways do people work in forestry?

"Well, logging, calculations, planting. All the things he needs to do with his forest."

"You mean he owns the property?"

Pappa did own the forest together with four brothers, so that wouldn't be a lie.

"Yes, he does."

"And where did you meet Anita?"

The question was a sneak attack. Alvar immediately began to hiccup.

"We met at the riding . . . club."

His face flushed immediately. Alvar Svensson af Björke was definitely a rotten liar.

On the other side of the table, Anita clenched her jaw, and he could see her thoughts churning furiously. "It was so embarrassing, for Alvar, Mamma," she said quickly and laughed. "He can't ride at all, but when he got there, he had to try, and they really were laughing at him."

Her mother nodded mistrustfully and turned back to Alvar. "Why were you there, then, if you can't ride?"

"It was one of the entertainment evenings—" Anita began but was cut off.

"I'm talking to Alvar."

Alvar swallowed and hiccupped. He kept on sweating profusely. *The hard way is always the easiest in the end,* his mother had said. *You should always tell the truth.*

"I'm a musician. I play bass. So I play at those kinds of entertainment evenings and parties and . . . other places."

Mrs. Bergner was looking at him as if he were telling lies, and he blushed because of that. She bored her gaze directly into his dishonest eyes, curled her lips, and nodded. This was not at all why he had come here. Why was he here?

"I saw the bomb," he burst out.

Mrs. Bergner's peering eyes opened wide. Anita's became as round as plates.

"The Russian bomb?"

"Well, I couldn't tell if it was Russian, but the entire Eriksdal Theater is gone."

Nobody said a word. Mrs. Bergner's expression of curiosity

showed Alvar how much she resembled Anita. Anita took a deep breath.

"I biked over here," Alvar continued when nobody said a word. "I thought maybe Anita might be frightened or . . . well, I came here just to see you, Anita. I wanted to make sure you were all right."

Anita laughed and exchanged a look with her mother. She cocked her head. "That was incredibly sweet of you. Alvar is always so sweet, Mamma, just like a little brother."

Mrs. Bergner seemed to be thinking hard and she looked them both over as she listened to Anita's words. Especially the last three, Alvar suspected, as her gaze fell directly on him while Anita spoke. Anita was twenty-three now. Could a nineteen-year-old ever be mature enough for someone who was already twenty-three?

Anita's mother spoke the words he didn't really want to hear. A real man would never have been allowed to accompany Anita to her room.

He could not escape that feeling when he was alone with Anita. It was there, just like when you took a walk in the forest and the trees suddenly opened to a glade. Fighting for a place in a swing band, conversing with Aunt Hilda about the decay of today's youth, and biking through the city with errands from Åkesson's grocery: all that was real life and demanded effort. With Anita, he could close his eyes and feel his pulse slow. He sat down on a chair. She sat down at her desk and turned toward him.

"Do you think the war has come to Sweden?"

Alvar did not want to talk about the war, but this was the day when a bomb had fallen. He thought back to his emotions near the crater that had been Eriksdal Theater. Then he thought about his mother and father and the soldiers at the Norwegian border.

"The war has already been here a long time. Normal windows don't look like that."

He nodded toward Anita's well-crafted blackout curtain. She got up and walked over to him and ran her hand through his hair. Their roots sent tingles down his entire body. What had he just thought about a lowered pulse?

"Come." She sat down on her sofa and patted the empty seat beside her. "I don't want Mamma to hear us."

They sat next to each other. Any thought of bombs felt far away now. It was as if they no longer existed, even though they'd fallen just last night. Even though he could still feel them vibrating through the floor.

"You are like my little brother."

"I am not your little brother."

"Well, I know I have lived longer than you have. And I ought to know more about life, but all I feel is lost."

Those words *little brother* were still ringing in Alvar's ears, but he tried to ignore them and concentrate on what Anita was saying.

"I'm twenty-three years old and I should have already moved out and married. Mamma is always bringing over people like bank directors for me to meet. The kind of men she wants me to marry, you know."

Alvar didn't know, but he knew enough to keep quiet and listen.

"And Ingmar . . . yet *you* were the one who came here. The bombs fell and you came here. Why didn't Ingmar come?"

"Maybe he was scared."

"Scared of the bombs?"

"Scared of your mother. She scared me."

Anita smiled briefly, as if he were joking. He took in her smile.

"I know Ingmar likes me. But he's so difficult. It's not easy to talk to him. I always feel like I have to be . . . that kind of woman."

She said *that kind of woman* with such an intonation that he didn't need to ask for further explanation.

She sighed. "He always seems evasive somehow. And all those strutting bank directors—they're old. Not always in age, but in their minds."

Alvar looked at her. One of her hands was scratching the other, as if picking off an imaginary scab. He took a deep breath. "I'm young."

She was pulled out of her thoughts, looked at him and laughed. "You're extremely young."

Her eyes glittered as she said this. He believed that it was not just his imagination. Somewhere inside her, Anita liked the fact that he was young.

A step forward.

# – CHAPTER 22 –

The teenage girl had left. Her brown eyes and deep thoughts were gone from Sunshine Home. Did he ever look that serious when he was fifteen? Hardly. But he remembers feeling just as lost inside his growing body. It took time to learn how to use it. He still remembers how growing pains had felt in his legs and how he kept getting taller and taller. Steffi is not as lanky, but she moves as if her body and her head existed in two different worlds, until she had started to listen to swing. If he were twenty years younger, he'd teach her the jitterbug and her entire self, body and soul, would then be united. All right, thirty years younger. All right, forty.

He tosses and turns. He prefers to lie on his back when he rests, but sometimes it's hard to swallow that way, so he has to turn his head to the side until his neck stiffens. The last few days, he'd felt the tension even more. He had had no idea how badly Steffi was suffering under her tormentors until he'd seen the decapitated bass guitar. It was as if he'd been refusing to see it, as if it did not manifest itself until he'd seen it in reality, in the physical form of a broken instrument. He could be dense, sometimes, not at all like his mother had raised him. She'd told him to think about those who were weak, and she'd said it so long ago that by now he ought to have forgotten her exact words. His neck is aching. He shifts.

Right after the bombs hit Stockholm, he'd gotten a letter from his mother. She'd asked him to be a good boy and to be careful when it came to the war.

*My dear boy,*

*I hope you are well and that Hilda is also well, of course. Don't forget to be kind to her. She must have great difficulty with her legs.*

*I was so extremely frightened when I heard that bombs had fallen in Stockholm. You weren't nearby, were you? You listen to what people tell you and stay away from dangerous places, won't you? And you make sure that you have blackout curtains at home and don't start fights with people in uniform.*

*I don't know what to warn you about. I would like you to bury yourself somewhere safe with some food and water until this unpleasantness is over, but you know that is my mother's heart speaking. Go ahead and live your life. But don't forget there's a war on.*

*Here in Björke, Elsa has had a baby girl, Hjördis, and the baby was born with so much hair that people gathered at the hospital to take a look. Kalle Svensson was arrested for public drunkenness again. Young Karin Berntsson in Lysvik, if you remember her, they say she's found a German in Fryksdalen on the other side of the border, but if you ask me, it's just a rumor. And the boys in Torsby IF soccer have made it to division three and that's all your brothers can think about right now.*

He smiled as he read this last bit. The war, jazz music, bombs, and theaters that turned into gaping holes—and all his brothers could think about was soccer. He could see his mother in her clumsy handwriting. He could imagine his father, gruff but gentle, in the room beside her. He had been away from them for so long that he'd forgotten how their voices sounded, but he still knew exactly how they smelled. He'd have to go home. Soon. But first, he had to substitute again, for the second time, at Nalen. And make Anita understand that he was a man.

He'd started writing a song to win her heart. It grew from his guitar, even in the evenings as he sat in Aunt Hilda's kitchen. He'd dampened his strings so it wouldn't bother her. Sometimes she began to talk with him about it.

"What kind of noise is that?" she'd scream at him, as if he were the one who was deaf.

"It's Beethoven," he'd say. Then he'd have to repeat it, louder: "BEETHOVEN!"

Aunt Hilda had frowned skeptically.

"I can tell it's not Beethoven. I hope it's not that jitterbug music."

"Of course not," he said honestly, because it wasn't a swing tune.

"I absolutely forbid you to play Negro music in this house. You must understand this and take it to heart." Her voice trembled with emotion.

"I will take it to heart," he replied as he kept working on his composition.

He'd called his tune "A Girl and the Air," and it was a jazzy fox-trot. He called the music style Alvar-jazz. The lyrics were about how a girl could change the air just by coming into the room. Even if his English wasn't the best, he thought it sounded professional. He'd even found a rhyme: *air* and *near*.

---

He laughs to himself in his room at the Sunshine Home. *Never,* he tells himself, his forefinger in the air, *never tell Steffi that you once tried to rhyme* air *and* near. *She's a girl who knows a good rhyme, that one.* He turns his head to the other side, points his nose up, and starts to doze.

Hepcat never logs in to the computer at school. That would be insane. It's hard to keep to schoolwork when the assignment is *Information Searching and Source Review* and she's been able to answer all the questions in five minutes. For a while, she searches for electric bass guitars and tries to figure out how long she has to save until she can buy a Fender. Much too long. Depressingly long. Then her fingers turn to The Place.

Stephanie Herrera's page doesn't look anything like Hepcat's. They even have different colors. In the in-box there's no sign of any messages, but three are shown on her guest page. Karro never writes a message to Steffi. That would be too intimate. The whole point is writing something on the guest page so everyone can see. Clicking on the guest page would mean accepting the shit thrown at her. Still, she can't just let it go.

In addition, she feels hard as stone.

In addition, she's a hepcat nobody can reach.

Even if they break her bass and call her a lesbian slut.

She is hard.

Like.

Stone.

Karro has written the first contribution. *I forgot how ugly you are until you got to school today. I get why no guy wants you so you have to meet dykes on the net!!!!* Steffi clicks delete. Feels nothing at all. Reads the second contribution. *Slut.* Creative. As she deletes it, she thinks she really ought to ignore the whole thing. Every time Steffi deletes something, Karro probably believes she's been touched, as if she were soft and easily influenced, as if she went along with Karro's game. She looks absentmindedly at the acknowledgment: *Message deleted.* She's breathing quickly, exhaling Steffi's vomit-green web page and inhaling something, anything, even *Information Searching and Source Review.* She never should have logged in.

The third guest page comment is not from Karro. It's not from anyone else she knows, either. It's from somebody named Simon Kjellman, and at first she doesn't get it.

*Really nice friends you have there. Hope it's just some net trolls; otherwise they're seriously mental. Anyway, did you get a chance to listen to Avishai Cohen yet? ;)*

Avishai Cohen. At first she has a vague recollection of the name and then warmth spreads through her. She's back in the hallway at the music school. There are other boys and girls all around her and they're looking at her without seeing someone disgusting. The boy with the beret has looked her up on the net, and that means that he even remembered her name, and not only that, he's called Karro *seriously mental.*

To Steffi's surprise, she feels the warmth turning into a lump in her throat. She feels it pressing against her windpipe and there's hot tears welling up behind her nose. They're now starting to stream down her face so quickly she can't stop them. It's like a volcanic explosion and she has to run to the bathroom.

She's cried in the bathroom many times before, so that the feeling of the toilet under her thighs is the same as tears falling and dripping on her knees. She's an expert on crying silently and letting her nose run freely into toilet paper until she knows she can stop and flush to hide the sound of sniffling and until she's able to push the last bit of weeping deep into her stomach. But this bout of crying is something entirely different. It's like opening a door. It's someone holding up her heart so she can let the rest go. It would be a stupid lyric, she thinks in the middle of blowing her nose, but that's exactly how it feels. She's humming in her head as she walks home:

*This is how it feels when your tears run and your heart burns*
*You may think it's foolish, but that's how my world turns.*

It almost sounds like rap and she gets lost in the feeling of how rap and jazz would sound when played together. She thinks the right walking bass line would make it work, and she'd try it if she had a bass. She tries not to think about her decapitated bass guitar as she puts the key in the lock. She tries to focus on something else, like the guy who wrote her, Simon Kjellman with the beret.

Pappa is in Karlstad with Edvin to find a pair of glasses and Mamma is at work. Steffi was hoping to have the apartment to herself and maybe practice the clarinet for a while. But she sees shoes in the hallway, Julia's and Fanny's, thrown down like last season's style. Julia's door is ajar and they're talking about guys again. Steffi rolls her eyes—maybe Karro has a point and she really is a lesbian, because she finds all this boy talk ridiculous.

"What about David? He kisses like an electric mixer!"

"Like a mixer! But how?" Julia exclaims with excitement.

Silence. Steffi walks closer to Julia's door and wants to tell them that she's home and needs to study, but the silence makes her forget what she wants to say. Through the gap in the doorway, she sees how Julia's and Fanny's heads are close together, as if their lips were . . . but it's gone so quickly she could have misunderstood what she'd seen. Julia is giggling again.

"OK. I get it! Like an electric mixer!"

Fanny laughs.

"Yes, that's it! Some guys kiss like that."

"Actually," Julia says, leaning back against the wall. "Actually . . . girls are more attractive. We're better at, like . . ."

"We wax!" Fanny says with emphasis. "Such lucky guys who get *us*! Right?"

Julia glances at Fanny. Steffi can't stop looking. It's like she's watching an R-rated film and she's the child who'd sneaked into the movie theater. Julia looks like she wants to say something. She doesn't speak, but for a while she still looks like she's about to.

"Too bad we have to fall in love with them!" Fanny giggles.

Julia nods, but a part of her smile disappears. "Exactly. But . . . like, take Lukas for example. He kisses really well, like . . . wait, I'll demonstrate."

In the R-rated film in front of Steffi's eyes, Julia leans toward Fanny. Softly she puts her hand on Fanny's neck and then tucks a strand of Fanny's hair behind her ear. She leans forward and kisses Fanny. Steffi is well aware that she knows nothing about the mysteries of love, but she can tell, just by Julia's posture, exactly what Julia is feeling. The kiss goes on for so long that Steffi forces herself to look down and look at the door hinge for a moment. Then she hears Fanny laugh out loud.

"God! Now I know why you broke up with Lukas . . . *not*!"

Julia laughs, too, blushes. She says she'd rather have a guy with a car and then she starts to talk about kissing again, but Fanny changes the subject to a fan of fifties cars she'd met at a festival and who had a tree-shaped air freshener hanging in his tent.

Steffi backs away. She tiptoes to the kitchen and puts a slice of bread in the toaster and waits. When the toast pops out with its too-loud sound, it takes just three seconds for Julia to fly into the kitchen. Her question comes like the crack of a whip.

"How long have you been home?"

"A long time."

"How long?"

Steffi looks at her nervous older sister. The one who let everyone believe Steffi was a lesbian.

"Twenty-two minutes and five seconds," Steffi replies. "No, six seconds. No, seven seconds. No, eight . . . nine . . . ten . . ."

Julia shakes her head. "I forgot how crazy you are."

"Why do you care how long I've been home?"

Julia shrugs. "I don't."

"If you're wondering if I saw . . . what you were doing . . . in your room with Fanny."

Julia's usual tanned face turns bright red.

Fanny has come and is leaning in the doorway and now she laughs. "Were you spying on us?"

Julia is red, red, red.

Fanny is not reacting at all. "It's a good thing if she was listening. She'll learn how to avoid electric mixer kisses, that is, if she even likes boys."

She nudges Julia with her elbow, and this seems to give Julia the ability to speak. "To avoid something, you have to be able to attract it in the first place . . . that is, to get a guy you have to *attract* a guy."

That was the least effective insult Julia has managed for at least six months. Steffi puts cheese on her toast and begins to chew. The message on her Web page, Julia's burning red cheeks, Karro calling her dyke slut, and now Fanny, who has no clue about Julia's feelings. All of it is beginning to be too much.

# – CHAPTER 23 –

Fanny has gone home and Julia is in her room with her door firmly shut.

Steffi wanders back and forth outside Julia's door, but since she can't really think of anything to say, she finally goes back to her room and takes out her dismembered bass. Perhaps if she's really careful and takes off the strings first and uses some superglue, she'll be able to fix it. She starts by taking off the strings. Now only the body of the bass is lying there all alone. As she tries to position it next to the fingerboard, she realizes the whole thing's impossible. The saw has taken away almost two millimeters so that the fingerboard would be too short even if she could glue it back together. The notes on one half of the fingerboard have come completely off. She puts the strings back on just to make sure. Yes, this is not a slap bass but a loose bass.

In the silence of her room with her useless instrument, Steffi wonders if Julia is crying. It almost sounds like it through the wall, if it's not the water pipes. If Pappa were home, he'd go in to Julia and call her *Julita* and ask her what was wrong. Julia would never tell him, of course, but she might feel better anyway. Perhaps she's really not crying. Steffi listens closely. *Is* it the water pipes?

She's on her stomach on her bed writing down the lyrics that had come to her on the way home. She writes down the bass line that might work with it. The last words still don't work as well as she'd like. *That's how my world turns.* No matter how much she tumbles them around in her head, she can't come up with better ones.

Is Julia crying?

Steffi goes into the kitchen and cleans up the bread crumbs to make Pappa happy. Then she sits down on the living room sofa and flips through a magazine. Finally, she goes back to Julia's door. She listens, but doesn't hear anything. Knocks. Knocks again.

"Don't come in!"

"It's me, Steffi."

"I told you, don't come in!"

Steffi keeps standing there perplexed. She's prevented by the strict protocol of not entering a room without someone's permission. Then she knocks again.

"WHAT?"

When she opens the door, Julia is lying on her bed. She looks like she hasn't been crying at all. She doesn't have the puffy eyes that Steffi usually gets, but her eyes are somewhat bloodshot. And maybe she's frightened.

"I won't tell," Steffi says.

Julia looks suspiciously up at her, not moving from her position on the bed. "What are you talking about? There's nothing . . . I'm not . . . didn't you get what Fanny said? Or what?"

She grins with the effort and it looks more like a grimace. Steffi wonders if she should leave, but she sits down on the edge of the bed.

"I won't tell."

Julia turns over on her side. She doesn't look at Steffi or anything else either. Her mascara-rimmed eyes are focused on something invisible. When she takes a breath, it's shaky. Then she looks at Steffi. "If you tell . . . if you say one word . . ."

Steffi could have reached out and stroked Julia's hair like Pappa would have done, but she's only the little sister. Time stands still.

Julia breathes heavily. "You really won't tell?"

"I won't tell. I promise."

Julia turns onto her back. Her voice is thick and almost unrecognizable. "I don't understand why this is happening to me. Why me?"

Steffi lies down next to her. Like she used to do when they were small. A time so long ago, she's almost forgotten it. They lie there for a while.

"There's nothing wrong with being one," Steffi says.

Julia snorts. Or she's taking a deep breath. They're not looking at each other. Steffi looks at the ceiling. Julia looks at the ceiling.

"There's nothing wrong with you being you, either," Julia finally says after a long pause.

"I know."

Julia's words spread all through her body, although she'd already known. The words have the feel of a warm bath when she was small.

"You're good at playing your stupid instruments," Julia says with a giggle.

"You can be in love with your stupid—"

Julia's stare stops her. Now Julia is going to throw her out. Steffi can feel it. She shouldn't have spoken those words. But Julia just sighs. "Don't talk about it. Go play your stupid bass or something."

The ceiling in Julia's room is the same as Steffi's, but it still feels different to be staring at it here. Steffi looks from one corner to the door and then to the bed frame and then the poster with Justin Bieber. "They broke my bass."

"What?"

Julia sits up on her elbow. Steffi bites the inside of her cheek.

"They broke my bass because they think I'm a lesbian."

Julia doesn't reply. Steffi doesn't dare look at her. She just stares up at the ceiling and listens to the water pipes. Someone is flushing the toilet in the apartment upstairs. The streetlights have come on. She can see them through the window.

As Steffi is about to go to sleep that night, Julia comes in. She doesn't knock. She never has and she never will. She doesn't sit on Steffi's bed, either. She just stands there in her pink sleep shirt. "I thought of something. You can ask for another bass for your birthday."

Steffi shrugs, but her shoulders are beneath her blanket so Julia can't see it.

"I'm going to ask for money. I don't want them to know about it."

"OK. Well, I hope you get a lot of money, then, so you have enough."

Steffi has never said thank you to Julia. Julia has never said sorry to Steffi.

"OK."

# — CHAPTER 24 —

From: Stephanie Herrera
To: Simon Kjellman

I've had a chance to listen to Avishai Cohen now. I watched the video you sent. He's really good, although he plays too much fusion for me. Like all real musicians, it's like he's one with his instrument, if you know what I mean. And when I'm playing my best, it feels like that for me, too. You play guitar, right?

From: Simon Kjellman
To: Stephanie Herrera

It's real when you are one with your music, not with your audience. At least, that's what I think. Didn't know if you'd like the modern stuff, but talent is always talent. If you like funk, you should listen to Meshell Ndegeocello when she's playing bass.

Yes, I play guitar. Like everybody else at the auditions. So unique, I know.

From: Stephanie Herrera
To: Simon Kjellman

Have you heard from them yet? I check every day, even though I know they said not to expect a response until May.

By the way, it's not unique to play a different instrument than most people. You're unique when you are successful playing the same instrument as everybody else does, but in your own way.

From: Simon Kjellman
To: Stephanie Herrera

You're right. Infernally important if you want to be a real musician. And I'm not talking about a song in the Melody Festival but being a real, timeless musician. Like you. Honestly, when I saw you, I thought: here's a musician I can play with. I hope you get in. And I get in.

Steffi now has both Avishai Cohen and Meshell Ndegeocello on her mp3 player. When she plays them for Alvar, he snorts. "Yes, well, that's pretty modern, isn't it?"

"But listen! Listen to the bass! Wait . . ."

Steffi looks for a video clip on YouTube and shows Alvar her phone, but Alvar says he doesn't see that well and that the sound is strange, which is true, since it's coming from a phone.

Then he totters over to his record shelf and pulls out a record of Duke Ellington and his orchestra. "Have you listened to Jimmy Blanton?"

Steffi sighs, but there's something about rumpled old Alvar she can't be angry with. "Many times, but we can listen to it again."

Alvar glances at her as he puts the record on. His wild, bushy eyebrows are frowning almost admonishingly. "He died of TB, you know."

"He did?"

"Just twenty-three years old, still a kid. When I took the train to Stockholm, Jimmy Blanton was lying in bed coughing blood. I've often thought about it. Still, his music lives on whenever I play it on the gramophone. Erling often pointed this out to me."

In 1945, Erling started saying that they'd all die someday. "Just like Blanton. You never know."

He wound up his portable gramophone, which was given a place of honor in the middle of their rehearsal space on Åsö Street. The word *portable* was due more to the manufacturer's positive thinking than the real practicality of it, but as Erling had said while the two of them wrestled it down the stairs: twenty pounds weighs less than forty pounds.

"I'm only twenty," Alvar said. "He was twenty-one when he recorded this song."

Erling grinned.

"That's the whole point, Big Boy. Do you think you'd be able to play this a year from now?"

Anita snorted. "Of course he could."

"How would *you* know?" Ingmar demanded so quickly that it must mean something.

"All I'm saying," Erling continued, obviously irritated by Anita's interruption. "All I'm saying is it doesn't matter when we die as long as we've left something good behind us."

They all sat quietly a moment and thought about this while Duke Ellington's piano and Jimmy Blanton's bass were giving life to music none of them could play yet.

*I'd like to leave something really good behind me,* Alvar

thought. *I have to take every chance I get. Always say yes to Lulle Ellboj, Seymour Österwall, and Thore Ehrling.*

After his success at Nalen, they were all more eager to have him fill in as a bassist. He didn't dare tell Erling how many gigs he was starting to get or how much he was getting paid.

"Right now we're listening to Blanton, right?" Erling said as the record was reaching the end. "He's dead. Dead and gone. We'll be dead and gone one day, too, and long after we're dead, far into the next century, people will play an Erling Trio record! Then we'll be alive again, although in a different way. We'll be immortal. And people will say, 'Hey, listen to that bass player, Alvar Svensson of the Erling Trio! Listen to Ingmar's virtuosity on the piano!' "

Anita laughed. "And that Erling," she teased. "The greatest of them all!"

Erling laughed, too, slightly embarrassed but actually pleased.

Alvar stood. "I have a piece," he said, blushing at having told them. "I wrote it myself, that is."

Erling stood. He picked up his clarinet. "I don't know, Big Boy. I have to go to the printer's in an hour and we have to rehearse 'Sweet Georgia Brown.' We'll never get any serious gigs if we don't get it down."

"I bring it up every time." Ingmar got up, too. "If people are going to take us seriously, we can't play pieces nobody recognizes, you know."

Alvar didn't let anyone see his irritation. It was obvious that Anita wanted to protest, but she didn't say anything and so neither did Alvar.

Erling looked at Alvar and then at Ingmar's back as he sat at the piano. "All right, then! Let's take it from the top!"

—

As Alvar was getting ready to get on his bike and head back to Vasa Stan, Anita came up to him and gave him a quick and completely respectable hug.

"'Bye now!" she said loudly and then whispered, "Bike around the corner and then wait for me there."

Her warm whisper remained in his ear and intoxicated him so that he felt he was flying around the corner. He stopped and waited, as out of breath as if he'd biked for blocks.

Anita didn't come. She still didn't come. Alvar's breathing calmed down, but the warm feeling on his ear remained. Anita didn't come. She didn't come. And then there she was. "I really had to figure out a way to make sure Ingmar didn't walk me home." She laughed and Alvar laughed, too, and hiccupped, and fought for breath.

She was standing so close to him. It was March and all the headlines were about the concentration camps they'd found in Germany and everybody was talking about death. Perhaps that's why he felt so alive in the breathing space between his red nose and hers.

"I want to hear your piece."

None of them had a key for the rehearsal space, but that didn't matter. She knocked on the door and cocked her head at the doorman with the fleshy lower lip and they were let in at once.

"That would never work for me," Alvar said.

Anita smiled. "No, it wouldn't."

By now, Alvar had kissed four different women. Almost. One of them had wanted to kiss him, but he'd turned away and gotten spit on his cheek. Anyway, by now he was experienced. One girl had even compared him to the American movie star Ronald Reagan. But he still found it impossible to try to kiss Anita. She was too self-contained, and being near her went right to his stomach until he had no defense.

Now she was sitting on the piano stool waiting for him to play his piece.

"It's in English," he said, and regretted it immediately. He should have said there were no lyrics.

"I'm looking forward to hearing it."

Was she smiling at his nervousness? Was she pleased by it? He had no idea. But he took out his bass because she wanted him to play.

"It's in B."

"Go on."

"And it's not really finished yet."

"I'm listening."

"It's not all that great."

"Alvar! Just play it!"

At home, Alvar had used his guitar. Now it didn't sound that bad on the bass, either, but you had to imagine the other voices. When he got past the intro, he felt surer of himself and hummed along more loudly and dared let the words come out. It was just a song, not some confession that he'd have to back up.

> *"There is something else in the air,*
> *when she is near and I can feel the smell of her hair.*
> *Something in the air says to me that she is near.*
> *The air becomes so clear. Oh, the air becomes so clear.*
> *I think maybe I love her."*

He had barely enough courage to look at her as he sang the last line. Her face showed a good deal of emotion, but he couldn't make out which. After the second verse, she turned toward the piano and began to play along in B. If he'd been a different sort of man, he'd say it was special that the girl was playing the song about herself and she'd fallen for his words. But he was just Alvar, still feeling seventeen years old when it came to Anita.

She broke off in the middle of a chord. "Is this someone special you were writing about?"

*Very special,* Alvar thought.

"It's a jazz song," he said. "That's how it's supposed to sound."

Anita turned the piano stool so she could face him. She gave him a teasing, questioning look. "It sounds like *more* than just that."

She kept chatting away as they left the room to walk upstairs to the outside. When he blushed, she thought it was amusing; she giggled and recited the parts of the lyrics she remembered and improvised the rest.

"Is it Ulla?" Anita asked. "Is it Anna-Lisa? Kerstin? Britta?"

He was pushing his bike to her streetcar stop and was amused by the improvised English she used to fill the spaces in his lyrics.

"The air is everywhere, I have nothing to wear, the air and a bear, oh the fear and a spear! Is it Elsa?"

The streetcar was nearing from the crossroad and Alvar looked at the giggling girl rhyming to his song and he looked at her with everything he felt, straight from his heart. She fell quiet immediately. They were both silent and the streetcar would be there in two seconds.

"It's about you, of course."

Did he really just say that?

The streetcar stopped, the doors rattled open, and people streamed out and others streamed on. Anita was still looking at him. He threw himself on his bike and rode off so quickly he almost fell over and almost, but luckily only almost, crashed into a streetlight. The whole way home, his stomach bubbled and he kept thinking—did I *really* say that? He rushed on, laughed out loud, and then started singing to the city he'd now become part of: "The air becomes so clear, I think I maybe love her!"

The Jimmy Blanton has now played three times in a row and Steffi changes the record. She chooses "Honeysuckle Rose" with Louis Armstrong, but she holds the needle hovering over the record. "And what happened then?"

Alvar grins and she can see how he must have looked in the spring of 1945. "I thought you were going to criticize my rhymes."

"They were terrible. But can't you sing to me what happened next?"

He seems even more like a twenty-year-old, maybe even like a fifteen-year-old. He gets up with difficulty and starts to search through his records far up in the left corner. He has to reach high and still it seems he's not finding what he's looking for. His fingers move more frantically and Steffi steps toward him in order to catch him if he falls.

"Maybe it's not important," she says, but Alvar is not looking at her.

Finally he finds what he was looking for. The record has a red label, handwritten. The cover is made from a paper in a greenish color like mold and says *Your Own Voice.*

"Let's see," he's mumbling, and it's clear he's worked up. "Let's see if this old record still sounds like anything. But we'll have to change the needle for this one. . . ."

Steffi puts Louis Armstrong back into the sleeve and watches Alvar put the record with the handwritten label down in its place. He putters with the screw, and then replaces the needle with one he's found in a drawer, before he sets the new needle with great care onto the record. It begins with a lot of crackling.

Then there's a piano, a jazzy intro behind more crackling.

Steffi tries to catch Alvar's eyes, but he's closed them and he's far away. After the intro, the bass comes in, and although it's strange, she *knows* that this bass player is the same Alvar who'd played with the Karlstad Jazz Club. Steffi leans back in her chair and closes her eyes just like Alvar. She's not ready for it when his voice starts—an obvious Värmland accent singing "There's something else in the air" in English—right through all the crackling. She can't help starting to laugh.

"But that's you!"

Alvar opens his eyes. "Yes, I'm not the greatest jazz singer in the world," he says with a giggle. "But I could wail . . . now wait."

The song is coming to an end. After the last chord, a woman's voice speaks. "I think we don't have to do it again."

Alvar smiles. He's leaning his cheek on his wrinkled hand and just lets the needle rasp on the inner track until Steffi removes it.

"That was Anita, wasn't it? The woman who said that?"

Alvar moves his head in a way that is hard to interpret. "I'll have to tell you more some other time. Now I have to sleep and dream a beautiful dream."

Steffi is about to leave him with his beautiful dream when he calls to her.

"Steffi! It's a good thing that you're following the music of your own time. That Avishai Cohen, he's pretty darn good on the bass."

Steffi feels warm inside.

"You are, too," she says.

"Thank you. But nobody is *ever* going to be as good on the bass as one Steffi Herrera! Am I right?"

She nods in agreement and takes in his words.

Nobody.

# — CHAPTER 25 —

What a coincidence," Karro says. "I just pooped a long string of shit that looked exactly like you."

Sanja giggles hysterically. Jenny and another girl who had been walking away stop to take in the action.

"Just like you, it's shit brown," Karro adds, spurred on by having an audience. "Then it was slimy and bent, so I couldn't help assisting it with you."

Steffi meets Karro's eyes. They're filled with laughter, high on adrenaline and her debasing statement.

Steffi has to choose between keeping her mouth shut and responding. Part of her wants to say that Karro looks just like a pimple she'd popped this morning, but she sees problems with that strategy, one of which is introducing the topic of her pimples.

"Associate," she says.

"Excuse me, piece of shit, are you talking to me?"

Sanja is laughing so hard she has to bend over, repeating "excuse me, piece of shit" until even Jenny is giggling.

"When you were sitting on the toilet, you weren't assisting, you were associating. At the very least you should learn how to speak properly!"

Steffi could add that Karro can't even write a proper e-mail message, but then Hepcat's identity would be revealed.

Karro doesn't move a muscle. "*I'm* not the one who has to learn Swedish. You should go back to Cuba and eat bananas."

Steffi was born in the maternity ward in Torsby, but knows that facts don't mean anything in Björke School. Her eyes have begun to burn, no matter how much she tries to hold back the tears.

"I didn't know what to say," she tells Alvar.

Alvar is lying down on his bed because he's tired, but he didn't ask to be left alone.

Steffi gets up and runs her fingers along the cardboard covers of all the records on the shelf. They're rough against her fingertips, which have started to get soft since her bass had been broken.

"First of all, it was idiotic, saying I should go back to Cuba just because she couldn't say the word *associate* properly. But I don't know . . . I get so . . . I know I shouldn't take it so hard and stuff, but when she starts in on my pappa . . ."

Alvar is silent. At first Steffi thinks he's begun to doze, but when she looks at him, his eyes are open and he's chewing on the inside of his cheek.

"Those small insults," he says after a while. "They're not really so small. Every society has this kind of curse. Even big cities have people like that, people who are driven to find someone to pick on. . . ."

His voice disappears into a sigh, a sigh so deep that she has to answer it. "They're not picking on me because my dad is Cuban. The thing is, they just hate me."

Alvar grimaces.

"It's not that they *just* hate you," he says with sudden strength. He sits up to lean on his elbow. "It's not just that at all. Hating someone for no reason . . . no real reason at all. They have to be . . . unbearably unhappy, the people who do this. And everyone else just observes and doesn't interfere; we just watch. . . ."

He's rambling on just like the old ladies on the other side of the hallway. But it warms her heart to see him angry over what Karro has said, and Steffi hasn't even told Alvar the part about how Karro compared her to her own poop. Alvar is actually trembling.

"You're not just observing," she says. "You're here."

He sits up all the way. His blue eyes are looking at her, filled with heartbreak.

"You have to understand how in love I was with Anita."

"What?"

"You have to understand . . . you have to realize how much I needed her and I was just twenty-one."

"Alvar, what are you talking about?" She wants to tell him to pull himself together, but she doesn't. He looks as thin and fluffy as a baby bird, and whatever he wants to tell her, he really wants to tell her. He sighs and looks at the air, or at something that is not Steffi.

"So much was going on, in those days. I thought about Värmland, I did, but . . . especially when the war was over . . . there I was in Stockholm thinking about Värmland."

When the war ended, Alvar was at Erling's place. One of Erling's girls, the one called Hedvig, was also there, and the three of them so filled the studio apartment that there was hardly room for Erling's radio. They were all sitting and staring at it intensely, as if it might come to life and start to dance. Their hearts were beating as hard as Alvar's.

"Now!" the girl said, glancing at the clock.

"Shh!" Erling said.

The newscaster raised his voice: "Now our prime minister is going to speak. Per Albin Hansson."

Erling's mouth had fallen slightly open and the girl was biting her lip. Alvar started to wonder if Anita was also listening to the radio at that moment, sitting in her mother's fine living room. He was sure his mamma and pappa were listening up in Värmland.

"My dear listeners. I am sure the news that the war is over in our part of the world does not come as a surprise. We have been waiting for this moment and yet it still fills us with inexpressible joy."

Alvar felt it. A roar came from a window on the other side of the street, and then another one, and then all of Bonde Street was filled with jubilation, from the large families at Sofia on one end to the Kino Movie Theater on the other. Alvar was breathing heavily. The giddiness from the knowledge that the war was over made him light-headed, and he felt he had to move and get outside.

Alvar flew through the streets. They were filled with people and he had to zigzag on his bike between families with children and old men. Spring was everywhere in the air, even in the smoke from the printer's, and there was peace in Europe. And Mamma—it hit him like a wave to the stomach, so intense was his joy that he almost fell over—Mamma no longer had to worry about German soldiers and their Norwegian girlfriends. As he turned into King Street, he heard people singing the Norwegian national anthem and he let go of the handlebars and joined the song, his arms raised in the sign for victory. The street was filled with people as far as the eye could see. Homemade confetti whirled down from the windows as if the skies themselves were releasing it. Someone had written PEACE on a large piece of cardboard. Others waved the various Scandinavian flags, Swedish, Norwegian, and Danish, and as soon as someone started to cheer, twenty others joined. Norway's national anthem changed to the Danish national anthem, and although Alvar didn't know all the words, he sang along as best he could.

Anita was at the corner of Birger Jarl Street. In the almost supernatural atmosphere that had sent confetti from the heavens, it was perfectly natural that she would see him at once. Her usually serious expression had changed to a huge smile. A ripped-up receipt floated onto her face and she laughed as she shook it off.

"Did you hear the news on the radio?" she asked as he got off his bike to stand beside her.

"Yes, Erling, Hedvig, and I heard it at his place."

"Who's Hedvig?"

"Another one of Erling's girls."

She smiled again. "Five years ago, peace didn't mean much to me."

"I wonder whether Mamma is crying. I'm sure she's crying."

"I'm sure she'll be crying the entire day," Anita agreed.

Alvar could stand like this in Anita's smile forever. They would smile at each other, arms covered in goose bumps, just because there was peace; Anita would talk about his mother as if she knew her; and they'd always be surrounded by cheers of joy and waving flags.

Then it happened. A huge Norwegian flag fell across his head and blocked his view of Anita while everything turned red, white, and blue. As the flag swept onward in its triumphal journey, Anita emerged, standing right in front of him. She put her hands to his cheeks, pulled him close, and then kissed him on the lips. Then she laughed.

"For peace."

For peace.

He flew through Östermalm, Norrmalm, Kungsholmen, rode the wrong way, slid into a fine pile of gravel, ripped a marvelous hole in his pants, got a wonderful puncture, which he fixed joyfully and easily. He ran up all the stairs and lifted Aunt Hilda to the ceiling.

She looked at him in fear, so he put her back down and petted her wrinkled cheek. He smiled at her and thought she might have resembled his own mother when she was young, and therefore she had once been beautiful.

"Peace has been declared in Europe!"

"Well, then maybe we'll be able to get real coffee again!"

He laughed out loud and one corner of her mouth turned up into a smile. "May I call my parents?"

Later he could never remember all the details of the telephone call. He thought his father had picked up the phone; he had a vague memory of a laughing male voice and his mother's warm dialect, but it was all mixed together. The thing he remembered most clearly from that day was the fact that Anita had kissed him. Such wonderful excitement; how he would have loved to declare this wonderful news in his call. If he had called from Aunt Hilda's—he couldn't remember if she'd actually had a telephone. Maybe he'd called from a box in the street?

He *had* called, hadn't he?

---

"Hello?"

Steffi was waving a hand in front of his face. She's looking at him and brings his focus back to the room with its institutional curtains. Her backpack is on the floor, and he comes back to what was happening now, history being written today and tomorrow.

"There is nothing whatsoever ugly about you," he says.

She looks at him questioningly with her dark brown eyes and a face that still retains a child's quality. Of course it would not matter what a decrepit old man says.

"Those bullies are wrong about you," he says anyway.

"I know."

He can see in her eyes that she knows this but doesn't yet feel it. He wants to pick her up as if she were four years old. He feels he's been holding on to these words for a long time.

"They just want someone to pick on, you see, because they don't feel so good about themselves. Every single word against you is a word they actually want to use about themselves. They're small people."

He uses his thumb and forefinger to make a very small space and he peers at Steffi through it. "This small."

She nods and says, "I know. There are small people and big people. A small person hopes that another small person will just disappear. A big person hopes that the small person will grow up and become big."

This girl warms his heart. She looks indifferent on the outside, but inside there's so much going on.

"Wise words. Who told them to you?"

"Pappa. But he said it in a different way. He can't always use good syntax, but simple words . . . they're easy to say."

Yes, he understood that.

"I imagine sometimes you just want to punch them."

"Yes. Or, sometimes, I want to punch myself."

He feels as if gravity has grown stronger when he hears her say that. As if his entire mind had gotten heavier. He wants to disagree, but he's tried to explain away others' emotions before and knows it doesn't work. "I imagine you would have to feel that way sometimes."

Perhaps she's disappointed. Perhaps she's just blinking.

"But that's not any kind of real revenge," he continues.

He's tired. The fifteen-year-old, the four-year-old, the evil people, the good people who don't do anything, as when Steffi's classmates keep quiet, everything that happened to Svea, the peace in 1945, the kiss on the corner of King Street and Birger Jarl Street, which he can still feel deep inside, and *did* Aunt Hilda have a telephone or not? There's so much to think about when you reach the age of eighty-nine.

"I usually think I'm going to show them," she says. "They'll just stand there in amazement . . . like this . . . they will just be *amazed*!"

She's opening her eyes wide in a theatrical way as she says this. He giggles and she smiles. *She's balancing,* he thinks. *Balancing between wanting to punch them or punch herself. She's in a terrible state of balance.*

His thoughts clear up after she's gone. He now thinks about subject after subject more slowly, at his own speed. He puts on Stan Getz's "Ack Värmeland" on the gramophone and puts his thoughts in order. Anita. Peace. The four-year-old Svea. The fifteen-year-old Steffi. All the steps in between. His conscience. The boy he used to be.

When he presses the button to summon the nurse, she comes immediately and looks for him in the bed. She's surprised to find him sitting in his armchair.

"I just wanted to make sure the alarm button worked," he

says with a smile, and the nurse sighs in relief and shakes her head.

"But now that you're here," he says, making sure he doesn't draw her into a discussion on Stan Getz's wonderfully nonrespectful treatment of Värmland harmonies—the nurses usually didn't like those kind of discussions—"I actually have a request."

The nurse always has a great deal to do and he's aware of this—he can see it in the pulsing vein in her neck—but he forces her to listen to his words until she just has to say yes. He already knows that only one kind of person comes to work in retirement homes—angels.

# – CHAPTER 26 –

The next morning when Steffi wakes up, she is sixteen years old. She looks at herself in the mirror and tries to find the sixteen-year-old in there. Does she resemble the fifteen-year-old, the one in ninth grade at Björke School who had come home from gym class last February in soaking socks? No.

When Steffi gets to school, she's a whore's daughter and an Indian. Sanja has started up this thing about her being an Indian. Class 9B really enjoys Sanja's creativity.

"So what's your Indian name, then?" Karro smiles, with dancing eyes, right in front of Steffi. "Whores with Wolves?"

"Horny Buffalo," Sanja adds.

"Pops Pimples with Teeth," Leo says.

Karro explodes in laughter. "How does she do it?" she shrieks. "How the hell, Leo?"

"Indian magic," Hannes says.

He's standing next to Leo. Once Hannes and Steffi had played like professional musicians in the music room. He looks at Steffi as he says this, but not right at her, more like at her shoes.

"Yeeees!" Karro grins. "Indian magic! I was wondering how she could be such a slut without anyone wanting to sleep with her!"

Steffi has often wondered this herself, but she doesn't say anything.

In the classroom, they all sing "Happy Birthday to You" to her. Since they are in social studies, they sing in the most beautiful way possible. Sanja's honestly beautiful voice creeps under Steffi's skin like a germ.

Afterward, Bengt asks her how her project is going, and she says she's getting near the end.

"I'm writing about how they celebrated after they heard on the radio that the war was over. In Stockholm there was, like, a party in the streets. People were throwing confetti from their windows."

"What was happening in Värmland?"

"Oh . . . they were listening to the radio and were happy and . . . I don't know that much about what was happening here. My source was in Stockholm then."

Bengt nods. "If you have time, find another source, just for the sake of local interest. And it would be good if you could add something about the Norwegians under Quisling and the German influence on Norwegian-Swedish relations."

"OK."

"But what I've read so far seems fine. Although your writing style is still too informal."

"OK."

When Steffi gets to Sunshine Home, she's met by the woman whose mouth hangs open and the other one who chews on her cheek walking toward her. Between them, the strict nurse, the one Alvar told her was named Karin, has the arms of the two women, helping them slowly along the hallway.

"Hello, Steffi," she says.

"Hi," Steffi replies.

"Hi! Hi!" says the woman chewing her cheek.

Karin keeps looking at Steffi. Steffi can't figure out why. Karin doesn't say anything, but it is apparent that she's touched.

Alvar is in his room. He smiles widely when he sees her and she laughs out loud and exclaims, "Well! You are looking especially fine today! What a great hat!"

He's still grinning as he straightens his party hat over his tufts of hair. "I have one for you, too!"

She obediently puts on a green, glittering party hat. Alvar asks her to put on "Honeysuckle Rose."

"The one with Ella."

Ella Fitzgerald fills the room with her *do-do-be-do-le-do-le-do* and the piano trills in playfully and then the bass and then the brass. Alvar nods contentedly. "Now that's a great birthday song."

He puts two napkins on the table. He takes out two green marzipan pastries from a cardboard box.

"Much better than birthday cake, I believe."

"Me, too."

He lifts his pastry and they say *skål* and best wishes. He giggles. "What a party! It's as good as having a jazz club at a library!"

She giggles, too, and takes a bite of the pastry.

"I asked Karin to buy these for us," Alvar says. "So, in a way, she's wishing you a happy birthday, too. And a number of the other old folks in the building, the ones who remember that I told them you were having a birthday, they told me to tell you to have a happy birthday."

"That was sweet of them."

"Yes, most of them are a bit addled, of course, but they are sweet."

"Maybe not Svea. She's not what I'd call sweet."

Alvar hums to himself as he sweeps some marzipan crumbs into his napkin. "Since today is your birthday, you can ask me to tell you a story. Isn't that a good present?"

"OK, then I want to hear about when you were in the studio with Povel Ramel."

"When was that?"

"In 1946. Hjukström was on clarinet. Maybe you didn't care because you're so focused on the beautiful Anita. Hello? Don't you remember?"

Alvar nods and his party hat bobs up and down. "Of course I remember that. It was one of the best days of my life. But I can't tell you about that yet. It's too far ahead in the chronology. So wish for something else."

"Well . . . then I'd like to know what happened when you came home to Björke. Didn't you go home for Christmas or something else? Did you go see your mother after you'd been missing her for so long?"

"No, no, I can't talk about that yet, either. Can you turn the record over?"

Steffi turns Ella Fitzgerald over and sets the needle down in the groove.

"So what do you want me to ask for, then?"

"Maybe how it felt to play the Winter Palace? In 1945?"

"All right. What was it like to play the Winter Palace in 1945?"

"Well, let me tell you! It was not at all like playing Nalen!"

---

Playing the Winter Palace was nothing like playing Nalen. For example, jitterbug was forbidden.

"That's rotten," he exclaimed to Erling.

"Absolutely nuts," Erling agreed. "Jitterbug and jazz go together, but these gorillas have no clue about jazz or jitterbug."

The gorillas in question were two tough bouncers. They were there to keep the Winter Palace clean. The first time Alvar had come to play, he was barely able to get through the door because he was so nervous that they thought he was drunk. Finally he was forced to use his Värmland dialect, the one he called the bumbling and innocent one, and now he used it whenever he had to pass by the bouncers.

"I imagine they'd beat me to a pulp if I tried Söder slang," he said, laughing, to Erling, who laughed roughly back.

"Yeah, *you* speaking Söder slang!"

"Still, it's a fun place to play," Alvar said in the purest Stockholm dialect possible. "I don't think there's an orchestra I'd rather play in than Lulle's."

He shivered, thinking that at twenty, he could already say that. While he was wrestling his upright bass out of its case, he imagined how he it would be to mention this in passing to anyone who happened to walk by.

Erling was humming with a jealous note. "Too bad Arne Domnérus never gets sick."

Alvar glanced at him and grunted. He knew Ellboj would never take Erling on clarinet into his band, even if Arne Domnérus were on his deathbed.

But Erling was his friend and didn't need to hear those kinds of truths from him.

"You promised," Erling said.

"I promised to ask. I haven't promised what they're going to answer."

"You *promised*." Erling mimicked him with a half-smile.

Alvar got an A from the pianist and started to tune his bass.

"The trio is going to rehearse at one P.M. tomorrow," Erling said.

"I can't make it then."

"You can't?"

"I'll be at the Flame with Arne and his guys."

Erling lifted an eyebrow as he spit on the floor. "All right, all right, I get it. Message loud and clear."

"You can come. They have some new Roy Eldridge records."

"Thanks, but I have records of my own at home."

"Roy Eldridge records?"

Alvar didn't get a reply. He was tuning his E string as Erling got up and walked away. Alvar watched his back and thought it was as thin as a stray cat's.

Maybe he should go to rehearsal after all.

Erling came back when the orchestra began to play. Alvar tried to catch his eye and give him an encouraging look, but Erling never looked at him. Instead, Erling began to dance wildly until the Winter Palace bouncers came up to him and lifted him, energetically kicking, by the elbows to carry him to the exit. Ingmar met him at the door, and they went on out into the night. Then Anita appeared from the other side of the dance floor, as if she'd been hiding all that time.

When the last piece was over, she came up to the stage and leaned on it, her elbows on the edge. Arne looked at the trumpet player, Nisse, who shook his head.

"Hello, Anita," Alvar said, not able to hide his pride.

"You were really swinging tonight," Anita said.

"Not like those grandpas at the Bal Palais, right?" Nisse said, with a wink.

Anita looked at him with her head to one side. "One of these days, you'll just be fussy old men while the young guys are playing real jazz. Have you ever thought of that?"

Alvar laughed while he put his bass into its case. Nisse also seemed to be amused, and he came to the edge of the stage and squatted down.

"Some of us are going to grab a bite at Fiffe's place later. Want to come along?"

"Give Fiffe my regrets. I'm going to go on home now, in the company of Mr. Alvar Svensson."

The guys behind Alvar laughed heartily. "Yep, good to have a muscular guy like Big Boy Svensson along if there's trouble!"

"He'll scare off all the bad guys!"

Big Boy was pleased.

"I've decided I need to find a job."

The evening was warm, although fall was in the air. A clear white moon was looking down on them as they walked slowly through the labyrinth of Stockholm's old and new architecture.

"I can't be what my parents want me to be. So I think I'll take the secretary course and earn my own living."

"And here I thought you were going to marry an old, rich banker," Alvar teased her.

"That's what my parents think."

"He'd be blown away by your beauty along with your horseback riding skills and your secretarial independence."

"Be quiet!"

"You'd be an asset to his business!"

Anita laughed and gave him a pretend slap to the ear. "I told you to be quiet!"

They turned onto King Street and a sudden blast of wind made them pull their coats closer around themselves.

Anita stumbled and tumbled into him so he almost lost his balance.

"Oh!" he exclaimed stupidly.

She laughed. "Better have a muscular guy like Big Boy Svensson in case of trouble! Right?"

He blushed, but the weight of her body now leaning into his made it hard for him to think. They walked in silence for a minute.

"But what do you think about me getting a job? Do you think I'll make a good secretary?"

"Wouldn't you rather be a jazz pianist?"

She smiled and looked up at the white moon. "Maybe, if it were easier. But you have to be tough."

"Like Erling?"

She giggled, or perhaps snorted. "No, not like Erling."

Anita climbed up on the long wall along the road and stopped. They were almost the same height now, with her perhaps a few inches taller.

"Then you'd be like Alice Babs, just on the piano."

"You're so sweet." She ran her gloved hand across his cheek. "Lots of people think even the boys shouldn't be playing jazz. Have you ever thought how hard it would be as a girl to do the same? It would be really tough."

Alvar let the words sink in. He'd never thought other people, besides Ingmar, considered girls and jazz that way. As if it mattered if you were a girl, as long as you were good.

"I don't want to try to tough it out," Anita explained. "I just want to be free."

In her eyes he saw what she meant. He saw someone who lived differently, who thought differently, who came from somewhere very different.

"I want you to be free, too."

He heard how banal that sounded, but she put her hands on his shoulders and leaned her forehead on his.

"If everyone were like you, I would happily play at the Winter Palace. If I got the chance."

Her forehead was cool on his but still warm in another way. The tips of their noses touched. She was talking quietly for his ears alone.

"But in my home . . . I would like to have a piano . . . and I'd play piano for my family . . . all the children . . . and grandchildren." She giggled. "Can you imagine a grandmother playing jazz music?"

Perhaps the September air was making him brave. Or the darkness around them, the streetlights fighting against the foggy darkness with their round balls of light.

"Yes," he said. "*I'd* want to listen."

The tip of her nose slowly turned aside and the blond hair on her upper lip tickled him slightly and he felt them as warmth right before Anita kissed him. He'd always fantasized kissing her when they were on a park bench or a dance floor and that she'd be turning her face up to his and he'd be bending over her, but now she was up on the wall, at his height. She bent down to him.

The record is over. Alvar's gaze is in the distance again. Steffi removes Ella Fitzgerald and puts on Alice Babs. Alice Babs doesn't sound as tough as she must have had to be.

"I think Alice Babs was the free one," she says.

Alvar picks up a crumb from his napkin and pops it into his

mouth. "Yes, I thought so, too, but that girl had to endure some really hard stuff. Anita knew that. Some people made fun of us boys, too, but nobody called us names like 'loose woman.' "

"Who called her that? Ingmar?"

"No, not him. Eric somebody . . . the manager of music rights company. I forgot the name . . . he said Alice Babs should be smacked on the rear and sent home. At least, that's what he wrote in the newspaper."

Steffi lets the information sink in as she turns the record cover over to see if there's a picture of Alice Babs. There isn't one, of course.

"Well, I don't want just to play for my grandkids. Well, if I have any and they want to listen to me . . . but I want to write my own songs and have them be recorded and everything. Don't you think Anita wanted that?"

Alvar sighs deeply and sucks in his upper lip. "Yes, yes, I think a part of Anita, a large part, would have liked to play the Winter Palace, or even be recorded in a real record studio."

"Were you a couple then?"

Alvar looks at her with his old eyes. Alvar—*he's so serious,* she thinks.

"You know . . . she was a girl from a good family, and Ingmar came from the same place. I was just a country boy."

"But she kissed you."

"Yes, she did," Alvar said. His voice was slow. "It was a wonderful evening. One of the best evenings of my life."

Her family was waiting for her at home. They'd have sparkling cider and a birthday cake.

Steffi puts on her jacket and winds up the gramophone so that Alvar can hear the entire record if he wants to.

"Something is bothering me," he says, sitting on the bed.

"What?"

"You said you want to write your own songs and all the rest."

"Yes?"

"Well, I was wondering," he says. "How can you do it if you don't have one of these?" He lifts up the blanket and grins at her, a real big grin.

Steffi is about to say something, but she's lost her breath. She's looking at a four-string Fender bass guitar.

# – CHAPTER 27 –

This is a bass worthy of a hepcat. Retro brown and bone white with a sound that the poor decapitated one could never have made.

Only one month remains in the semester. Steffi will never take her Fender to school. Every day when she comes home, she goes into her room and puts the strap of her new Fender around her neck and plays the old songs like those by Ellington and Domnérus and Povel Ramel with Alice Babs. She plays along with Sonya Hedenbratt and wails along with her: *"Feet on the ground but a heart full of blues."* She plays along with Avishai, Malheiros, Ndegeocello, and all the other new bassists, the ones Simon in Stockholm calls the new funk movement. And she looks at herself in her Hepcat hat while she plays her bass. She wonders how she'd look in a suit, a white suit.

When she logs in to The Place, she still has her bass on her knees. The unreal Karro has written to Hepcat. Hepcat and Karro have absurd conversations about Karlstad, poetry, and imagined offenses at school, such as Karro's belief that her closest friend has betrayed her.

From: Karro N
To: Hepcat

God, I can't stand it. Like my best friend Sanja, she can be so mean. For example, yesterday we were putting on our makeup and she said I have SMALL EYES. What? Anybody can just look at me and see what kind of eyes I have. Or what do U think? U saw my pictures. (I posted two new ones, btw.) Plus, my pretend dad is supposed to work from home the next four weeks and we argue ALL THE TIME because he's so disgusting. Soon I'll move to Karlstad and move in w/ U. U'd like that, right?? Ha-ha!

From: Hepcat
To: Karro N

Nice of you to call me God. Sorry that your friend doesn't realize you have really, really big eyes, but nice that your spelling's getting better.

I've heard worse things than having "small eyes" (I don't know how things are in your innocent country school, but here in the city they use words like slut and whore to put down girls. So tasteless if you ask me.) It sounds worse to have to fight pretend dads. But you can't come to Karlstad, because then I'd have to tell you where I live.

P.S. Seriously, looking at your picture, your eyes are enormous. Almost scary.

Steffi reads over the message she just sent and decides that the words are not those of a big person. She probably should write and ask why Karro's pretend father is so disgusting. Perhaps she should care, even if she and Karro are enemies.

Instead, she picks up her clarinet, without slipping out of her bass strap, to search for a note she's been feeling inside the whole day. Happy when she finds it, she puts her amp on reverb so both instruments sound at the same time. She's starting to understand the clarinet. Maybe not like Erling did, and definitely not like Arne Domnérus, but she's starting to . . . feel it.

Steffi has brought that horrible clarinet. Alvar grimaces at it as if it were a scruffy dog or a three-legged table certain it can stand. He thinks he should have added a clarinet to the shopping list he'd given Karin when he sent her to run his errands in Karlstad.

Steffi is putting it together quickly and shoves the parts as close together as possible so there won't be a gap. She plays a note for him. "And I need an E as the bottom note of the chord. Can you hum an E?"

Alvar tries to hum a low E, but that ends up with both of them laughing. He loves listening to her laugh. It's a rough laugh and reminds him of Erling.

She pulls out that phone and pokes it. On the minuscule screen there's an even more minuscule keyboard, and as he touches it, it makes a *plink* sound. It's very entertaining.

"I'd like to see Charles Norman on this thing."

"But, come on, hum an E for me!"

He obeys the teenage girl frowning in concentration, sitting on the floor. He touches the smooth screen to hit an E. Her clarinet drowns it out completely and she grimaces.

"Well, you can imagine it, can't you?"

His fingers feel energetic, even impatient.

"It's not going to work," he says. "If you open my closet door there . . . no, the other door . . . we'll be able to make some decent progress."

He enjoys her expression when she discovers his upright bass behind the door. She bravely wrestles it out of the closet and into the space on the floor between the gramophone and the armchair.

"I hope I can tune it," he says. "It's been standing around for months."

Perhaps for years. It hasn't really been years, has it?

It's irritating that his fingers feel so stiff. As if they were old twigs compared to how supple they used to be back in the day. He can't be as quick as he used to be, either, but his feeling for the instrument is still there, and he feels no pain as long as he's playing. Two things strike him while he plays with Steffi joining in on clarinet, as she's trying things out and trying to imitate what they've been listening to.

"Can you try B-flat?" she asks, and immediately he knows that she has real talent.

If they can't see this at that school of hers, then they are idiots. This clarinet is in the worst possible condition and she's been trying to play it for only a few months, but she's getting syncopation, sevenths, and that indefinable swing out of it. She's laughing and then she's blowing until she's red in the face and then she calls out: "Again!" and he thinks that if the people she meets in Stockholm are not idiots, he's going to lose her to the big city.

The second thing that comes to mind is Erling. He tells her so after they've been playing for at least a half an hour and the strain on his fingers and back has become too great. She wrinkles her brow.

"I remind you of Erling? Because of the clarinet?"

"Believe it or not," he said. "There's something about you that reminds me of him."

She's not at all pleased to hear this.

What has he told her about Erling? "He was not a bad clarinetist," he tries.

"He was nowhere near as good as Arne Domnérus. And he was so nasty to you."

Alvar leans the bass against his bed and sits down in his armchair.

"It depends on how you look at it. Erling was the first real jazz musician I'd ever met. Have you forgotten the train to Stockholm? He could swing, you see, even though his technique never was the best. And a disposition to annoy the other guys . . ."

"But he didn't like it when you started to play at Nalen. A real friend would be happy for you. He wouldn't keep on nagging you about his trio."

Alvar thinks about this. He can still see Erling's face in front of him: his good-humored look, the almost movie star appearance of his face, and his hair always styled just so. Not to mention his worn-out suit.

"Erling," he said thoughtfully. "Erling was a working-class guy with big dreams."

Erling was a working-class guy with big dreams. He'd grown up in a one-room apartment with four siblings, a constantly exhausted mother, and a father he saw only the day before payday. When the first state apartments for large families had been instituted, he was fourteen. He had moved into one with his family, just one kid among many in patched clothes who stole into the movie house through the back fence. But all that time, he knew he'd make something of himself.

"You see?" he said as he peered over his pilsner at Alvar. "I always knew that I would make it playing jazz music. I started long before you got here, Alvar. Erling's Trio started in the thirties! I'm not like Ingmar or some damned Thore Ehrling. Or that

Tersmeden guy; he's someone who shouldn't have bothered to come to Stockholm."

He snorted. Tersmeden was a composer whose musical pieces had been given professional arrangements and were often played at the Winter Palace, chiefly due to Tersmeden's willingness to pay for Ellboj's Orchestra's studio recordings. Alvar had to admit that Erling was right. If he had Tersmeden's resources, he would already be a soloist. But if you didn't have money, you needed to have technique.

"If you take more care when you practice, you'll be someone," Alvar said and regretted his vague encouragement immediately. "You'll be one of the very best."

Erling took a few deep gulps and wiped the foam from his lip. "I don't know. I'm starting to get tired. I'm getting tired working every night. It's just . . . I can't leave the band. Erling's Trio. Doesn't that sound grand?"

Alvar noticed the dark rings under Erling's eyes, but he saw those eyes light up when Erling talked about his trio.

"With you on the bass," Erling said, "we could really get somewhere." His enthusiasm returned. "I just . . . I have to admit that you're the one who is the real talent here."

Alvar had nothing to say to this. At least, not a direct reply. He took a gulp of his own pilsner. "I don't know," he said. Alvar had still not gotten used to the sour taste. There must be something wrong with him. "I mean, it's you and me and Ingmar," he said evasively. "I don't know if Ingmar and I are . . . such a good combination."

Erling tapped his bottle with his forefinger. "I shouldn't get into the middle of this," he said. "No, actually, I should. Two things. Number One. Watch out if Ingmar finds out about you and Anita canoodling behind his back. And Number Two."

Erling paused and looked at Alvar with a gaze that was

difficult to interpret. "I would never have believed that Big Boy from Björke could have ever captured the heart of a girl like that. I must have taught you a thing or two after all."

Alvar laughed, perhaps extra long and extra loud. Erling gulped down the last of his pilsner. When he turned back to Alvar, the darkness in the corner of the bar crept closer. Erling breathed out beer and the desperation of broken dreams. "If you would just ask Topsy, we could get a gig at Nalen, am I right?"

Alvar couldn't meet Erling's eyes. He couldn't tell Erling the truth. He couldn't insult a friend to his face. His chest tightened. Perhaps he should just ignore his own reputation as a musician and give Erling the chance his talent did not deserve. On the other hand, he'd come to Stockholm to be a jazz musician, and a real friend should see that he, too, had dreams he had to chase, ones that were just as important to him.

A sharp bang made him jump. Erling had slammed the pilsner bottle on the table. His film star eyes were filled with disgust. "I never thought you'd be such a coward!"

Two days later, Alvar found retribution come creeping up on him. Erling's words had started to seep under his strings and made his playing wishy-washy and out of tune. Hadn't Erling taught Alvar everything he knew about jazz? Didn't Erling deserve a band, even if it was just a trio? The director at the Winter Palace noticed the change and asked Alvar if he'd lost his drive. His jazz was sick. No, his concentration was back at 140 Åsö Street.

He heard the music all the way from the street. He threw down his bike so quickly it almost crashed against a drainpipe. He stumbled down the stairs. Perhaps he'd go to Topsy after all. It never hurt to ask. His jazz fingers began to feel better as he used them to open the basement door. He was about to yell "I'm going to ask Topsy . . ." but he never got any further than "I" as Ingmar shot up from the piano stool. Alvar had never thought about how big Ingmar was, and the way Ingmar now jumped up made it look as if he loomed as high as the ceiling. Ingmar's usually blank eyes were thunderously black, and the darkness spread across his face.

"You little rat!"

Alvar didn't fly across Stockholm. He stumbled, panted, leaped between streetcars that seemed ready to block him or even kill him. He lost his breath and couldn't get it back. The men in his band used to joke that they were musicians, not built for athletics, but Ingmar was motivated by rage and self-righteousness.

*He's so big, I'm so stupid,* a small voice peeped inside his head. *He's so big! He's going to kill me! Mamma! Help!* But his mother was in Värmland and Alvar had to catch his breath. He stopped in front of a streetcar, feeling dizzy. Ingmar was catching up now, with a roar. Alvar deserved it; he knew he deserved it. "Ourfatherwhoartinheaven," he began but gave up asking for God's forgiveness at the last minute in preference to the streetcar. Perhaps it was his prayer, perhaps God gave him the strength to leap up on the streetcar that almost ran him down. Ingmar's roar behind him reminded him of a bassoon.

"You damned rat! You're DEAD, do you hear me? Go ahead, run away! I'll find you and you'll be DEAD! YOU RAT!"

"It's just like I said."

Alvar opens his eyes, which he'd closed for a moment. "What?"

The sixteen-year-old in his room bends over and plucks one of the strings on his upright bass. It gives a dull thud when she releases it. "I told you Erling was nasty. You said he wasn't and then you told me even more about how nasty he was to you."

Alvar is lost in his own thoughts for a moment. Had he been intending to defend Erling when he started? He didn't remember. Well, if he had, he certainly chose the wrong anecdote.

"We'll get there," he says and he hopes he will.

There was a place in his heart where he remembered the betrayal of a working-class guy who'd had dreams. For some reason, he really wants her to understand this. But not today.

"Steffi," he says. He'd taken a good look at the calendar that morning. "When will you get your letter?"

"In May! In May and today is the first of May!"

Today is the first of May and she'd forgotten all about it. She'd forgotten to check the mail ever since she'd gotten her new Fender bass. She runs the whole way home and calls into the kitchen: "Is there a letter for me?"

There was no letter for Steffi. But it was May now. The letter might even come tomorrow.

# – CHAPTER 28 –

In reality, he hadn't caught the streetcar that day. What really happened was that Ingmar had caught him and beaten him to a pulp. *Steffi doesn't need to know that,* Alvar thinks, and as he looks back, he remembers what had really happened.

The streetcar had pulled away and Ingmar's fists had pounded him so that the whole world seemed to turn bloodred and throbbing. A blow to his eye. Blows to his chest. Blows to his shoulders as Alvar had managed to get back up on his feet and run for the next streetcar. When at last he'd finally tried to sneak into Aunt Hilda's apartment, his shoulders ached and his left eye was swollen and black and blue. He'd hoped she was asleep.

"Alvar Svensson!"

Her voice struck him like another blow. Aunt Hilda's consonants were getting sharper as each year passed. She was holding a newspaper, and it looked as if something must be upsetting her, but when Alvar came in and she saw his condition, the newspaper rustled to the floor. "Oh, dear heavens! Sit, dear child, sit down!"

She sighed and went to the kitchen to wet a handkerchief that she held to his throbbing eye. His mother would have done it differently. While she pressed the handkerchief to his forehead, Aunt Hilda rocked back and forth and muttered incomprehensibly.

"That it has come to this! That THIS is what it has come to! No, I said right from the beginning, I said it, didn't I tell you?"

The handkerchief pressed hard against his forehead stung more than it helped, but he didn't dare say anything about it.

"What, Aunt Hilda?"

She dropped the handkerchief and tilted his head so he could see her. She was obviously no longer concerned about his injury. She stared stubbornly into his uninjured eye.

"I said from the very beginning that you were not to have anything to do with that jazz music as long as you were living under my roof. Did I or did I not make myself clear?"

Her eyes were those of an old, angry hawk. This scared him more than Ingmar's fists.

"But I . . . but I haven't—"

Aunt Hilda interrupted him as she picked up the newspaper.

"Don't lie to me, young man. Lies also do not belong in this house. And see, this is how far things have gone!"

His eye was throbbing so hard he could almost hear it. He couldn't say he hadn't lied, because that would be another lie. But he couldn't say anything else, either.

"What's wrong, Aunt Hilda?"

He would never forget what came next. Her wrinkled fingernail tracing the headline, his aching body, and the words he was reading.

Karin comes in. She has to change his sheets. He likes it when they change them when he's still in the room.

"Do you want to hear what they wrote about me once upon a time in the Stockholm newspaper?" he asks.

"Only if you tell me the short version," she replies with a quick glance in his direction.

She has a sense of humor. Karin keeps it secret, but inwardly, she's a good woman with a real sense of humor.

"You really know how to encourage a guy," he says and smiles the way Erling taught him. "Well, this is what they wrote: '*Among the really great Swedish jazz musicians we also must mention Alvar Big Boy Svensson, who has come from the forests of Värmland to supply the Winter Palace and The National, better known by the nickname Nalen, with real swing. He's a rock in the studio and a fresh breath of wind in any orchestra.*' "

Karin rearranges his pillows after she's changed the pillowcases. She is unbelievably quick.

"Those were nice words," she says. "To think you still remember them after all these years."

Even though she's already heading out of the room, Alvar replies: "Yes, to think I do."

If she'd stayed a moment longer, he would have told her that those nice words had gotten him thrown out of his aunt's apartment in Vasa Stan.

# – CHAPTER 29 –

Steffi is doing an experiment. She *is* Hepcat, though nobody knows it.

When Karro calls her "the daughter of a whore," Hepcat makes a mental note: "Gal calls her classmate the daughter of a whore."

She looks over the whole class and notes: "One guy is jealous of another guy's iPad."

She calls them "guys and gals," as if she were living in the forties. Her idea of a curious hepcat fills her mind: she could write a song! *A Hepcat Visits the Twenty-first Century.* She opens Word and can already hear the walking bass line in her head. After a moment's thought, she changes *hepcat* to swing player.

*The swing player's in town*
*What do these kids have on the table? What kind of class is this?*
*Where are all the telephones? Why don't they swing to jazz?*

*Why do they always need more?*
*Why do they call this girl whore?*

Though Steffi is not sure people actually used the word *whore* in the forties, she suspects that Alvar has cleaned up his stories a bit. She'd have to ask him.

"That doesn't look like research to me."

The computer teacher, Elin, always sneaks up on kids, and you never know when she'll catch you when you're in her class. But she always winks, and that makes it easier to handle.

"It's lyrics from a song," Steffi says quickly, and changes the window to Internet Explorer. "I'm doing research on the forties."

"May I see?"

"It's not important. I just wanted to check it. It was about some musicians." She shows the picture of Lulle Ellboj that has appeared on the screen. He's smiling, dressed in his suit and tie. "He wasn't the best musician in the world, but he could keep a band together. And his father was an engineer, so he wasn't exactly a working-class guy."

"It sounds very interesting," Elin says. "But I thought Bengt said your project was on the Second World War?"

"And jazz music. They belong together."

Elin nods. "I can imagine. Jazz came from America, so, absolutely, there was a political dimension."

"Jazz music was forbidden in certain countries during the war. Though people still played jazz—they just called it by another name. The politicians didn't figure out it was the same music."

Elin almost looks impressed. She pats Steffi on the shoulder and moves away to sneak up on the next unsuspecting student.

Steffi concentrates on Lulle Ellboj's black-and-white photograph. He looks young in this picture. He *was* young when

Alvar played in his orchestra. That very face, except alive and in color, was the one Alvar watched when he played the Winter Palace.

She searches for Alvar Svensson although she already knows there's no picture of him. Wikipedia mentions him, in a few articles on various bands, but there's nothing about Alvar himself, except that he was a jazz musician. She clicks *edit* and she feels somehow invasive, but that's how Wikipedia is supposed to work.

*Alvar Svensson is from Björke in Värmland,* she writes and hits save. Then she searches for Erling, but none of the Erlings she finds on Wikipedia are described as jazz musicians. She just finds skiers and Norwegian princes. Did Alvar ever mention Erling's last name? What did Erling say to Alvar when he introduced himself?

"Erling . . . ," she mutters. "Erling *hum hum*. Erling . . ."

*Karlsson!* She types in *Erling Karlsson* into the search engine because Wikipedia seems not to know him. It appears there are many Erling Karlssons in the world. Most of them are not the right Erling. Then she finds a blog.

It's called "In My Own Words," and the author describes herself as a retiree interested in genealogy, crime novels, and Swedish handicrafts. The chapter that Steffi finds is entitled "What Happened to My Sisters and Brothers." The chapter starts with a man named Rune Karlsson, born in 1917, who, *unfortunately, fell victim to the bottle just as his father had. He was some kind of foreman at the printer shop for a short time and this was the high point of his career. He had been fired and had to support himself by small jobs (not all of them within the limits of the law, I believe, God rest his soul, as these were not easy times).* The blog continues with the story of a sister named Britt, who was adopted by a childless couple in Nyköping out of the family *and she did very well for herself. She became a teacher and eventually married the principal of the school.* Erling is the next sibling in line.

Steffi waves her hand to catch Elin's attention. "May I print something out?"

Alvar is visibly touched when she tells him what the printout is. Either that, or he is tired today, too. He takes a deep breath and lies back on his pillow as he looks up at the ceiling. "Could you read it for me?"

Steffi reads: *"Erling Karlsson was my second brother. He was born in 1920 at our home on Skåne Street. Both Liselott and I idolized him. He was bitten by the jazz bug, as the saying goes, and although it was not yet popular elsewhere, jazz was something we liked in our part of town. Rune, who was still a foreman in those days, helped Erling get a job at the printer's. Erling held on to his job much longer than Rune did, but every free moment was dedicated to jazz music. He played clarinet at many of the city's dance halls. During the fifties, he met every jazz musician who came to town (and there were a number). He envied 'the Negroes' as he called them, but the word was used differently then. He only had admiration for them. To his sorrow, his musical career never took off. For some time, he didn't even want to continue playing anymore. He left the printer's for a better job at Bergners, where he remained until cancer took him in 1984. He spread happiness wherever he went and I miss him to this very day."*

Alvar's eyes are closed. Maybe he fell asleep. But then he makes a humming sound that whistles through his nose and he opens his eyes. "Well, that was news."

"What?"

"Well, I thought he must have . . . obviously he would have . . . and why would anyone have told me, anyway?"

"You didn't know he'd died?"

Alvar sucks on his lip and shakes his head quickly. "It would be strange if he hadn't. Anita would say about him: *that man will live himself to death.*"

Steffi studies his face as he talks about Erling. It is a sad, almost sorrowful face.

"Do you miss him?"

"Erling . . . Erling might have been able to help me when I was suddenly homeless. He would have shared his one-room apartment."

He's jumped the gun on his story. *Homeless?*

"Weren't you living at Aunt Hilda's apartment?"

He shudders. "Didn't I tell you? Aunt Hilda was all in a rage when she found out . . . she read it in the newspaper . . . didn't I tell you? I thought I told you."

"No, you didn't."

"She read in the paper that I was playing jazz music at the dance halls. She told me she'd never allow any Negroes or hooligans in her house. But I told you that, didn't I?"

She wants to pretend that he has. His blue eyes seem to be wandering back and forth from images in the forties to today.

"Seriously? She threw you out because you played jazz music?"

"I should have gone to Erling. But that's not the way I saw it back then. Erling was furious about the success I was having and Ingmar wanted my head on a platter."

"And Anita?"

"Anita was just sad."

Alvar could see that Anita was sad. Even though she tried to hide it, he could tell.

"Oh, Alvar," she said. Her eyes went from him to the entrance.

He'd been standing outside the door of Nalen like the worst dime-store detective. When he saw Erling and Ingmar go off to the restaurant, he sneaked inside. They could return at any moment.

*Anita, I know this might sound hasty, but would you marry me?*

The question was on the tip of his tongue, and when it reached his lips, he realized he couldn't ask it. A homeless jazz musician asking this of a girl who lived in a house with crystal chandeliers. She still was Ingmar's girl, and who was he? A lost boy from Värmland, even though his hair, for the moment, was still covered in Brylcreem. He couldn't even ask her if she knew of anyone with a room to rent. It was 1946. Nobody had an extra room.

"I'm going home," he said instead. "I'm going home to Björke. Thanks so much for . . ."

His voice became thick. He could feel her eyes on him as he turned around and left. Perhaps she called his name, filtered through the sounds of "Shake the Blues Away." Seymour's orchestra was playing. As Alvar made his way through the crowd, on both sides, girls were dancing. He's joked with these girls, kissed some of them, and there were guys he'd loaned his bike to and listened to records with and they were part of the frame of his life here. Once upon a time, he was a jazz musician in Stockholm. They were still dancing, but he was leaving that scene.

"A boat with bananas."

Steffi stares at him as if he's lost his mind.

"See whether you can find it," he says, waving his hand at the record shelf. "It's by Harry Brandelius."

He smiles as she puts the needle onto the record. It's hard to hear what Harry Brandelius is singing, but Alvar is singing along: *"A boat with bananas arrived at last, we can eat them again like we did in the past."*

It's not jazz. It's not even in four-four time.

"What kind of a song is this?"

"Listen!"

"It's a waltz, right?"

"Girl, listen! *We stood in line not for meat but for fish! Now we eat meat and it's delish!*"

She does what he says and listens. When he's done singing, she has an analysis. "It's a postwar song, isn't it? About how you don't have to ration food anymore."

"Yes, and that song always comes into my head when I think about my trip home to Björke. It was constantly on the radio that year."

"So you went home?"

"Yes, that's what I just said."

"But I thought . . ."

She'd thought his farewell to Anita was part of a longer story. He'd tell her how everything worked out in the end.

Alvar nods. "Perhaps that's why this song stuck in my skull. My adventure in jazz was over. It was time to go back to the waltz, the schottische, and the hambo."

Something in his voice reminds her of the feeling she'd had when she'd found they'd sawed her bass into pieces. She always had to remember her new bass right away to shake off that feeling. *Did Alvar finally make it big, get into the papers, and then head home to Björke to listen to the hambo?*

"After all those years in Stockholm you just up and left?"

"Almost four years."

—

It had been almost four years since Alvar had been sitting on the same kind of bench on the same kind of train. Then he'd been mesmerized by a jazz clarinetist who had a clarinet at home and one for traveling. A clarinetist who showed no respect for angry ladies and replied with "Doo-be-doo-be-doo" to make a sad girl smile.

Alvar had the same suitcase he'd used then, but nobody could mistake him for the same Alvar Svensson who'd left Björke four years ago. His hair was stylishly combed, as it should be beneath a stylish fedora. His woolen suit fit him well and kept him warm, although his wallet was painfully low on cash. A few girls, perhaps sisters, glanced up at him from their bench opposite.

He smiled at them and one of them leaned forward. "Don't you play at the Winter Palace?"

At least three other travelers turned their heads toward him, some more discreetly than others.

"Yes, I've played there a few times."

"I've seen you at Nalen, too," another sister added with pleasure.

What was he supposed to say to that? "Yes, I've played there, too."

They looked at him with expectation. He hoped they didn't think he was going to leap up and start playing for them right in the middle of the train. He had his upright bass stored in the baggage car.

He cleared his throat. "How . . . nice that you recognized me. And that you like to go to Nalen."

It seemed to work. The sisters looked happy. Strange how he could still be nervous in front of a few girls. Part of him felt like he was seventeen again. Perhaps it had to do with being on the train. A rumbling train had not seen Alvar since he was little more than a boy.

The only people who seemed to have something against jazz music were an elderly couple who glanced almost fearfully in Alvar's direction. They said nothing, however. Mostly the train was filled with young people. They wore winter coats and fancy hats in an attempt to impress the relatives back home with the sweet life in the big city. The fact that they all traveled third class told a different story.

"What's in your suitcase?"

"Just clothes, records. Presents for my relatives."

The girl looked disappointed. What did she think? That his bass could fit in a suitcase?

"For my mother, my father, my brothers, and my grandfather," he added. *And another present that was a secret.*

"What about for your sweetheart? Or do you have one?" The girl smiled flirtatiously. The other one giggled.

"No," Alvar said so abruptly that the giggling stopped.

Alvar's mother screamed with happiness when she caught sight of him. She ran up, touched his cheeks, pulled him close, and then pushed him back as if she couldn't decide whether to hug him or to look at him. She laughed and turned to his father. "Look what a man he's become!"

"Yes," his father agreed. "Good to see you, my boy. But what's that on your head?"

Alvar laughed and straightened the brim of his fedora. "That's the hat people wear in Stockholm."

"Well, well!" his father said heartily. "And I imagine they've never seen a tree, either!"

Alvar smiled halfheartedly at his father's joke. You don't need a hepcat hat working in the forest.

"Alvar's here!" Mamma started yelling to people walking by. "Alvar is home from Stockholm! It's my boy Alvar!"

*We go back to life the way it was*
*The way things were just because.*

# – CHAPTER 30 –

Steffi is silent so that Alvar can talk about his parents for a while. But there's one thing she has to ask him. "Did people really say 'Negro' back then?"

Alvar coughs—no, he's laughing. "That was the word people used, even in the newspapers, back then. Especially in articles written about jazz music!"

Steffi is staring at him.

He clears his throat. "Yes, in those days, everybody said Negro and it wasn't particularly derogatory. Everyone wanted to play like the Negroes did. You would even see it in the ads: *Svensson's Band with the NEGRO Joe Wilson, Saturday at eight* P.M., for example."

"But, today, it's a word you just don't use."

"So I've heard. Many times, in fact. And I'm not going to argue about it . . . not everybody back then admired the Neg . . . the black musicians the way we did. So I can understand why the word went out of favor. But, remember, I'm an old man."

He pats her on the head. Wants to get rid of the conversation's unpleasant feeling.

Steffi scratches her head. "Did anyone call anybody names like 'slut' and 'the daughter of a whore'?"

Alvar sighs. "All too many called people bastards and children of whores. Especially where the living conditions were poor."

Living conditions were poor in the backwoods. In Björke, there were the people who owned timberland and the people who worked it. There were some people who were neither the one nor the other but still showed up at church cleaned up. And then there were the families living out in the woods. Some of them had never owned anything to speak of, while others drank everything away.

*Sending your child to a family in the back of the woods was a desperate move,* Alvar thought, and shivered.

He didn't have to search long to find Knut and Elna Storfors. When Alvar was a child, he and his brothers used to run all over the woods. Sometimes they had errands and other times they were up to mischief. But this time was different.

He took off his hat as he knocked at the door. He knew how the disrespect of leaving it on might provoke them. He bowed when Knut opened the door. Knut's nose was red from drinking and he was surprised to see Alvar.

"Hello. Merry Christmas," Alvar said.

Knut looked him up and down. "Merry Christmas yourself."

Alvar held up the bag of baked goods his mother had sent along as a Christmas gift. "A present from my mother, Kerstin Svensson."

Knut appeared even more surprised, but took the bag and let

Alvar inside. The hall smelled sour. Either Kurt's smell had soured the air or vice versa.

"Who is it?" yelled Mrs. Storfors from the kitchen.

Alvar could hear the shrieking and yelling of children's voices on the other side of the house.

Alvar fumbled with the knot in his tie but peered along his arm into the room. There was a big boy, perhaps eleven. Two girls, around seven, and a toddler.

One of the girls was glaring at the toddler. "Shut up! You're nothing but the daughter of a whore!"

"Bastard child!" yelled the other girl.

The toddler stared at them, crying.

"He didn't do anything to you—just this!" The first girl pinched the toddler's arm.

The toddler screamed and the boy grinned.

Mrs. Storfors came running from the kitchen. Her face was bright red and filled with words she hadn't time to say before she saw Alvar.

She stopped and blushed even redder. She wiped off her hands on her apron. "Yes?" she asked as she curtsied while taking Alvar's hand.

The children's screaming was silenced. Four heads were now turned toward Alvar. He forced himself to smile wholeheartedly. "I have a small Christmas present for Eleanor."

Both Knut and Elna Storfors stiffened, and he could see the muscles of Elna's neck tense up.

"There is nobody by that name in this house," Knut explained.

Alvar smiled as best he could, even though he felt his heart was being dragged over gravel.

"Perhaps I misunderstood the name," he said. "What's your name, little girl?" He bent down to the toddler.

"She's a whore child!" one of the girls said, grinning, and her mother boxed her ear.

"We don't talk like that!" Elna said, and she hit the girl again when she started to say, "But you do—"

Alvar kept his smile through sheer willpower. He looked the little girl in the eye and she looked right back. He could tell she was already starting to resemble her mother. "I have a present for you from Stockholm, from your—"

"No, that name is not mentioned here," Knut said roughly. Alvar felt a hard hand on his shoulder.

"This nice present is from Alvar Svensson," Elna explained almost as roughly. "He is much too kind to you bringing a present all the way from Stockholm, but that's all I'm going to say about it."

There was candy in the bag, which the other children immediately took for themselves. There was also a butterfly in silk paper and a little muff, which the other girls grabbed. Only a small rag doll with braids was left.

The toddler picked it up and looked at its button eyes. Alvar's chest had filled with anger, but he forced himself to smile.

"What's your name?"

The girl hugged the doll. Soon it would smell as sour as everything else in this cabin, but at the moment, it was something from outside. A Christmas present from a very nice man. She looked at the doll as she answered his question.

"My name is Svea."

# – CHAPTER 31 –

Steffi can't let go of the thought that the little toddler had been Svea. She can't wait to go see Alvar again to talk about it. She wants to see Svea and ignore her torrent of insults to look for the innocent four-year-old behind them.

But right now she's in school with no one to talk to. She checks the door to the computer room. Elin is teaching, but the door is open. A few seventh graders are chasing a fat, buzzing fly with a newspaper. Elin comes silently up behind them and stops them.

Steffi finds an empty place at the back of the room so as not to disturb the lesson. She logs into The Place under her own name, but changes her mind. Nobody can see the screen where she's sitting. She feels the excitement of doing something forbidden as she logs in as Hepcat. In school!

Karro has written to Hepcat again. She always writes to Hepcat.

From: Karro N
To: Hepcat

*I didn't SAY my eyes were enormous, but thanks. If u don't give me ur address, I'm going to go to Karlstad and search for u house by house. Hee, hee, no, but seriously, I can't stand living here. My pretend pappa is disgusting and all my mamma does is gamble on the net. My siblings are idiots and everyone at school is mental. u r the only one I know who's OK.*

Steffi reads this a few times. This very morning, Karro had spat onto her math book. Thready mucus, along with a note: "You can use this to clean yourself up."

Steffi doesn't owe Karro a thing. Spitting on somebody's math book should disqualify you from decent human interaction for all time.

She reads the message again. *U r the only one I know who's OK.* She runs her hand through her hair. She rubs her forehead. She wants to escape the feeling that life is complicated.

From: Hepcat
To: Karro N

I also want to get away from here. My family is nothing like yours. But the people around here have trouble accepting people for who they are. I'm tired of being spat on. And I know there are people who only care about one thing: making music swing. Their feet on the ground, their hearts filled with blues.

In what way is he disgusting?

P.S. Life is complicated.

As she sends her reply, she notices that Karro is logged in. Steffi looks around the computer room among the seventh graders fighting for the word processing programs and teaching portals.

Karro is on the other side of the room. She's staring at the screen with a sullen expression. She clicks, sighs, and suddenly she lights up. Not terribly noticeable, but obvious if you're watching her closely. Steffi looks at her own screen. *Message read.* Four minutes later, the reply comes in.

From: Karro N
To: Hepcat

Well, in how many ways can he be disgusting? All right, one is he ALWAYS comes into the bathroom when I'm taking a shower. He gropes me when he hugs me. He calls me things. Totally disgusting, like I told you! Right now I'm in the computer room at school and making sure nobody is reading this or I WILL DIE!!!! Thanks for being there. It means a lot to me.

Steffi peeks at Karro again. Ponders her own existence. Her body exists IRL, where people judge each other by what they see. Online, she exists through her thoughts, not her body. She is Hepcat. Which existence is more real, the body or the mind? Is it fair to say that Karro hates her in the real world, but online, she is deeply thankful? What's the truth?

Hepcat replies to Karro. Hepcat says that it must be against the law for her stepfather to do those things. *Film him secretly when he comes in the bathroom and calls you stuff. It's a violation of your rights.* Sending the message gives her mixed feelings. She feels good, because big people are helpful. She feels bad, because Karro is still disgusting.

As she gets up to leave the room, Karro is getting up, too. For a few seconds, they stare right at each other. A breathless break without a solo. Not even the fly on the ceiling moves.

Alvar has been thinking about Anita a lot the past few weeks. Whenever Steffi goes back home, he's back in Stockholm and he's dancing through the streets with Anita again. They respond when older people tell them that the jiggerbug is destroying the young. He with his youthful energy, Anita with her lively arguments. They've gone to Gröna Lund amusement park with his song—the one he wrote about the air and the girl. At Gröna Lund, there's a recording studio open, called Your Own Voice. Anita spurs him on. She tells him it's good. She refuses to sing it. "You sing as well as anyone," she tells him. When he says she should play the piano, she blushes with delight.

They stand in a long line in front of the Your Own Voice recording studio. In front of them is an overly lively man who prattles incessantly on how surprised his wife will be when she listens to his voice. "As if she can't hear it already!" a person in the crowd calls out. Everyone laughs. The man has red, freckled ears. Two finches are hopping on the roof of the booth. The air is sweet from the scent of cotton candy. Alvar is tall and strong and Anita's hand in his makes him feel ten feet tall. As a song reaches them from the stage, he takes a few Charleston steps and Anita laughs and does the same. They dance the Charleston waiting in line for Your Own Voice and the people around them begin to clap in time to the music. When they finally get their chance to record in the booth, Anita is praised for her swinging piano playing. The man recording them tells her that she's "a cooler version of Alice Babs." Anita lights up at the praise. She's happy about it for the rest of the day, and the rest of the week.

She dabs his nose with cotton candy and laughs.

---

He wants to tell all this to Steffi. It's important that he doesn't forget. His bursting heart tells him that someone will have to remember Anita.

But when Steffi shows up, she wants to talk only about Svea. "So, I've been thinking," she says. "When Svea screams 'bastard child'—why does she do it?"

Alvar would much rather talk about Anita, but Steffi is serious and wants to know what he thinks. "It's not strange at all," he says. "Since that's how people treated her."

It makes him feel bad just to say it. Who knows what kind of a person Svea would have become if he'd taken her out of that cabin in the woods? Or just told her mother the truth about what was going on?

"Yes, yes, I know," Steffi says impatiently. "But *why* does she say these things now? Do you think it makes her feel better? Or . . . why?"

Alvar tries to shake away his bad conscience and give Steffi a clear answer. "It's projection," he says. "A way to wipe the dirt from her mind."

"So when she calls other people names, deep down it means that's how she sees herself, and want others to feel it, too?"

"I don't think she even knows why she does it anymore. I believe she's afraid. She has dementia and she's afraid and feels totally out of control over even her own life. The most spiteful people are ones who are actually trying to defend themselves from their own reflection."

"Pappa says that, too." She's silent for a moment and then picks up his magnifying glass. "It's strange how you can know all this, about why people act the way they do, and still take it personally."

He doesn't know if she's still talking about Svea or about somebody else.

"What about the kids in school?" he tries. "The ones who are mean to you. Any chance they're from the Storfors family?"

She shakes her head. She's looking at the tracks on Thore Jederby's "Boogie-Woogie" with the magnifying glass.

"So, perhaps they're from the Färne family?"

She looks up from the record. "Karro's last name is Färne."

"Karolina Färne. She's related to little Knut Färne."

"Who's that?"

"Well, he's not so little anymore. Today he must be . . . well . . . over sixty, I imagine. He also lived in a cabin in the woods. They were neighbors to the Storfors. Knut was born nine months after the Zoo Circus had played in Torsby."

He thinks back. It's difficult to relate all the intertwined links going back in time.

"He seems a likely victim of Svea. She felt helpless, so she took it out on him."

Steffi picks up the magnifying glass again. It's heavy and has a metal edge. *Over sixty,* she thinks, counting backward. This is like a game of dominoes. One person calls another a "bastard child" and that person calls the next one the same and so on and so on—from pinching a toddler to spitting in people's math books.

"So, if those kids hadn't called Svea a whore child," she says, "Karro might not be running around spitting on people's books."

Alvar sucks his lip. "If wishes were horses, beggars would ride," he says. "But sometimes . . . I wish I had intervened on Svea's behalf. I never even told her mother in Stockholm how she was being treated. I didn't want her mother to feel even worse than she already did." He's rubbing his forehead and looking out the window. "I was stupid," he says.

He's looking so sad. He's not even grimacing. His cheeks are drawn down and puffy.

Steffi looks at him through the magnifying glass. He's an upside-down version of himself. "But it really wasn't your fault," she says.

"But I was here," he said. "Or, at least my body was here."

His body was in Björke. His body put on boots and walked across deep green moss through the forest, inhaling the scent of the woods. The tree trunks around him were silent.

"Look at that!" his father exclaimed time and time again. "No trees like this in Stockholm! We'll cut this one down in two years. Are you looking at it?"

Anita would never recognize him if she saw him like this. The cap he was wearing, for starters.

"Aren't you looking at it?" his father repeated. He threw his arm up toward the high branches. "My grandfather planted this tree so we'd have something to harvest seventy years later."

He was boasting to Alvar. Alvar stood with his hands down at his sides and tried to look impressed. Sure, it was hep to have a great-grandparent who planted these enormous spruce trees with his own two hands. He wondered whether Anita would be impressed. He wondered if Duke Ellington had released a new record.

"We'll be back in time for *Gramophone Hour*, won't we?" he asked.

"Look over there," his father said. "On the other side of the ridge. Trees never grow well there. There's something wrong with the soil."

Alvar did his best to feel a connection to the trees and the soil beneath his feet. He felt he was standing back in his own childhood; he felt he was sinking, in his boots, into all the dark green moss the train to Stockholm had once liberated him from. This evening he'd listen to *Gramophone Hour* on the radio, and in another universe Lulle Ellboj would be rounding up his band members to tune their instruments.

"That's the way it is," his father, Inge, continued. "Some trees grow better in one place and not at all in others. That's just the way it is."

His father's words seemed to carry two meanings, so Alvar had to look at him to see if his father was winking, as if his father was criticizing him, as if he were the bad soil, the soil that could not understand the trees like his brothers did.

But Inge Svensson had already plodded on. He had started to talk about the woodpeckers.

His mother was the one who recognized that only her son's body was in Björke. They'd all finished dinner, but Alvar was still in the kitchen with his guitar. His guitar fit in with the sounds of pots and dishes being cleaned.

"So, you can go with them tomorrow and you can stay overnight, all three of you," his mother was chattering on while the sounds of pots and dinnerware continued. *Clink, clank,* the brush against the pot, the porcelain against the sink.

It wasn't exactly a brass section, but he could hear the rhythm of a fox-trot in it. A few words came to him, a new song lyric. He played the bass line on his guitar. *I am so blue, so blue without you. You are free, so free, like a melody.*

"That will be good, won't it?" his mother asked him.

Alvar could hear Anita's voice singing over his bass line. Her voice would carry great emotion, even if it didn't always hit the note. *So free, like a melody.*

He hoped she'd found freedom. He hoped she'd found a job as a secretary and had gotten rid of that violent idiot Ingmar. Her voice was in his mind. *I can't take it. I want to be free.* Her giggles, her bubbly voice, her way of making fun of his lyrics, quite rightly, actually. *I am so blue, you are you, I am I, like a pie. . . .*

"Alvar?"

Alvar jumped. His mother had come from the sink and all the pots to put a damp hand on his shoulder.

"Where are you?"

He looked up into her eyes. They were like his; they even shared the same color. "I'm right here."

She shook her head. She sat down on a kitchen stool in front of him. "Your body is here. But where are *you*?"

Alvar has reached the age of ninety and it's been almost half a century since his mother had passed away. He still remembers her scent, her face, the way she studied him that evening. He remembers all that much more clearly than what he had for lunch yesterday.

"That evening," he says to the teenage girl in his room, "that evening I showed her the difference between having rhythm and having drive. And she tried to understand me."

Steffi had taken out her phone. She's pecking at it with a finger, but he keeps talking, he keeps telling her the story anyway. He's talking to the walls, and for the part of Steffi's ears that might still be listening.

"She didn't understand me until I got to Anita. And told her about Ingmar."

Steffi looks up. "What did she say?"

His heart is warm in his sunken chest. To think you could remember words said so many decades ago. To think you could remember exactly how they were spoken.

"She said: 'Listen, Alvar, and think carefully about what I'm saying. Did you move home because you were homesick? Or did you just want to run away and hide?' "

# – CHAPTER 32 –

The sun was shining through the cold Stockholm air as Alvar stepped off the train. It was the seventeenth of February, 1947, and he was a musician returning to town. He was definitely a homeless musician, but at least he'd had the presence of mind to take a copy of the Stockholm phone book to Björke. He had called everyone he knew until the saxophone player Gunnar Liljebäck had finally agreed to let him sleep on the floor in his apartment until he found a place to live.

Here was Gunnar, stepping out of the crowd to help Alvar with his suitcases and his upright bass. Casper Hjukström was with him. Alvar peered discreetly around behind them to see if Anita was there. She'd said she might meet him at the station. Anita had been happy when he'd called to let her know he was coming back. Alvar was absolutely certain she'd been happy.

"Hey there, guys!" he exclaimed as they thumped him on the back in greeting. "Casper, are you on Gunnar's floor, too?"

Casper laughed out loud. "We need a bass player," he said. "We've got a studio session on Wednesday, but Thore won't be back in Stockholm for two more weeks." He added, "You're going to like this gig!" He picked up one of Alvar's suitcases. "We're backing up Alice Babs!"

By the time he'd spent his third evening on the mattress on Gunnar's kitchen floor, Alvar's heart was beginning to ache. He'd had no chance to talk to Anita, that wonderful vision. *It's all or nothing,* he'd written to her in a letter. He'd decided to tell her: "I have loved you from the day you saved me from the doorman at 140 Åsö Street."

She'd smile, and she'd understand what he meant when he'd go down on one knee. Her eyes would shine.

Three days later, he'd changed his mind. A new idea had come to him as he wrestled his bass up the stairs to the recording studio: he'd sing for her. He even knew the song he'd choose and he'd sing it softly into her ear once they were alone. *All of me. Why don't you take all of me?*

She'd understand before he'd even go down on one knee, and her eyes would shine.

The atmosphere in the studio was calm, almost subdued. Usually there were more people around, running up and down the stairs and having opinions about the recording sessions. But this was a Sunday. Outside the windows, fluffy snowflakes were drifting down and collecting on the windowsills.

It wasn't the first time Alvar had played with big names. He'd played with them at the Winter Palace and at Nalen and in the parks the past few summers. Still, it was different to be standing in a recording studio surrounded by walls, snow, and a hungover city, listening to Alice Babs's every whisper. He heard Casper

Hjukström warming up with scales over in a corner. He listened as Miss Babs began to quietly sing to Charles Norman's accompaniment on the piano as the studio techs were getting everything in order.

He should have been overwhelmed with sheer adoration. If his seventeen-year-old self could have seen what he was doing today with all these musicians in a recording studio, he would have burst. But that's how it goes with such moments in your life. You can't know until you're in them how you're going to feel.

The next time Casper took a break, Alvar called out to him. "Casper! Wasn't Anita going to be here?"

Casper shrugged. He didn't know.

"She does know we're here today, right?" Alvar insisted.

"Bass player! Can you take your place?" announced a voice from the control booth.

"That's Big Boy Svensson," a younger man said.

"Big Boy Svensson, could you stand on the tape mark over there?"

There were four spots of tape on the floor. Alvar put himself and his bass on the right one. Casper stood between him and Alice Babs, who was frowning in concentration, while Charles Norman and the piano were in the usual place in front of the drummer, who was the farthest from the microphone.

"Take it from the top!" one of the oldest techs said from the booth.

Watching Alice Babs take the microphone was seeing a professional at work. Alvar had read that she was just a year older than he was, but she'd been a film star when he was still a country boy of seventeen. She kept an eye on the techs to see if she needed to stand closer to or farther back from the microphone and yet she sang with great feeling, as if they'd already begun to record.

Casper was doing the same with his clarinet. Alvar was glad he didn't have to move his bass around. His music stand was filled with scribbled sheets of music: holds and harmonies, breaks and solos, all in his crooked handwriting. Educated musicians like Ingmar would laugh at his improvised notation, but one bandleader had told Alvar that he scribbled in his music the way the great Satchmo had before he recorded his songs. "Nice of him to say that," Anita had wryly commented afterward to make Alvar wonder if the bandleader had just made it all up. Anita was a sharp one. Sharp and nice all at the same time. Hardly anyone was like her.

"Keep playing," the tech said while he shifted the musicians with their instruments around the studio. "Take it from the top, Mister Norman! Hey, Pelle, does this sound better?"

The kid in the control booth gave a thumbs-up. The older tech made a few more adjustments before he was satisfied. Alvar kept studying his handwritten notes and then it came to him that he should have written his letter to Anita on a typewriter.

"Alvar!" Charles said and winked at him. "Time to swing!"

And so they played a last run-through before it was time to record. Alvar was eternally grateful to Charles Norman for those words bringing him out of his thoughts and onto one of the first recordings ever made of Sweden's greatest jazz musicians. He felt the vibration of the rhythms in his bones with Alice Babs, film star, right in front of him the whole time, Charles playing behind him on the piano, and the most modern microphone in the world hanging from the ceiling. They played perfectly; hit the notes "on the spot," as Erling would have said.

"All right, then, we'll record," the studio tech said. "Everyone ready? Three, two, one . . ."

When the drummer hit the next-to-the-last beat Alvar was still completely caught up in the music they'd all just been creating. With the last beat, he caught a movement through the window and he craned his neck to see. The blood rushed right to his heart, because wasn't that Anita herself coming down the hill? He didn't care how charmingly Alice Babs was smiling or how the drummer, content with how they'd performed, asked him for his telephone number. He didn't care that he'd just played with Norman on the piano and Hjukström on the clarinet. The girl on the way outside the window, this wonderful apparition, went by the name Anita Bergner.

She was laughing as she came through the door. She was covered in freshly fallen snow. Alvar helped her brush it off and proudly introduced her to the other musicians who hadn't yet met her. He had *the* letter in his coat pocket and his coat called to him from its place on the coatrack. He would pull out the letter and read it to her. Then he'd ask his question. No, first he'd ask and then he'd pull out the letter.

"Oh, what are you thinking about, Alvar?" she asked. She laughed at his confused expression. "Weren't you listening? Charles was just inviting us all out for a bite to eat."

Alvar nodded, thought, tried to think. "Later. Let's take a walk first, shall we?"

"In this snowstorm?"

Anita was looking at him quizzically, but then she nodded and wrapped her scarf back around her neck. "He's a country boy," she said, winking at the others. "The weather never bothers *him*!"

He let them laugh at him because he had the best woman of all holding his hand. She held it naturally and tightly as they walked down the stairs. He was hers and she already knew this.

Still, he found it impossible to get the words out. Anita was talking about Charles Norman, jazz, the snow, her boss, her work as a secretary. She'd had her job for a month and a half.

"So that's why I had to work on a Sunday," she said. "He never lets me leave until all the work is finished. But if I take the tiniest little break, he writes it up in his book. Yes, he keeps track of every single minute I work. Though, to be fair, he writes up all the extra hours as well, so I guess it works out in the end."

Alvar hummed something as the snowflakes landed on his eyelashes. He blinked them away as his brain worked furiously. Was he really going to start wailing "All of Me" in the middle of the street? It had seemed perfect in his imagination, but he hummed a note and it sounded like the howl of a dog. Anita turned to him and raised an eyebrow.

"What did you say?"

"No, I . . . it . . ."

She stopped. "Are you feeling all right?"

What had he intended to say? Plan A, what was his Plan A? All he could pull from his imagination was the image of Anita's eyes shining when he went down on one knee and asked her to marry him.

She was looking at him with worry. "Alvar?"

He'd have to improvise. If Carl-Henrik Norin could improvise, so could he.

"No, I . . . there's no problem . . . I mean . . . nothing wrong with me . . . I just want . . . to ask you something."

Then it hit him—he should have bought a ring! How could he have forgotten such an important thing? He was about to propose without a ring! It was like asking someone to dinner and not having any food in the house.

Anita cocked her head. Were her eyes shining? "What is it, Alvar?"

"No, well . . . if . . . I . . ."

He couldn't breathe even though they were standing stockstill in the falling snow. He found he was also sweating. Anita deserved a better proposal, perhaps even a better man to make a proposal.

She looked up at the sky. "Look," she said. "What a wonderful feeling."

He obeyed because any other alternative was gone. From far, far away, from the dark, endless realm of space, snow was falling down on them. Anita's arms came around his thin body and she was still looking up at the sky, her chin nestling on his chest. "What did you want to ask me?"

"Just if you . . . not just, I mean, but . . . if you wanted to marry me."

She wasn't surprised, unlike the scene in his imagination. She didn't take a deep breath and burst out *Yes, yes, Alvar! Oh, yes!*

The snow was melting on her forehead and she smiled warmly at him. "I guess this means you'll have to find us a real apartment."

He laughs as he relays her reply.

Steffi thinks it's terrible. "That's not romantic at all! How could she say such a thing!"

He chuckles. "Romantic! Do you know what's romantic? When someone decides in all seriousness to spend the rest of her life with you! Look for Billie Holiday and you'll have a record . . . no, not that one. The one next to it."

Steffi pulls out the record, takes it from its sleeve, and winds up the gramophone.

"Listen!" Alvar says. "Anita bought this record for me! Listen!"

Steffi sits down on the floor near the horn. Alvar leans back in his armchair.

Billie Holiday starts to sing:

*It's very clear. Our love is here to stay.*
*Not for a year, but ever and a day.*

"What's she singing about?" Steffi can't catch all the words.

"Well, she's singing that the radio and the telephone and the movies we like so much are going to disappear one day, but our love will be here forever."

He nods, closes his eyes, and smiles. "Anita was romantic in just the way she was with everything else. Thorough. Thoughtful. You have to remember she had her worries, too, just as I had mine. She was twenty-five and she was not yet married. How would it work out with a younger man, a bass player, who didn't even have a place to sleep but Gunnar Liljebäck's kitchen floor? She was probably . . ." He coughs. "She was probably the braver one of the two of us."

Billie Holiday has finished singing. The needle scratches on the last groove. Steffi gets up and flips the record over.

She hears Alvar chuckling behind her. "So now you know."

"What do I know?"

"What happened in 1947 when I played with Hjukström on the clarinet. The story you wanted to hear on your birthday."

She turns toward Alvar. He seems content, even though he's told the story all wrong. "You played with Povel Ramel."

"No, no, Alice Babs."

"You told me you played with Hjukström on a Povel Ramel record in 1946."

"Oh no, it was really Alice Babs."

Steffi is looking at him. Was he just making up a story? Is he just as forgetful as the old ladies in the hallway? She can't really ask him directly.

"I see," she says.

Billie Holiday starts singing again. After a moment, Alvar

gets up and looks for a record from his shelf. His old fingers trail along the records filed under *A*. He pulls one out. "Take a look."

The record label says: *Alice Babs, Charles Norman & Co.* On the dirty gray sleeve, written in blue ink: *Charles Norman, Casper Hjukström, Gunnar Ohlsson, Alvar Svensson. February 1947.*

Steffi reads it over and over.

After Steffi leaves, Alvar wonders what she's going to think of him years from now. He puts on the record he'd made with Alice Babs and can still see Steffi standing in front of him. In time she'll be nineteen, then forty-two, then . . . and she's going to stop in the middle of what she's doing and think: just a minute! That old man got me to listen to him by pretending he'd played with Povel Ramel! Then he told me this long story about Anita and finally he'd admitted he never played with Povel Ramel at all! What a cunning old man he was.

He giggles at the thought and looks out the window. Everything is turning green. The plants are growing as fast as they possibly can.

And another day, he thinks, another day she's going to stop and think to herself: *That Fender electric bass!* Maybe he only gave it to me because he had a bad conscience.

He doesn't even know himself why he gave it to her. Things are always more complicated than they seem.

He thinks about it for an hour or more and manages to listen to Wingy Manone and Blue Lu Barker and ten other songs on his gramophone. He finally decides it doesn't really matter. He gave her the bass just because. And now it's bedtime—he should go and say good night.

# – CHAPTER 33 –

Jake Berntsson never should have become a teacher. He has ten more days to figure out the grades for all his students. He has to make sure they are impartial and based on the curriculum and its objectives. He should already have comments for each and every student in his logbook, but there aren't any yet. There are three girls in his eighth grade class he has never learned to tell apart; they all have identical blond ponytails and none of them play any instruments. He certainly can't write that. He's definitely going to have to buckle down.

He doesn't notice when Steffi enters the music room. She's just there in the doorway. Her dark eyes are studying him calmly and, as usual, make him nervous. He knows why the other kids tease her. It's the same reason people want to break into a locked cupboard. Sometimes he wished he could talk to her about it, but he can't figure out how to bring these thoughts into a conversation.

Steffi lifts up the old clarinet. He gives his friendly teacher's laugh that's supposed to remind him that he is the grown-up.

"Oh, yes, you had the clarinet," he says.

"You said you wanted it back in May for the eighth graders."

Her eyes are looking at him searchingly. Her demeanor is not that of the average teenager returning something; perhaps she wants to talk to a grown-up.

He clears his throat. "So, did you find it useful?"

She nods. "My bass got broken, so I've been playing on it instead."

"That must not have been easy."

She barely moves a muscle. Another student would have shrugged or laughed or at least smiled. The only thing Steffi moves is her fingers, which play on the clarinet's keypads. "It was actually kind of fun."

Jake Berntsson is not good with people and probably never should have become a teacher. Still, he keeps trying. And he can tell when someone wants to play an instrument.

"Let me hear it."

Already from the first notes Steffi plays, he knows that she is more of a musician than he will ever be. Five years ago, he would have found this unjust. That's when he thought he was just teaching until he made his big breakthrough. Steffi's talent would have brought out feelings that he would not want to recognize. Now he just laughs.

"Wow, Steffi, who taught you all of this?"

She smiles now. "Do you know Alvar Big Boy Svensson?"

He likes her smile. There's nothing like seeing an otherwise sullen teenager break into a smile. Perhaps he was meant to be a teacher after all.

"I recognize the name," he lies.

"He lives here," Steffi says. "In Björke."

"Oh, I didn't know that," Jake says, which is not a lie.

She's weighing the clarinet in her hand like a question. He makes a gesture that is supposed to look generous but it comes out merely vague. He smiles to compensate. "You can keep it until the end of the year."

"Are you sure?"

"I'm just happy that there's finally someone who can actually play the thing."

He shouldn't have said that. As a teacher, he shouldn't accuse the other students of not being able to play the instruments. On the other hand, Steffi laughs for the first time ever in his music room. A really bad teacher would never have gotten her to laugh.

Steffi is singing. Not out loud, of course, as that would be dangerous at school, but inside her head. She waits in the building until she sees Karro and Sanja disappear down the slope from the schoolyard. Through a gap between the social studies and home ec buildings, she can see the road all the way to the crosswalk. Once they've turned to the left and they've disappeared behind some birch trees that are in the midst of leafing out, Steffi runs with the clarinet in her backpack and her song in her head. It's been May for a while now and the acceptance letters may already be in a postal truck on the way to the ninth graders. Jake had told her she had talent. This means she might really have a chance to get in. On the way home, she swings past the Sunshine Home.

As soon as she walks in the entrance, she stops. Svea, with her cane, is standing right there. She whirls around when she hears the door shut. Her eyes turn to evil slits.

"Bastard child!" she hisses and lifts her cane like a weapon.

Luckily, Svea can't hold her cane up for long without losing her balance, so it's nothing more than a gesture. Steffi looks at Svea and tries to see the four-year-old inside Svea's eyes and all the other people who were mean to her. She's trying to wipe off the dirt, Alvar had said. This means that Svea is really talking about herself.

"You are not a whore child," Steffi says as calmly as she can manage.

Svea pounds the floor with her cane, so Steffi jumps.

"Whoooooore child!" Svea says more slowly, with a raspy and witchlike voice.

"You're a good girl," Steffi says. "You are a nice girl, Svea."

Svea looks at her, perhaps surprised, perhaps in suspicion. "Whore child," she says, but at a whisper.

"No, you're not," Steffi says, and shakes her head. "You're nice, right?"

Svea doesn't say anything else. She glares at Steffi and follows her with her gaze as Steffi walks away down the hallway. When Steffi reaches Alvar's door, she turns around.

Svea is still looking at her in complete silence.

Alvar is humming and nodding as Steffi tells him of her latest Svea encounter.

"Haven't I always told you that you're a smart girl?"

"You did?"

"Sure, I did! Well, at least, I've always thought so."

"Svea was completely surprised."

He grins. "I can imagine. But the next time you see her, she'll have forgotten all about it."

"Then I'll have to say nice things again."

Alvar starts humming again.

"Alvar?"

"This building is full of forgetfulness," Alvar says. He looks right into her eyes. Then he gets up and pulls out a new record.

"You're the only one who remembers," Steffi agrees.

He points at his head. "You and I are the only ones with everything in order up here!"

He lets the air out in a long sigh as he winds the gramophone.

Steffi thinks maybe she shouldn't have mentioned Svea. "Alvar," she says quickly. "When Anita wanted to marry you, what did her parents say?"

"I don't want to talk about this today."

Steffi doesn't know what to say to that. "I'm sorry."

"Oh, that's just what they said. It was the same week coffee rationing returned."

Director Bergner said, "I don't want to talk about this today."

He looked as sulky as a child, but his voice was as authoritative as ever. Alvar looked at Anita, who looked at her mother, who sighed.

"Alvar," she said. "You are a sweet boy, but . . ."

She almost laughed, as if it were just a joke. It was like a spike right through Alvar's heart. Mrs. Bergner looked back at Anita.

"You can't be serious."

Alvar swallowed and swallowed but couldn't clear the thickness from his throat. Was he really such an unthinkable son-in-law?

Anita tensed her jaw and her voice was controlled. "Read his letter at the very least. He deserves that much consideration."

They waited and it was horrible. At first it was bearable, because he was waiting with Anita. She held his sweating hand in hers, and for the first time, hers was just as sweaty as his. Then Mr. and Mrs. Bergner called her into the room and he was all alone at the dinner table. His heart was pounding so hard it should have echoed through the large room. He could see two portraits of gentlemen in cravats hanging on the wall and they seemed to be looking down on him with censure. He changed his seat so as to avoid looking at them. He could hear a few words from the salon, mostly from Anita's insistent voice. Once or twice, he thought he heard her parents say Ingmar's name.

He looked at his hands. Anita's parents were right. Hands like his did not fit on this beautiful, polished table. Was he crazy, thinking he could make her happy? He felt the angry glare of the portraits hitting the back of his neck. The chair itself seemed to be rejecting his bony backside and the rug on the floor seemed to say, "Be worthy and do not ever dance."

Finally they returned to the dining room. They all sat down silently. The slight sound of chairs against the dining room rug moving toward the table was the only sound. Alvar tried to calm his nervous breathing, but in vain. Mr. Bergner drilled his eyes into Alvar.

"Our stubborn daughter Anita," he began. "She never listens to her parents." He leaned back in his chair but did not release Alvar from his glare. "We have no reason to believe she will change her mind this time, either. Therefore, we will not attempt to convince her to change her mind, but we will turn to you instead."

"We have a request," Mrs. Bergner added.

Alvar's gasping was getting worse and worse. He had tried to prepare himself for any eventual outcome of this meeting, except the one where Anita's parents would turn to plead with him directly. What was he supposed to say? "I am sorry, honorable director and honorable Mrs. Bergner, but I cannot resist your daughter." He kept silent and waited.

Mrs. Bergner put her elbows on the table, in a manner contrary to her normal behavior. She looked right into Alvar's frightened eyes. There was a place inside Mrs. Bergner that appeared sympathetic. "A boy who only plays jazz music could never support our Anita," she said. "Anita understands this as well, if she thinks about it."

Alvar wanted to exclaim that he earned as much as an average worker with his music these days and he did two shifts at Åkesson's Grocery as well, and they'd never had as hard a worker as Alvar Svensson. Not a single word left his lips.

"In short," Mr. Bergner said, "there's an open position at my good friend Malkolm Brink's firm, and I would recommend you. If you are willing to take this position, we will give our consent."

Was it a test? Or a joke? Or a psychological experiment? The truth sank in slowly, very slowly, as if he'd inexplicably won the lottery. He had to swallow three times before he replied. "Of course."

The Bergners had always been tough businessmen and they were society, so they do not reveal their thoughts, but Alvar could still see the relief in their expressions.

He still could feel the fear running down his back, but it was departing from his body as he contemplated his new life.

Mrs. Bergner looked him right in the eyes. "You wrote a beautiful letter."

Steffi realizes she's been holding her breath. Time has passed and the Emil Iwring record had fallen silent some time ago. *Just as Alvar had been forced to do,* Steffi thought. She looks at him, disturbed. "How could you stop playing after all you went through?"

His sly old-man look went right to her.

"Whatever makes you think I stopped playing? Put on Lill-Arne's swing. We need something upbeat."

Steffi finds the record while Alvar explains that Lill-Arne brought jazz to the accordion.

"You see, Steffi," Alvar says, "the most important thing for a man who wants to play jazz music is not to refuse any chance of obtaining lucrative work. It is to make sure he marries a real jazz crazy girl."

"Like Anita." Steffi smiles and sits down in the chair.

"I did have to say no every once in a while when a gig conflicted with my position at Brink's. On the other hand, I was able to afford a telephone. And a real bed. And, eventually, a piano."

"I imagine that made Anita happy."

Alvar smiles from ear to ear. "Happy as a clam."

Steffi laughs at his clown smile and takes out her phone to snap a picture.

He keeps on smiling as he starts to speak again. "I have regretted many things in my life, but I have never regretted marrying Anita. She was the smartest, funniest, and most beautiful girl you ever could imagine. Not to mention the most impudent and bold, if she needed to be. We . . ."

Alvar sighs and doesn't finish his sentence. His smile seems to go out.

Steffi wonders whether or not she should ask. Then she just asks.

"When did she die?"

Alvar looks at her strangely and then scratches his chin. "Oh," he says. "Oh, she's not dead. She lives right here."

# – CHAPTER 34 –

Their walk through the hallway seems like a walk through time. The gramophone is still playing Lill-Arne's swing as they close the door, becoming an echo of the forties. But as they reach room 16, Alvar shows his nearly ninety years.

Steffi holds her breath as he opens the door so she can finally see the woman who'd made Alvar weak at the knees the first time he saw her. It's as surprising as it is obvious.

It's that white-haired lady who mistook Steffi's broken bass for a dog and who told stories about old toilets.

Her face lights up when they open the door. When she sees Alvar, she reaches out her hand and Alvar takes it.

"Hello, Anita."

"Hello, sweetheart."

Steffi has to giggle. If it was difficult to see a sad four-year-old behind Svea's angry face, it is easy to see the jazz crazy girl behind Anita's wrinkles. Steffi should have figured this out weeks ago. She should have figured it out when she heard the old lady speak with a posh Stockholm accent.

"I have to tell you something," Anita says, opening her gray eyes wide. "I just saw . . . something that wasn't a camel or a horse. It wasn't a cow, either."

Steffi glances at Alvar. Perhaps animals are the only things Anita can talk about these days.

"It was a llama," Alvar says. "We saw a llama when we were in America."

"I see," Anita says. She turns to Steffi. "It was such a tall beast, you see. And our little Christina . . ."

She begins to laugh right in the middle of a sentence. She laughs so heartily that Steffi had to smile.

"Christina wanted to pet it, but we didn't dare let her! Those llamas spit, you know!"

Steffi laughs. Anita laughs. Finally Alvar laughs.

"Who's Christina?"

Anita looks at Steffi and puts a wrinkled hand on hers.

"That's our baby girl," she says. Then her eyes get worried. "Where is she?"

Alvar pets her calmingly on the shoulder. "Christina is in Malmö."

Alvar turns to Steffi and says, "Christina moved there a while ago to be closer to her grandchildren."

Anita's voice is still nervous. "Is she going to be all right? How will she manage? She's so slight for her age."

"She's doing just fine. She's in the best of health."

When Anita's worried look does not disappear, Alvar changes the subject as well as his accent. He speaks as if he were in Stockholm. "Look, Anita! This is my friend, Steffi! She's wondering how much you remember about Nalen!"

Anita's face glows. "How could I ever forget Nalen? Oh, Nalen! What a place! And one day, Alvar was going to play there for the first time! With Seymour Österwall! Erling was so angry! I thought it turned out to be a very pleasant evening."

It was a very pleasant evening. Of course, it was cold and the snowflakes were as large as quarters and if you turned your face toward them, the snow mixed with the stars and fell on your face in small, damp fluffs.

The night was magical, and Anita could feel in her whole body that Alvar had an important question for her. When he tried to ask, he was so nervous he turned red. His laugh was so nervous, she couldn't let him suffer any longer.

"Come on," she said and took his hand. "You know how to dance, don't you?"

She noticed when they got out on the dance floor that he didn't know how to dance at all, but she could see he had rhythm in his gangly, tall body. What a sweet boy he was! He was honest; you could see the honesty in his eyes. He had such nice lips and he was so incredibly young.

*Don't even think of it, Anita,* she told herself. Her heart was pounding as she moved even closer to him. Now there was nothing between them at all, and Mother and Father weren't at home, and she was supposed to be with Ingmar instead. Didn't she feel something for Ingmar and wasn't he far more suitable?

"Do you play?" Alvar asked her and gestured to the sheet music on the piano.

"How do you know I play the piano?"

"I don't know, that's why I asked. But you usually—"

He interrupted himself. His lips were close enough, how would they feel on hers?

"What do I usually . . ."

"You like music so much. Perhaps you play the piano, I thought."

Everyone had gone home, except for Seymour Österwall himself, who had gone somewhere to change.

"You have to try," Alvar said. "It's a fantastic experience. You have to feel these acoustics."

She looked at the piano on the stage, infinitely tempted. Finally she yielded, lifted the lid, and played a trill. The walls and the ceiling amplified the sound, and it alarmed her and delighted her. Think if she could play here every single evening!

Alvar started to play a walking bass line on his upright and he laughed in delight with her.

And then she looked up and it was by a fence, a little beyond where they were standing, and it was the most remarkable beast she'd ever seen. It wasn't a camel or a horse and she had never seen anything like it.

Part of the story was that when Alvar had come to Nalen all changed, with his hair slicked back and a suit that actually fit him, she'd said that Alvar had been *Erlingified*. But she realized that he looked more like a man than a boy now, even though he was still much too young, crazily too young.

But who was this girl?

"Who is this girl?"

Anita cocks her head. Alvar bites his lip and hopes that Steffi isn't disappointed. This Anita is the one who doesn't remember things, when he'd let her get to know the *real* Anita.

"This is my friend, and her name is Steffi. She's visiting me today."

"Oh, hello! Welcome!" Anita says, her gray eyes shining. "Have you ever been to Värmland before?"

Steffi nods. "Yes, I was born here."

"You know," Anita says. "I saw something so strange. It wasn't a camel or a horse. It wasn't a cow, either."

Steffi glances at Alvar before she asks, "Was it a llama?"

"Oh, yes! That's exactly what is was! A llama!"

Alvar gets up. He knows the best time to leave is when Anita is happy.

"I'll see Steffi out," he says. "You are such a hard worker, Anita, all your duties here at home and you take care of everything so well! So you just rest while I show Steffi to the door."

Anita smiles gratefully and winks. "You're such a sweetheart."

*Anita is just fragments of herself,* Alvar thinks as he closes the door behind them. Just pieces that have fallen apart, and she keeps trying to put the pieces together every day and they're all mixed up. She's the memory of a person, a mosaic, a potpourri. He still loves her, but nobody should think that this mosaic was really *her.* How can he explain this to a sixteen-year-old?

"Oh! She's so sweet!" Steffi exclaims once they've left.

This warms his heart. "Yes, but you should have met her ten years ago, when her head was still clear."

Steffi opens the door to his room. The gramophone has stopped playing a while ago. She puts on a record with Kai Gullmar on the piano and winds up the gramophone. "I still can see the person she is," Steffi says.

Alvar doubts this. He knows who Anita had been in real life. "You do?"

"Yes, she's kind, she's smart, she's funny."

He watches her concentration as she lowers the needle onto the outer track. Steffi Herrera, what will time make of you?

She turns toward him as the record starts to play.

"Does she still play the piano?"

"You mean Kai Gullmar?"

"No, Anita, of course."

Alvar misses Anita. He says good morning to her every morning and good night every evening. He often holds her hand as her fragmentary memories touch reality. He does as much as he can bear. And yet, even when he is with her, he misses her.

"We used to live on Klaus Street," he says. "When my parents got older, we moved back to Björke. We had a grand piano in our house on Klaus Street and Anita used to play it. When Anita started to get really bad, we sold the house and moved in here."

"But there's a piano in the dining room."

He doesn't know how he can explain to Steffi about how much he misses Anita. "It's locked," he says instead.

Steffi stares at him. "If it's locked, someone has a key."

"I don't think so."

He's lying even as he's telling the truth. There is no key to Anita, not any longer, and Steffi cannot comprehend how it feels to lose the key to the one you love. Steffi is still a child, and she's looking at him with her wise eyes and is speaking right to his old man's heart.

"Anita and I are the same. She has a heart of jazz, a heart full of jazz."

Alvar thinks so slowly these days, and he wants to make sure everything he says to Steffi is correct. Anybody can say anything without putting thought into it.

Finally he says, "That's good. Remember her just like that."

She has a great amount of remembering to do, Steffi thinks as she leaves the Sunshine Home and the spring weather hits her. *Heavenly remembering.* She likes the sound of the two words together and writes them on her phone.

"You have to remember all of this," Alvar had told her. He looked directly into her eyes. "You must remember Anita."

The warm air is tinged with the scent of honeysuckle. The Isakssons have planted honeysuckle all along their driveway. She's looked up the English word *honeysuckle* in her dictionary and found the Swedish was *kaprifol*. The English lyrics she'd heard still didn't make any sense to her. Still, she hums the song to herself as she reaches her family's driveway.

She opens the door and stops. Two white envelopes are waiting for her on the doormat. Silent, magical, addressed to *Stephanie Sophia Herrera*. Her heart pounds as she picks them up. One is from the music school in Karlstad and the other one is from the music school in Stockholm.

At first Steffi thinks she's the only one home, but then her mother calls to her from the kitchen.

"Hello," Steffi calls back and then sneaks into her room.

Which one should she open first? If she opens the one from Karlstad first and knows she's gotten in, then it might help her over any disappointment if she opens the one from Stockholm. But if she opens the Stockholm letter first and doesn't get in, maybe she'll be that much happier when she opens the letter from Karlstad. She waits for a few seconds, trying to decide what will give the maximum happiness and minimal disappointment. Then she rips open the letter from Stockholm. Holding her breath, and as the sheet of paper trembles in her hands, she reads:

*Congratulations on your acceptance into the music school!*

She reads it over and over. Her hands are now shaking uncontrollably. She reads it at least twenty times. Finally she continues to read the rest of the letter. Her eyes are blurry, she's started to cry. The letter is dated the fourteenth of May. There's a signature in ballpoint pen. Steffi wipes her nose and rubs her eyes but more tears come. Finally she goes out to her mother.

Mamma rushes over. "Oh, Steffi!" She hugs her. "Oh, my poor dear! You didn't get in? Sweetheart, things will work out somehow. . . ."

Steffi rubs her nose on her mother's collar. In the doorway behind her mother, Steffi sees Julia has come out, looking lost.

"You didn't get in?" Julia asks.

Steffi shakes her head, then nods, and then wriggles out of her mother's embrace. She waves the sheet of paper. They can read it for themselves.

"I got in!"

# – CHAPTER 35 –

It's the last school day for the ninth graders. Half of Steffi is already in Stockholm. Half of the other students are already on the beach. Half of the other teachers have their minds on summer vacation in Greece or Spain. Except for Bengt. He's 100 percent still in school. Everybody has already received report cards. He believes that the last day of school is the perfect day to give a lecture on the future of the ninth grade class.

"In every class of twenty students," he says, "one person will go to jail. Two people will become alcoholics. Seven will complete an upper-level education. Three of you will start smoking and one in ten of all smokers will get lung cancer. Twelve of you will leave Björke, but only three of you will leave Värmland."

*One of us three will be leaving Värmland this fall,* Steffi thinks.

"Some of you will become Social Democrats and others Moderates. Some of you will be doctors, others welders, and still others business owners."

*And one will be a musician,* Steffi thinks.

"You have choices. Some of those choices will define the rest of your lives. Think before you choose! And good luck!"

Semlan starts to applaud from a corner of the classroom. The whiteboard has the message: *Have a Happy Summer and a Wonderful Future!*

Semlan walks up to Bengt and shakes his hand. "And now," Semlan says. "We're going to hear from a girl with talent! She's been admitted to the Karlstad Music School and she's even sung with our local band, Lard Heroes! Perhaps 'singer' should be added to our list of careers? Let's give a warm round of applause to Sanja Eriksson!"

Class 9B applauds for Sanja. Karro squeals as if she were at a rock concert, and two guys whistle.

Using the interactive whiteboard, Sanja selects the backup music and starts to sing "Umbrella" into one of the microphones from Jake's music room. Steffi thinks about all the times she's fantasized about standing there and showing everyone else what she can do. She realizes now it would be all wrong. They're not really celebrating the shining future of these people. They're thanking the retiring queen bees. She applauds for Sanja when she finishes. *Bravo. Tomorrow you're a nobody.*

Everyone receives the gift of a sketchbook and a rose. Semlan is crying. The girls are wearing white dresses that barely cover their thighs. The boys have tried to wrestle their gangly bodies into suits. Steffi's wearing dress pants and a vest. She feels Björke School losing its hold on her the way she loosens a string on her bass. It already feels like *the school I used to attend.* One day she might walk past the building and say: *Once there was a school here.*

Karro is hugging all the other girls. Soon she'll be lying on the beach. "Now our lives are really starting!" she's probably saying to them, and it's like she doesn't even notice Steffi at all.

Finally, she picks up her sketchbook and her rose and is ready to go home. She stops right in front of Steffi. "Bye forever, you stinking rat," she says.

Steffi looks right at Karro. Right into Karro's mean soul.

"I know everything about you," she says. "I know what your pretend father does to you. I know you invite yourself to strange boys' houses on the Internet."

Karro stares at her, but Steffi can't stop. "Your mother gambles and your cousins back in the woods are all alcoholics," she says. "I know who taught you how to say slut and whore."

Karro collects herself and is about to say something nasty and call her a pathetic liar, but she isn't fast enough.

"Don't you recognize this?" Steffi takes out her fedora from her bag. "Yeah, that's right, I'm Hepcat."

People start to gather around them. Karro's face is white, and for once she can't say a word.

Steffi is on fire and all the words she has built up inside come out and she has to raise her voice. "I could spit on you, because you never had trouble spitting on me," she says. "But you're not even worth my spit! Go to hell, we'll never see each other again."

At least, that's how things play out in Steffi's imagination.

In reality, she looks right back at Karro. She looks right into Karro's mean soul.

"You're a rat's cunt," Karro says.

Steffi can see Karro in the Sunshine Home seventy years from now. She'll be shaking her cane and hissing at all the visitors walking in the door.

Steffi hears her heart beating inside her vest. "I hope you have a pleasant summer," she says.

Then she turns around and walks down the hill, away from the schoolyard, for the last time. She glances back. Nobody is following her. As she walks away, she notices how the rosebush has started to bloom.

She's going to tell Alvar what happened with Karro. What she wanted to say and what she really said. How it felt nice and also irritating not to confront her. Perhaps Alvar would say, "You're a good human being, a mature person." And she'd just say in return, "No, I really just didn't care anymore."

Outside the Sunshine Home buildings, roses are growing along the supports. When she reaches Alvar's room, she can't hear any swing music through the door. He's usually in his room. He's always in his room at this time of the day. And he knew this was the last day of school and she was going to come by.

On the table, the magnifying glass is lying beside a folder and a small calculator, and an envelope with the words MISS STEFFI HERRERA is propped up. She puts down the rose she's still carrying and takes up the envelope. A frightening thought churns through her stomach. Perhaps she has no reason to be frightened. Perhaps it was like the last time, when he was in the dining room. But when did Alvar ever make the bed?

Her hands are shaking as she opens the envelope. She thinks, *Alvar Big Boy Svensson, did I ever tell you you're the best old man in the whole wide world? Did I ever tell you? Or did I forget?*

If she closes her eyes, she can hear his old fingers pluck a bass line as if he were still just a boy.

*Some day you will meet*
*The friend you need*
*Don't wait . . . time doesn't allow*
*Many moments for the dance.*

# – CHAPTER 36 –

It's as if Alvar is with her. She's listening to Ella Fitzgerald and there's a family with children across from her. They're eating sandwiches. The girls are looking at her with round eyes and she puts one hand on the largest of her suitcases. Yes, these are my suitcases. Yes, I'm traveling all by myself.

But not all by herself, because, in a way, Alvar is with her. He's seventeen, and as she gets on the train, so does he. A heavyset man of about fifty offers to help her with her luggage, but she's able to wrestle them into the luggage racks herself. She and Alvar find her place together, since it's not the forties any longer and all the train seats are numbered and have comfortable upholstery. She sits at seat 22 and checks her ticket again. She shoves her hand baggage against the wall by her feet.

Nobody is curious about why she's going to Stockholm. They're not staring at her electric bass guitar case or the other case she has with her. They don't exclaim: "Please, play something for us!" They're all looking at their phones and run their fingers over shiny screens. All the music they could ever want in the world comes through their earphones.

She wishes someone would look at her smaller case. She would say, "This is my clarinet." She wouldn't be lying. She'd be just like Erling. "I got it this summer as a graduation present. But I didn't know it right away."

Steffi didn't realize she was getting a clarinet when she got it. It was in its case propping up the envelope she'd just picked up. She was too busy thinking about the old man who was not in his room to realize what it was. She didn't know why he was not in his room, but his empty armchair and perfectly made bed didn't feel right and she wanted to run home and pretend she hadn't even noticed. But this letter was for her. She opened it with a breaking heart. The handwriting was in cursive and somewhat shaky, but if she read slowly, she could make it out.

*Congratulations on your graduation!*

*This is your clarinet. Put it together and go to the visitors' room.*

*Then let's see if Erling's Trio can't come back to life!*

*Your friend,*
*Alvar*

The lump in her throat dissolved at once and she felt excited as she snapped open the case and pulled out the shiny black parts of a brand-new clarinet. She was so nervous, she fumbled as she assembled the pieces. She wet the mouthpiece just like Jake had taught her and produced her first note, which sounded so much better than the old clarinet that she had to laugh.

She realized, as she walked through the hallway, why it

seemed so quiet. There was nobody around. Neither old ladies with canes and walkers nor old men with gaping mouths. Not even resolute nurses with hearts of gold. The Sunshine Home was empty.

Karin was at the door of the visitors' room. When she saw Steffi coming, she called something into the room and soon Steffi heard Alvar's familiar voice.

"Povel Ramel once wrote . . . all of you know Povel Ramel, don't you, even if you've forgotten everything else?"

An energetic murmur came from the visitors' room, in response. Steffi had now reached the door. She saw that all the tables had been lined up against the wall and all the residents of the Sunshine Home were lined up in their chairs and wheelchairs. Even all the staff was there.

"As Povel Ramel once said: *This old guy is still singing!* Or, in our case, still playing!"

It was hard to tell if the audience members, all with hair in various shades of gray and white, were laughing at his joke or at his enormous clown smile. Alvar told a few more jokes and then wrapped a chivalrous arm around Steffi's shoulders. "Our soloist on the clarinet is Steffi Herrera, a young star rising in the sky of jazz, as Topsy Lindblom would have said. Let's all give her a warm round of applause!"

The applause in the Sunshine Home was much different that the one class 9B had just given Sanja a few hours ago. Nobody yelled, nobody whistled. If they had tried to whistle, they might have suffered lack of oxygen. But it was a round of applause given by hands that once had put up blackout curtains, hands that were raised in fists against the German occupation of Norway, hands that had comforted small children who had grown up and now were even retired. These hands had stuffed thousands of sausages, cut down thousands of trees, gently touched the cheeks of their own children and elderly relatives, as they themselves slowly began to acquire wrinkles on their own faces. Now they were clapping for her.

Alvar gave her a wink as she came up to the piano. Then he looked to the right. "On my other side, we have a real virtuoso on the piano!"

Anita laughed and twisted on the piano stool and Alvar added a few more words: "Anita Svensson, Sweden's answer to Nina Simone and Duke Ellington together! Watch out, folks, this is one jazz crazy girl!"

The crowd was smitten by Alvar's enthusiasm, and one of the old ladies started to clap again.

"Why are you using that Stockholm accent, Alvar? We know you're here from Björke!" called out one of the gray-haired ladies. Many people laughed.

Alvar picked up his string bass, and in the curved posture he probably would never have been able to do in his advanced age, except that it was so familiar to his body after all the decades of playing that his body took to it naturally, he was ready to play.

"Ladies and gentlemen! Erling's Trio! Steffi 'Hepcat' Herrara, Anita 'Jazz Crazy' Svensson, and myself, Alvar 'Big Boy' Svensson, would now like to play for you our version of 'How High the Moon.' "

Steffi leans her head back. The train has already passed Kristinehamn and through the window she sees a cormorant landing on a lake and quietly swimming on. She smiles as she thinks of Anita's back and her curly white hair that bounced as she hit the keys. Her fingers didn't always hit the right notes, but she'd never forgotten the chords.

One thought strikes Steffi, and she pulls out her notebook from the outer pocket of her bass guitar case:

*That old lady may be mixed up but we get her glimmers.*
*Holds a thought for a few seconds, but a melody forever.*

She writes quickly and almost illegibly and the lyrics come easily, as her muse is with her. In the future, when this song is played on the radio, she'll call Alvar and tell him to tune in.

*She's always been a jazz crazy girl of highest class.*
*Her feet no longer on the ground and her heart is full of jazz.*

Steffi can already hear the walking bass line.

## SWEDEN, VÄRMLAND, AND JAZZ MUSIC DURING THE SECOND WORLD WAR

Stephanie Herrera, Class 9B

The Second World War began in 1939 when Hitler invaded Poland. War did not break out over the entire world at the same time, but it was still called a "world war" because so many countries were parts of alliances that fought one another. Sweden was neutral, which means that Sweden did not officially take part in the war. But it was still difficult to be neutral, because all the countries around Sweden were fighting.

Because Hitler decided to send Jews, Gypsies, and homosexuals to concentration camps in order to either work them to death or kill them outright, Danes and Norwegians often helped these people escape from their countries and into neutral Sweden.

Many Germans were in Sweden during the Second World War. This was because when Germany attacked Norway, the German troops were allowed to travel by train through Sweden. Some people think that Sweden wasn't really neutral because we let the Germans through to Norway. The relationship between Sweden and Norway became very bad because of this. When Germany successfully occupied Norway, the relationship between Norwegians and Swedes got worse.

One thing happening in Norway at this time was the rise of a Norwegian politician named Quisling. He was working with the Germans and he took power in Norway after Norway was occupied. The Norwegians were afraid of the Germans and despised the Swedes, but, most of all, they hated Quisling.

Since Värmland lies right on the Norwegian border, people felt that the war was nearby, even if Sweden was neutral. Many Swedish soldiers were stationed at the farms, ready to protect Sweden if we were attacked. At the same time, German soldiers were on our trains, and there are elderly people still alive today who say they could see Germans on the other side of the border. They were so close that you could wave to them.

There was a nervous atmosphere in Sweden during this time. People were afraid that Sweden would be attacked, and many people did not want to talk about the war at all while it was still going on.

People tried to live their normal lives, but nothing was the same. There wasn't any gasoline, for example. It was forbidden for individuals to drive cars between 1939 and 1945. You had to either find a car that took wood gas or stop driving. So there weren't that many cars on the roads during this time, and in Stockholm, many people rode bikes or took the streetcar instead.

It was also difficult to find various items such as coffee. People drank a great deal of coffee in Sweden before the forties, but all of a sudden there wasn't any. This was difficult for many people. You got thirteen grams of coffee per person per week. You could buy it with a coupon. These coupons were used for all kinds of things, like sugar, meat, and cheese. This was the most difficult part of the war for most people in Sweden.

Once, the Swedish military shot down a German plane, even though it was probably just lost on the way to Norway.

This happened in Torsby, very close to Björke. Another time, a bomb fell in Stockholm. It was the evening of February 22, 1944. You could hear the boom throughout the city. The next day, all the papers said that war had come to Sweden and people were terrified. Today we think the Soviet Union bombed us, but we still don't know why. Some people think it was because Sweden had jailed a Soviet spy named Vasilij Sidorenko. Others think the bomb was a mistake and the plane had intended to bomb Finland. At any rate, nobody died and no other bombs were dropped.

A new style of music had come to Sweden during this time. It was called jazz music and it came from the United States. Since the United States was in the war starting in 1941, there was a great deal of propaganda against jazz music coming from Germany and others who were against the United States. They wrote in the newspapers that jazz music led to loss of morals in the youth and they also wrote many racist things about Jewish people and black people. Everything they thought was bad, they tried to tie to jazz music, but the young people never stopped listening to jazz.

The best jazz music was smuggled into Europe on gramophone records. Sweden also had its good jazz musicians, such as Arne Domnérus, Gösta Törner, Alice Babs, and lots of others who would play at Nalen and the Winter Palace in Stockholm. They were inspired by American musicians like Artie Shaw, Lucky Millinder, Glenn Miller, Barney Bigard, Duke Ellington, and Charlie Parker. After the war, many American jazz musicians came to Stockholm and played with Swedish jazz musicians at Nalen. For example: Lucky Thompson, Donald Byrd, Sonny Rollins, Quincy Jones, and Thad Jones.

One source I spoke with told me that this was a lively time in spite of the fear about war. I am going to finish my essay with a quote from him: "It was wartime in Europe and war is always a reminder of death. If you are always confronted with death, you want to live life to the fullest. That's what we did with jazz music. When I look back to the time of the Second World War, jazz music is what I remember best."

*Good work, Steffi! You've brought together different events from the war with individual experiences. I don't see some specific terms, such as "rationing" (the term for the limits on food and other items) or "through traffic by special permit" (used for letting the Germans travel through Sweden). The last paragraphs about jazz in Sweden don't really belong with the rest of the text, but you managed to bring it into context. Grade: Satisfactory*

# HISTORICAL NOTE ON SWEDISH JAZZ MUSICIANS

Jazz music arrived in Sweden from the United States after 1910 in the form now known as "ragtime." Jazz music spread through recordings and tours of American musicians throughout Europe. In the twenties, many people interested in new music discovered "free form" jazz. The strong elements of improvisation and the new syncopated rhythms contrasted starkly with traditional Swedish music. Many conservative people at the time hated jazz music, but musicians and young people felt they'd discovered something new and exciting.

During the thirties and forties, jazz and its many variations, especially "swing," took hold. Dance halls were filled with young people jitterbugging. Louis Armstrong and Duke Ellington were two of many jazz greats who came to Sweden and played with Swedish musicians. Swedish jazz was heavily influenced by America, and the jazz scene reached its peak during the fifties. The National, nicknamed Nalen, was the heart of the jazz scene. All the international stars played there, and many Swedish people discovered at the Nalen the new trends in exuberant dance and musical styles.

During the sixties, interest in jazz music waned as rock and roll claimed a bigger spot in the hearts of young people throughout the world. It was the end of the heyday of jazz music, but Swedes never lost their love for jazz. New Swedish jazz musicians keep appearing on the scene and experiment with, improvise, and continue the inheritance of jazz music into the future.

**Povel Ramel** was a magician with words, known throughout Sweden for his intricate lyrics. He assembled variety shows that have become an unforgettable part of Swedish music, comedy, and entertainment, and he was also an excellent jazz pianist and composer. He was born in 1922, and his father was a lawyer and his mother was very supportive. He had a happy childhood until his parents died in a car accident in 1937. Povel Ramel took punning to a new level and added it to his passion for music, especially jazz music. On YouTube and other video sites, you can find his video "Var är tvålen" ("Where's the Soap"), where Povel and his friends sing about a missing bar of soap.

**Alice Babs** had her big breakthrough with the film *Swing it, magistern!* (*Swing It, Teacher!*) in 1940, when she was seventeen years old. She was in over twenty movies, often musicals, and worked with Charlie Norman (still called Charles during the forties) and Duke Ellington, who was a great inspiration for Alice. Alice Babs was born in 1924 and died in 2014. On YouTube, you can find her music video from the movie *Swing it, magistern!,* which is about a few young people who provoke their more conservative peers by singing and playing jazz music.

**Thore Ehrling** was born in 1912 in Stockholm. He started a jazz band while he was still in school and had a long career as a trumpet player and bandleader. He studied at the music conservatory in Stockholm and started his own orchestra in 1938.

Thore Ehrling's Orchestra became known for their concerts at the open-air museum Skansen, and from 1943 onward, he was commissioned by Sveriges Radio to produce regular telecasts of modern dance music.

**Arne Domnérus** played the alto saxaphone as well as the clarinet. He led an orchestra and received the nickname "Dompan." At the age of seventeen, he played at Nalen and became an international figure with his work with the Swedish orchestra, known as the Paris Orchestra. When the American Charlie Parker visited Sweden, he played a few concerts with Arne Domnérus. This collaboration was talked about for years within the Swedish jazz world. Later he also played with the trumpet players Clifford Brown, Art Farmer, and Quincy Jones.

**Gösta Törner** was one of Sweden's best jazz trumpet players. He was born in Söder, Stockholm, in 1912. He received his first gig when he was seventeen and led his own orchestra. In addition, he played with the Paris Orchestra in 1949. During the fifties, Gösta Törner played at famous New York nightclubs. He was inspired by Louis Armstrong, Bix Beiderbecke, and Bobby Hackett. During the sixties, interest in jazz waned and Gösta Törner had to support himself as a security guard and as a caddy for a golf club.

**Casper Hjukström**, born in 1911, was a saxophonist and composer who played in all the major Swedish dance orchestras. He even played with Povel Ramel and Alice Babs, and he made a number of recordings with his own sextet. He was born in Sorsele, in Lappland, the most northern part of Sweden, but moved to Stockholm—most likely so he could devote himself to jazz music.

# ACKNOWLEDGMENTS

I would like to thank Povel Ramel and my family for brightening my teenage years.

A great thank-you to Lasse Odenhall, for your boundless knowledge about jazz, jazz musicians, and instruments! Without you, Alvar would have played "Indiana" in the wrong key. Thank you, Sofia and Anna, for asking the right questions. Thanks, Mattias, for all the books about Povel Ramel. A special thank-you to my publishers around the world for your confidence in me and in my books—for the English translations, Flatiron Books and Allen & Unwin. Thank you, Laura Wideburg, for translating this novel into English with great commitment—especially for taking the time to translate lyrics and finding the right slang and music terminology! Translating Povel Ramel into any other language is in itself an impossible task.

Last but not least: thank you, children and teenagers, sitting in schools all over the world, thinking about chords, shading, pi, medieval aesthetics, adverbs, metaphysics, Neanderthals, lace-making, chromatics, and making flambés, instead of letting schoolyard pecking orders get to you. Your time will come.

Recommend

# WONDERFUL FEELS LIKE THIS

for your next book club!